Erle Stanley Gardner and The Murder Room

>>> This title is part of The Murder Room, our series dedicated to making available out-of-print or hard-to-find titles by classic crime writers.

Crime fiction has always held up a mirror to society. The Victorians were fascinated by sensational murder and the emerging science of detection; now we are obsessed with the forensic detail of violent death. And no other genre has so captivated and enthralled readers.

Vast troves of classic crime writing have for a long time been unavailable to all but the most dedicated frequenters of second-hand bookshops. The advent of digital publishing means that we are now able to bring you the backlists of a huge range of titles by classic and contemporary crime writers, some of which have been out of print for decades.

From the genteel amateur private eyes of the Golden Age and the femmes fatales of pulp fiction, to the morally ambiguous hard-boiled detectives of mid twentieth-century America and their descendants who walk our twenty-first century streets, The Murder Room has it all. >>>

The Murder Room
Where Criminal Minds Meet

themurderroom.com

T0352211

Erle Stanley Gardner (1889–1970)

Born in Malden, Massachusetts, Erle Stanley Gardner left school in 1909 and attended Valparaiso University School of Law in Indiana for just one month before he was suspended for focusing more on his hobby of boxing than his academic studies. Soon after, he settled in California, where he taught himself the law and passed the state bar exam in 1911. The practise of law never held much interest for him, however, apart from as it pertained to trial strategy, and in his spare time he began to write for the pulp magazines that gave Dashiell Hammett and Raymond Chandler their start. Not long after the publication of his first novel, *The Case of the Velvet Claws*, featuring Perry Mason, he gave up his legal practice to write full time. He had one daughter, Grace, with his first wife, Natalie, from whom he later separated. In 1968 Gardner married his long-term secretary, Agnes Jean Bethell, whom he professed to be the real 'Della Street', Perry Mason's sole (although unacknowledged) love interest. He was one of the most successful authors of all time and at the time of his death, in Temecula, California in 1970, is said to have had 135 million copies of his books in print in America alone.

By Erle Stanley Gardner
(titles below include only those published in the Murder Room)

Perry Mason series

The Case of the Sulky Girl (1933)

The Case of the Baited Hook (1940)

The Case of the Borrowed Brunette (1946)

The Case of the Lonely Heiress (1948)

The Case of the Negligent Nymph (1950)

The Case of the Moth-Eaten Mink (1952)

The Case of the Glamorous Ghost (1955)

The Case of the Terrified Typist (1956)

The Case of the Gilded Lily (1956)

The Case of the Lucky Loser (1957)

The Case of the Long-Legged Models (1958)

The Case of the Deadly Toy (1959)

The Case of the Singing Skirt (1959)

The Case of the Duplicate Daughter (1960)

The Case of the Blonde Bonanza (1962)

Cool and Lam series

The Bigger They Come (1939)

Turn on the Heat (1940)

Gold Comes in Bricks (1940)

Spill the Jackpot (1941)

Double or Quits (1941)

Owls Don't Blink (1942)

Bats Fly at Dusk (1942)

Cats Prowl at Night (1943)

Crows Can't Count (1946)

Fools Die on Friday (1947)

Bedrooms Have Windows (1949)

Some Women Won't Wait (1953)

Beware the Curves (1956)

You Can Die Laughing (1957)

Some Slips Don't Show (1957)

The Count of Nine (1958)

Pass the Gravy (1959)

Kept Women Can't Quit (1960)

Bachelors Get Lonely (1961)

Shills Can't Cash Chips (1961)

Try Anything Once (1962)

Fish or Cut Bait (1963)

Up For Grabs (1964)

Cut Thin to Win (1965)
Widows Wear Weeds (1966)
Traps Need Fresh Bait (1967)
All Grass Isn't Green (1970)

Doug Selby D.A. series

The D.A. Calls it Murder (1937)
The D.A. Holds a Candle (1938)
The D.A. Draws a Circle (1939)
The D.A. Goes to Trial (1940)
The D.A. Cooks a Goose (1942)
The D.A. Calls a Turn (1944)
The D.A. Takes a Chance
  (1946)
The D.A. Breaks an Egg
  (1949)

Terry Clane series

Murder Up My Sleeve (1937)
The Case of the Backward
  Mule (1946)

Gramp Wiggins series

The Case of the Turning Tide
  (1941)
The Case of the Smoking
  Chimney (1943)

Two Clues (two novellas) (1947)

The Case of the Turning Tide

Erle Stanley Gardner

An Orion book

Copyright © The Erle Stanley Gardner Trust 1941

This edition published by
The Orion Publishing Group Ltd
Orion House
5 Upper St Martin's Lane
London WC2H 9EA

An Hachette UK company
A CIP catalogue record for this book is available from the British Library

ISBN 978 1 4719 0950 4

www.orionbooks.co.uk

FOREWORD

THE RELATIVELY few persons who have had first-hand dealings with real murder know that truth is not only stranger than fiction, but is much more exciting.

As one who has had intimate contact with several murders, who has also done some writing and some reading, I tried to find out just why this was so. I haven't found all the answers, but I think I have found some.

It is the difference between milk and meat.

Our so-called "murder mysteries" are escape fiction, and have become highly standardized through too much usage. Attempts to "create suspense," "plant" clues, and above all, to "surprise the reader," have robbed the reader of far more than they have given him in return.

In this book events are permitted to stream across the page in just about the way they would have happened in real life. Such clues as the reader will find are the ones that are there naturally. And if the reader isn't "surprised" in the conventional manner by having the characters who seem painted the blackest with the brush of guilt turn out to be the most innocent, while the real murderer is the one person who has seemed "as pure as the driven snow," I hope he will at least be entertained.

Reading it over, now that it is finished, I can find numerous technical errors—according to the standards of escape literature. I find that I also get some of the thrill which was inevitably associated with every real murder case on which I ever worked.

If the reader can get a taste of this "meat" he will feel compensated and I will be amply rewarded for the extra effort this book has cost.

Erle Stanley Gardner

CAST OF CHARACTERS

CHAPTER 1

TED SHALE walked along the hard-packed sand which had been left by the outgoing tide. He walked with the leisurely manner of one who has no definite destination in mind. To the south, the ocean was a sheet of deep blue. Above it arched the cloudless vault of the sky. The sunlight reflected from the water as from a burnished mirror. Behind him and to the north, the city of Santa Delbarra cuddled against the hazy blue slopes of the mountains. The sides of its stucco buildings were white in the sunlight. Green palm fronds splashed color contrast against red tile roofs.

It was Sunday. The sound of church bells, mellowed by distance, drifted through the balmy air. Out in the bay, some two dozen yachts swung to their moorings. On one of them stood a girl in a tight-fitting white bathing suit decorated with green and brown figures. The morning sun touched her smooth, bronzed skin. Her body was smooth, supple, and desirable, and she was fully conscious of that fact.

There was no other sign of life on any of the yachts.

A hundred feet or more beyond the yacht on which the girl was standing, the *Gypsy Queen* floated in regal splendor. The exhaust from its Diesel motor, disguised as a funnel, gave it the appearance of a miniature liner. Glistening with mahogany, brass, and white enamel, it dwarfed the other yachts in the harbor. Shale's interest centered on this yacht. From time to time, he shifted his eyes to it. Aboard it was Addison Stearne, who controlled, among other things, a string of Pacific Coast hotels. The sales manager of the Freelander Pasteboard Products Company had sent Shale to Santa Delbarra with instructions to get an order from Stearne.

So far Shale hadn't even been able to see the man, let alone talk with him.

Shale was only too well aware that Sunday might be an unpropitious time to make an approach, but, talking with some of the crew of the *Gypsy Queen* who had been on shore leave, Shale had learned that Stearne had left orders the yacht was to be ready to put to sea at three o'clock Sunday afternoon.

Shale's investigations had further disclosed that every man on the crew had been given overnight shore leave, had, in fact, been warned to stay ashore and not come back to the yacht. That had included even the cook. Obviously, Stearne would require some breakfast, and Shale intended to approach the man the minute he set foot on the landing float at the yacht club. Whether the time was propitious or not, Shale determined he was going to have a try at it.

It was as yet too early for many people to be at the beach, but a few family parties were gathered near the wall which served as a windbreak. Three or four children ran along the hard-packed sand. As they played, they shouted shrill little cries which spread out over the water and were lost. Farther down the beach, a flock of shore birds, moving in unison as though following carefully rehearsed maneuvers, ran up and down the sand, eagerly searching for food at every receding wavelet, turning in leg-twinkling retreat as another wave splashed up the beach.

Ted Shale regarded the girl in the bathing suit with surreptitious appreciation. She had chestnut-colored hair. Her waist was small. Her hips had a long slope which was pleasing to the eye. She had been swimming, and water glistened in sun-reflecting drops from her arms and legs.

There was no faintest breath of wind. Dead calm made the ocean flat as a floor. The pennant atop the clubhouse clung to the short pole. Along the landing float a cluster of small boats were tied in a confused tangle.

Abruptly a figure debouched from the cabin of the *Gypsy Queen*. A young woman ran to the rail. She wore a white sailor shirt and blue dungarees. As she bent over the rail, her hair, a shock of spun gold, fell down about her face. She made a feeble motion with her left hand as though to brush the hair back from her forehead, then her arm fell forward, dangling toward the water. Her head dropped limply. For a moment she hung precariously, then slumped over the rail and splashed into the water.

Ted Shale shouted to the girl in the bathing suit. She turned, regarding him with the cold indifference of one who rebuffs an advance. Ted shouted again, and pointed. She lifted her chin and turned away.

Ted Shale sprinted across the soft stretch of sand which lay between the low tide line and the entrance to the yacht club. For a dozen steps, the powdery sand tugged at his ankles, then his feet were pounding down the yacht club float. He made a quick survey of the small boats, found one that had both oars and oarlocks, jumped in and jerked the painter loose.

Shale gave the skiff a quick push, and kept a precarious balance while getting out the oars. A few seconds later, he was rowing with quick, sure strokes. From the corner of his eye, he saw the girl in the bathing suit arch cleanly from the deck of the yacht, knife the water in a graceful, effortless dive, and start swimming. She stroked a well-timed crawl which sent her cleaving through the water.

Ted Shale gave the oars everything he had. The blades bit cleanly into the water as he flung his weight against them, pulling first with the muscles of the back, then snapping himself erect with a quick motion of the arms, twisting his wrists and feathering the blades as he sent them skimming back into position for another stroke.

He beat the girl to the site of the splash by a matter of seconds.

At first he could see nothing save the bluish green water, with reflections from the sun glancing from the wavelets to dazzle his eyes. The momentum of his small craft carried him past the spot where the girl had gone down. He grasped at the yacht's mooring chain to check his progress. The cold slime of the metal slipped through his fingers. Water trickled along his wrist and up his sleeve. He saw a commotion in the water near the side of the yacht. A drifting blob of golden hair floated up near the surface. He heard the glug of sinister air bubbles, then, as the head started down once more, the hair floated up toward the surface, like golden fingers reaching for the sunlight.

Ted whipped off his coat and went overboard.

He braced himself for a struggle, but she was limp in his arms. Only once did he feel her stir, and then she gave a quick convulsive half-turn which helped him more than it hindered

3

him. He rolled over on his back, slid her head up on to his abdomen, and swam with a powerful backstroke, holding her body clamped between his knees.

The girl in the bathing suit came splashing up to overtake Ted and his burden with quick businesslike strokes. She flung her head back, shook hair from her eyes, said very calmly in a voice so well-modulated that it might have been trained for the stage, "Making it all right?"

Ted met the clear hazel of her eyes, turned to get his bearings. "I'll need some help when I get to the skiff."

The girl in the bathing suit said nothing, but swam quietly along, using a breast stroke now which enabled her to keep her eyes well above the water.

"Don't try the sides," she warned. "Get around to the stern or the bow."

Ted Shale's voice held a trace of sarcasm. "Thanks for telling me." He worked around toward the stern of the skiff, where it was lower in the water than at the bow.

"Can you hold her until I get in?" he asked.

"Certainly."

"Be careful she doesn't come to and start struggling. If she does, she'll try to grab you and . . ."

She echoed the tone he had used with her as she repeated his words. "Thanks for telling me."

Ted passed the limp body over to her by a deft leg motion, turned in the water, raised a right arm, his wet shirt hampering the motion, and caught the stern of the boat. He swung up his left, pulled himself up, then dropped back so that he pulled the boat down in the water, at the same time getting all the body buoyancy possible from his immersion. He heaved himself up, and managed to get that essential upward crook in the left elbow. Two seconds later, he was sliding smoothly over the stern, conscious of the water which was pouring from his trousers legs, of the wet garments which clung to him with hampering insistence.

"All right," he said, "let's get her up."

He reached over the stern, anchored his hands under the armpits of the limp figure, raised her until her hips were level with the water.

The girl in the bathing suit matter-of-factly swung up a glistening arm to the edge of the boat, placed her shoulder under the girl's hips, said, "Here we go," and Ted saw lean, sinewy muscles ripple under the bronzed skin of her arm as the dead weight of his burden was lightened. A moment later, he had the unconscious young woman dragged into the boat, where she lay, a soggy inert mass. Her blouse had been pulled loose from the yachting slacks, and had wrinkled up under her arms. Her wet hair plastered golden strings against her forehead.

Ted felt the boat sway, and saw that the girl in the bathing suit was pulling at the stern, trying to lift herself in. She couldn't get quite high enough out of the water to throw her left elbow into that bend which would give her enough purchase to come up over the edge.

"Just a minute," he said. "I'll give you a hand."

"You don't need to." She tried again.

Ted saw that she was getting weaker. He waited for her third ineffectual attempt, then bent over. She made no objection when he clasped fingers around her wet wrist, placed his other hand beneath her armpit, and lifted her high enough so she could slide in over the stern.

Once she was inside the skiff, Ted looked around toward the other yachts and toward the shore. Apparently the rescue had attracted no attention. The children still ran up and down the packed sand. The family parties that were grouped around lunch hampers lounged in the balmy morning sunshine. The float at the yacht club seemed deserted.

"Well?" the girl in the bathing suit asked.

Ted indicated the yacht, which was only a few feet away. "She evidently belongs on board," he said. "There's a landing ladder over on the starboard beam. If you'll keep an eye on her, I'll go aboard and make inquiries."

She nodded, and Ted, picking up one oar, sculled the skiff over toward the landing ladder. The girl, who had shifted her position to the bow, caught the deck of the yacht, and held the skiff ready. Ted stepped aboard, conscious of his grotesque appearance, of the little puddles of water which marked each squishing step.

"Hello," he called tentatively.

There was no answer.

"Ahoy!" Ted shouted, and, as he was greeted only with silence, walked over to an open companionway, and looked down into a sumptuous cabin.

It took a moment for his eyes to accustom themselves to the dim illumination of the interior. At first, he could see only splotches of sunlight where the sun poured through portholes, to splash vivid ovals on the carpeted floor.

One of those splotches of sunlight turned suddenly crimson, and Ted frowned as he watched it move slowly across the floor with the slight roll of the yacht. Then he saw it turn crimson again. His eyes slowly adjusted themselves to the relative gloom of the cabin. He saw something huddled on the floor, a grotesque something which sprouted out an awkward leg. Then he saw an arm, another leg, and still another leg. Two bodies lay sprawled on the cabin floor. A face stared upward with glassy, filmed eyes, and the slow swing of the yacht sent one of the oval splashes of sunlight across the death-distorted features.

Ted abruptly whirled and sought the open air.

He was hardly aware that his groping progress took him toward the landing ladder.

"Well?" the calm voice of the girl in the bathing suit asked.

Ted looked down at her. "We're going ashore."

"No one there?"

Ted didn't trust himself to answer this question until he had descended the steps of the landing ladder, and thumped his weight into the stern of the skiff. His stomach felt cold and heavy.

"Well, don't be that way," the girl in the bathing suit said. "What is it?"

Ted said, "Two bodies."

At that moment the golden-haired girl stirred uneasily, moaned, opened her eyes, and sat up. She stared vacantly at Ted, then with a purely mechanical reflex, clutched at her blouse and pulled it down over her body. "What . . . what . . ." Abruptly her eyes widened with panic. Her lips stretched until Ted could see the pink interior of her throat. Her scream knife-edged across the water.

"Shut up," Ted said. "Take it easy. It's all right."

She looked at him again with unseeing eyes, and screamed once more.

Ted said, "Do that again, and you'll pull my nerves out by the roots. Shut up."

He saw by her eyes that his words had failed to reach through to her consciousness. She opened her mouth again. Ted leaned forward, and slapped her hard across the side of the jaw.

He heard the girl in the bathing suit give a quick exclamation. She stood up in the boat. "This is where I came in," she said.

"Sit down," Ted said. "You've got an appointment."

"Oh, yes? With whom, may I ask?"

"The police."

CHAPTER 2

FRANK DURYEA rolled over in bed, stretched, yawned, and turned so that he could see the face of the alarm clock.

From the pillow beside him, Milred said sleepily, "Go on back to sleep. It's too early to wake up."

Duryea looked at the clock, knuckled his eyes, said, "It's nine o'clock."

"Well, it's Sunday."

"Take a look outside, hon. See the sunlight around the edge of the window shade."

His wife kept her back toward the window, refused to turn her head. She said, "That's always the way. You start me arguing, and that wakes me up. Go back to sleep."

Duryea got up, crossed over to the windows, and raised the shades, letting in a flood of sunlight. "Look, sweet, it's the dawn of a new day. It's Hollywood!"

"No, it isn't. It's the same day it was at two o'clock this morning when I wanted you to come home and you wouldn't."

"Come on, uppy-up! We'll take a walk in the fresh air. How about a glass of tomato juice?"

Milred sat up in bed. "All right, we'll argue about it."

"About what? The tomato juice?"

"No, your marital manners. They're very, very bad. Just because you wake up is no sign you should waken a bed mate."

"Have you been reading books on bedroom etiquette, or are you drawing on your past experience?" he asked.

She stretched and yawned. The silk nightdress matched the skin of her supple body. She was good looking, brunette, twenty-seven, a tall girl with the knack of keeping her youth, her figure, and her husband.

Frank Duryea, taller and five years older, was beginning to put on weight. For three years now he had been district attorney of Santa Delbarra. He stood looking out of the window at the sun-swept vista. "How about that tomato juice?"

"You've made a sale, but don't put too much Worcestershire in it."

Duryea went into the kitchen, filled two large tumblers with tomato juice, and poured in a generous helping of Worcestershire.

"Some lemon in mine," Milred called from the bedroom.

Duryea was adding the lemon when the phone rang.

"Want to get that, Millie? My hands are sticky."

"Get them washed then because it's some woman whose husband has left her, and she wants to invoke the law."

Duryea washed his hands at the kitchen sink. "Don't make my career sound so stodgy. Last Sunday it was the woman who had a stray horse on her front lawn. Remember?"

"At seven-fifteen," Milred amended, and said into the telephone, "Hello. . . . Yes. . . . Oh, yes. Just a moment."

She pushed the palm of her hand over the mouthpiece and said, "It's Sheriff Lassen, Frank. He's excited. Bring my tomato juice when you come."

Duryea brought in a tray with the glasses of tomato juice. She sipped her drink while Duryea, standing with the telephone in his left hand, his tomato juice in his right, said, "Hello, Pete. This is Frank. What is it?"

Lassen said, "Been a double murder on a Los Angeles yacht, Frank. Man by the name of Stearne who owns the yacht, and a friend of his named Right. I've notified the coroner and the chief of police. Better get down here right away."

"Where are you now?"

"At the yacht club."

"What's the yacht?"

"The *Gypsy Queen II*."

8

Duryea said, "Okay, I'll be down directly," started to hang up, then said, "Oh, hello, Pete."

"Yeah."

"Where are the bodies, aboard the yacht?"

"Yes."

"Who's there? Anyone?"

"Yeah. Art Perrin, and—and here's Sam Krause coming."

Duryea said, "Don't let them move anything until I get there. Any witnesses?"

"We've got three people who know something about it. They've all been in the drink."

"All right, hold them," Duryea said.

He hung up the telephone, and finished the last of his tomato juice.

"As important as all that?" Milred asked.

"Uh huh. A double murder."

"All right, go ahead. I'll be a dutiful wife, and give you first crack at the bathroom."

"No shave, no shower," Duryea said, peeling off the coat of his pajamas, and pulling his undershirt on over his head. "Pete Lassen has pulled his usual stunt of notifying me last. The coroner was just driving up as he telephoned, and Art Perrin, the chief of police, is already on the yacht. That means he called them about half an hour ago."

Milred pulled Frank's pillow over behind her head so that she could prop herself up in bed, and said, "Hasn't he been doing a lot of that lately?"

"Uh huh," Duryea said.

"Put some powder on your face if you're not going to shave, Frank. You look ragged."

"Can't help it," he said. "Three witnesses, and all of them have been in the water."

"How did that happen?"

"I don't know. Pete didn't say."

"Frank, is it true that Oscar Romley is going to run against you?"

"Darned if I know," Duryea said, knotting his necktie. "There's been some talk of it. There are half a dozen potential candidates who'd like the job."

"Frank, that shirt's been worn and looks it. Can't you . . ."

"Haven't time to break out a clean one," he said, opening

the closet door and jerking his coat off a hanger. "What about Romley?"

"Oh, nothing. Only I saw Romley and Jerry Bellinger holding a low-voiced conversation on the street. They gave the impression of having their heads together. They started when they saw me—a guilty start like small boys in the jam when mamma opens the pantry door. Better watch your step."

"Okay. If I'm not back in a couple of hours, take the car if you want it."

"I don't want the car. I want to go back to sleep. You take the car."

Duryea said, "Be seeing you."

"You left your hat on top of the radio when we came in last night," she told him, snuggling back down into the bed. "Are you going to pull down those shades, or do I have to?"

"You have to," Duryea said. "If I'm gone all day, it'll be the only exercise you'll get." He went out through the dining room, grabbing his hat off the radio, and slamming the front door.

Quite a crowd of people were gathered at the yacht club float, staring out at the yacht. One of the city police officers was on guard, saying occasionally, "Keep moving, folks. Keep moving. Don't block the road here. Keep moving."

No one paid him the slightest attention.

The officer saw Duryea, nodded, and said, "The chief's out there with the sheriff. Guess you can take any one of these boats."

Duryea felt unusually conspicuous as he cast loose the line of a small dinghy. He wasn't particularly accomplished as an oarsman, and realized keenly the loss in political prestige which would come from catching a crab in front of this silently curious crowd.

Duryea's progress to the yacht was awkward but safe. He worked the oars entirely with an arm motion. The horizon seemed suddenly possessed of a desire to spin around in crazy circles, but eventually he reached the yacht, tied up the dinghy, and climbed aboard.

Sam Krause, the coroner, A. J. Perrin, the chief of police, and Bill Wiegart, a deputy sheriff who handled fingerprints and photography, were all on the yacht.

Duryea said, "Hello," and, although he had seen all of these men within the past forty-eight hours, went through the formality of shaking hands, as though a murder had in some way interrupted their relationship and made this meeting something in the nature of a reunion.

He went down into the cabin and regarded the two sprawled figures. His stomach, never very strong in the morning, became decidedly squeamish. He knew that presently he was going to be sick.

"Where are the witnesses?" he asked Lassen.

"In the pilot house up forward."

"I'll go talk with them," he said, and it sounded to him as though the words came through his clenched teeth. He turned and hurriedly sought the air; but even the freshness of the ocean breeze and the warm sunlight couldn't erase what he had seen from his mind. He didn't want to talk with the witnesses. He didn't want to talk with anyone.

"Kinda tough," the sheriff said, joining him.

Duryea nodded, said, "I hadn't had breakfast. It's too much for an empty stomach. How many witnesses are there?"

"Three: man by the name of Shale, a salesman; girl by the name of Harpler from another yacht—she's the one in the bathing suit. Girl by the name of Nita Moline, easy on the eyes, came up from Los Angeles on invitation to join Stearne on a yachting party. Knows both of them, has an alibi, if what she says is true. They've all been in the drink. Guess I'd better go in with you and introduce you. Addison Stearne was the man lying on his back with his eyes open. The younger fellow was C. Arthur Right. Okay, let's go."

The sheriff performed the introductions.

Duryea said wearily, "Tell me what you know. Hit the high spots. I'll ask questions about details. Which one of you is Miss Moline?"

The golden-haired girl nodded.

"You first," Duryea said.

"I'm acquainted with both Mr. Right and Mr. Stearne. I'm —we were all good friends. They came up here yesterday. Addison told me he was going to give the crew twenty-four hours' leave after he tied up. . . . Listen, I've got to go get some dry clothes on. I'm cold."

"In just a minute. What time did you get here?"

"An hour or so ago. I don't know the exact time. The skiff

for the yacht was tied up at the float. I got in and rowed to the yacht. I rather expected someone would take the painter and help me aboard. No one showed up. I got aboard by myself, and tied up the skiff. I thought at first they were all asleep, then I looked down in the cabin and—I came up. I—I remember leaning over the rail. The next I remember I was sitting up in a boat. These two people were with me."

Duryea asked, "When did you last see them alive?"

"I hadn't seen Arthur for a couple of days. I saw Addison yesterday morning just before he left. I drove him down to the yacht harbor. . . . I simply can't stand these clothes any longer!"

"Why didn't you come up on the yacht?"

"I had an appointment at the hairdresser's and some other things to do. I've told the sheriff all this."

"What time did you leave Los Angeles?"

"It was real early, right around six o'clock."

Duryea turned to the other young woman. "You're Miss Harpler?" he asked.

"Joan Harpler."

"What do you know about it?"

"Nothing."

Shale met Duryea's eyes. He said, "I think this is a damned outrage, keeping us here while we're all sopping wet. I can tell you my story in a few words. I got up early this morning, went down to the beach to take a walk, saw Miss Moline come out of the cabin and fall overboard. I grabbed the first boat I came to that had oars and oarlocks in it, and rowed out to rescue her. Miss Harpler got there just about the same time I did. Together, we got her in the skiff. I knew she belonged on this yacht, and thought there was probably someone here who'd be interested in what had happened. I went aboard to find out, and saw the two bodies down in a cabin. I didn't go down. That's all I know."

"You don't live here?" Duryea asked.

"No."

"Where do you live?"

Shale hesitated, said, "I travel."

"A salesman?"

"Yes."

"Whom are you with now?"

12

"The Freelander Pasteboard Products Company."

"What brought you here?"

"Business."

"Now when you came to the yacht, was there any small skiff or boat . . ."

"Yes, that one tied up to the rail."

"That was the one in which I came aboard," Miss Moline said. "And if you don't realize it, it's *dreadfully* cold here."

"Just one or two more questions," Duryea said. "The yacht came up here yesterday?"

"That's right."

"Was Mr. Right aboard when you drove Mr. Stearne down to the yacht club at Los Angeles?"

"No. He hadn't showed up then, and I didn't wait. I had a beauty-shop appointment."

"I suppose you can prove all of this."

Her eyes were scornful. "Naturally."

"Where can I reach you, Miss Harpler?"

"I'll be aboard my yacht, the *Albatross*."

"You, Miss Moline?"

"As soon as I can leave here, I want to go back to Los Angeles."

"What's your residence there?"

"Six-o-nine Maplehurst Apartments."

"And you?" Duryea asked of Shale.

"I'm at the Balboa Hotel."

"How long do you intend to remain there?"

"Not very long."

"You'll be there all day today?"

"No. I'm leaving."

"I'm going to have to ask you to stay over at least one more day."

Shale said, "It costs money to stay here. I can't afford to . . ."

Duryea said, "I can probably make arrangements with the hotel. The county isn't very generous with me on such matters. The supervisors adopt the position that we maintain a proper boarding house."

"The jail?"

"Yes."

"Surely, you're not going to . . ."

"That's just it," Duryea said. "We have a wing on the jail we call a detention ward, but it's part of the jail just the same. You're a material witness. I don't want you to leave here until after I've checked into this a little more fully."

"There's not much chance I could walk along the beach and kill . . ."

"I'm not accusing you of anything. I'm simply telling you I want you to stay as a material witness."

"For heaven's sake," Miss Moline said, "quit arguing with him. I'll pay your expenses at the hotel. Listen, there's some whiskey in the liquor closet, and . . ."

"I don't think it's wise to touch anything," Duryea said.

She flared at him, said, *"You* wouldn't!" stamped a soggy foot, and raised fingers to the fastening of her slacks. "I'm going to get out of these clothes right now."

Duryea said hastily, "That's all. You may all go."

Joan Harpler said to Nita Moline, "Suppose you come over to my yacht. I can fix you up with some clothes."

"Thanks. They'll be more than welcome," Miss Moline said.

There was a moment's silence. Joan Harpler looked at Ted Shale. "I suppose there's no way I could—I'm sorry."

Ted laughed. "Forget it. I'm on my way to the hotel."

CHAPTER 3

FRANK DURYEA stopped in at a restaurant on the road home for a cup of coffee. He noticed that his hand was shaking slightly as he poured a spoonful of sugar into the steaming liquid. Well, after all, he told himself, he'd been up until three o'clock, had rolled out at nine, and then had this murder case dumped into his lap. He felt pretty shaky. The hot coffee revived him somewhat.

Driving home, he found himself thinking of a dozen questions he should have asked the witnesses. However, it wouldn't have been wise to keep them there in their wet clothes. If one should turn out to be suspect, a clever lawyer could make a grandstand play to the jury by harping on how the accused had been kept standing in wet clothes while being interrogated, first by the sheriff, and then by the district attorney.

Duryea rounded the corner, swung wide for his driveway, and then, with an exclamation of surprise, slammed on the brakes and stopped the car. A somewhat dilapidated-looking automobile and a house trailer which bore the unmistakable stamp of being what was known in the trade as "a backyard job" were parked in his driveway.

Duryea parked his car parallel to the curb, got out, and walked up the steps of his bungalow, regarding the visiting car and trailer dubiously.

Milred, attired in sharkskin slacks, came to the door. Ignoring the fact that he already had his latchkey in the lock, she made quite a ceremony of opening the front door.

"Why, hello, Frank! I didn't expect you'd be back so soon. Guess who's here?"

Her voice was raised sufficiently to be distinctly audible to a visitor who was in the living room, and she accompanied her question with the distress signal of a lowered right eyelid—a wink so violent that it twisted up the right-hand corner of her mouth.

Duryea winked back and raised his voice. "Gosh, I don't know. *Who* is here?"

"Gramps."

Duryea looked blank.

"You remember. Grandfather Wiggins. I've told you about him. You never met him, though. He was down in Mexico when we were married. Remember? He . . ."

Duryea heard quick steps coming across the living room, then an under-sized man with twinkling eyes, white hair, a close-cropped white mustache, and quick motions, so spry they seemed birdlike, came bearing down on him.

"It's all right, my boy! She's trying to break it to you easy. I'm bad news, but I ain't goin' to stay. Got Milred up out o' bed on a Sunday when she wanted to sleep, that's what I did! Just a damned old nuisance. She said you'd been up until three or four o'clock this morning makin' whoopee. More power to you. Didn't think you had it in you. Thought you was pantywaist. Heard you was district attorney, an' thought you'd be somethin' of a stick. How are you, son?" Grandpa Wiggins shot out his right hand, shook hands, said, "Turn around to the light. Let's have a look at you."

Duryea saw twinkling blue eyes surveying him through

steel-rimmed glasses, eyes framed in a network of kindly crow's-feet. "Look all right," Wiggins said. "Damn it, you look human. Had any breakfast?"

"Not yet," Duryea said. "We'll go out and get something. The maid's off for a couple of days, and . . ."

"Have breakfast with me," Wiggins said. "No use spendin' money at a restaurant. I'm the black sheep o' the Wiggins family, but I'm a good cook. I'll go cook up some breakfast. Good idea—mighty good! I'll get out an' Milred'll give you the dirt on me. I've been a heller, an' I ain't reformed yet. I'm the rollin' stone that's gathered no moss. All right, folks, when you hear me beatin' on the bottom of a fryin' pan, that'll mean breakfast's ready. Nothin' fancy, now. Just plain wholesome grub, but it'll do you good."

He nodded three or four times, beaming at them, then turned and darted across the living room, through the dining room, and out to the kitchen. Duryea had a departing glimpse of fast-moving legs, of baggy, somewhat frayed trousers, surmounted by a completely disreputable sweater.

When the bang of the back door announced their guest had left the house, Milred looked up at him. "Well, that's it, Frank. *That's* the family skeleton in the Wiggins closet."

Duryea asked, "What do we do with him?"

She said, "We don't do anything with him. No one ever has yet. The question is what he's going to do with us. He's capable of darn near anything. Honestly, Frank, I never thought you'd have to see him. That's why I never told you more about him. He doesn't like cops or the law, and, knowing you were a district attorney, I thought he'd give you a wide berth."

Duryea grinned. "What's he done?"

"Oh, everything and nothing. I think he did a little bootlegging once. He hates conventional things. He likes people who are—well, sort of on the fringe. He's always getting chummy with some down-and-outer. The last time I saw him, he was telling about a bank robber he knew, said he was a splendid chap—that the only difference between whether you robbed a bank or whether the bank robbed you was which one got there first. He's simply impossible, Frank—and yet he's likeable."

Duryea said, "I thought he had some mining property down in Mexico."

16

"He did. They took it away from him. He has some sort of an annuity that keeps him going. He just doesn't care enough about money to be bothered with it. Frank, I'll get rid of him by tomorrow, but if it isn't too much, can you put up with him today?"

Duryea slid his arm around her shoulders. "Sure thing, hon. Why shouldn't I put up with him? He's your family."

"I know, but he's so thoroughly unpredictable, and—gosh, you just can't tell what he'll do. I remember Dad telling stories about him. Dad was methodical and prudent, and—well, I think Grandfather hated him—said he took after his mother's side of the family."

"Where in the world did he get that trailer?" Duryea asked. "And where's he been?"

"He made the trailer himself, and he's been everywhere. I tell you, Frank, he has the weirdest assortment of friends and cronies scattered around the country, and . . ."

Duryea patted his wife's shoulder. "Listen, babe, you're all worked up. Sure, I'll like him—only we'll have to put him in the guest room, and get that trailer out of the neighborhood."

"You won't get Gramps Wiggins out of the trailer," she said. "That's his. It's his home."

"Been in it yet?" Duryea asked.

"No. He only got here about half an hour ago, and I kept him waiting while I bathed and dressed."

"Reminds me, I'm going to shave."

"You'd better hurry," she warned, "because Gramps moves like chain lightning. He's never able to stay put. Heaven knows what he'll cook for breakfast, but it won't be long before he'll be beating on the bottom of that frying pan."

Her husband made a grimace. "And me with a head," he observed. "Better go out and head off that frying pan business, Milred. The neighbors might not like it."

"Okay, you hurry with your shaving. I'll do my best. But if he says he's going to beat on a frying pan, it's my own private opinion that he's going to beat on a frying pan."

Duryea went into the bathroom, ran an electric razor quickly over his face, took two aspirin tablets, and was combing his hair when he heard the unmistakable sound of a heavy spoon beating against the bottom of a frying pan.

He hurried out through the kitchen to find Wiggins standing in the door, grinning. Milred was holding his arm. "Please don't do it any more, Gramps."

"Why not? What's the matter?"

"The neighbors might not like it."

"Why not?"

"Well, it's—you see, Frank has a position to maintain."

Gramps Wiggins surveyed the district attorney of Santa Delbarra County. "Shucks," he said, "come on in, son, and sit." Duryea entered the trailer.

It showed unmistakably that it was purely a masculine contraption, but it was scrupulously clean. The interior had been arranged with great efficiency and gave evidence of unusual mechanical ability on the part of its designer. Every inch of space was utilized to advantage. A gasoline stove was hissing a blue flame under a battered teakettle. On the table were three cups, three plates containing bacon, scrambled eggs, and buttered toast. Wiggins poured clear, golden-brown coffee from a tin coffee pot. "Milred tells me you're feelin' kinda low."

The district attorney nodded.

Wiggins swooped down under the table, jerked open a closet door, came up with a bottle, and poured a generous portion into Duryea's coffee cup, dumped a similar load into his own, and looked inquiringly at Milred.

"What is it?" Duryea asked suspiciously.

"Fix you right up," Wiggins said. "Put it in coffee, and it makes you feel good right away. How about it, Milred?"

She made a gesture of surrender. "Go to it, Gramps."

He poured some in her cup, shoved the cork back in the bottle, and dove down out of sight. During the interval while he was storing the bottle, Milred leaned over and sniffed the concoction in the coffee cup, then she looked up at her husband and rolled her eyes.

Wiggins popped up into view. "All right, folks, let's go! Food's gettin' cold. Sit down and dig in. Don't stand on formality. Drink your coffee first. It'll warm you up."

Duryea tried his coffee. The smell of rich brandy mingling with the coffee odor soothed his nostrils. He tasted the concoction, said to Wiggins with sudden respect in his voice, "Say, what *is* that stuff?"

"Best brandy on earth," Gramps said. "A friend o' mine

18

mails it to me. Got a vineyard up in Northern California. I'm on my way to see him. This is old, old stuff. Keeps it just for his friends."

Duryea took a deep swig of the coffee, picked up a wooden-handled fork, and tentatively tried the eggs. An expression of pleased surprise came over his face. He raised a piece of toast and conveyed a large forkful of eggs to his mouth.

"Told you he'd like it," Wiggins said to Milred, then to Duryea, "That's my own private recipe for scrambled eggs."

Duryea said, "Don't think I'm a dissipated hulk, Gramps, just because I've got the shakes this morning. My stomach's been looping the loop. You see, I was called out early this morning . . ."

Milred coughed.

Duryea stopped, thinking over what he had said. That cough was certainly a warning signal, but it couldn't have been because of anything he had said. He wondered if it was because of something he had done.

Grandfather Wiggins was waiting, with his head tilted slightly on one side as though to hear better. "Yep," he said, "you was called out this morning. What was it?"

"A very gruesome double murder," Duryea explained. "The bodies were . . ."

"A murder!" Gramps Wiggins shrilled.

Duryea nodded.

"Gee gosh!" Wiggins exclaimed, then turned reproachfully to Milred. "Why didn't you tell me?"

She looked across at her husband. "Why, I didn't—I just didn't think of it."

"Didn't think of it! Me droppin' right in on a murder case, a real, honest-to-goodness murder case, an' you not thinkin' about it! Gee gosh!"

Milred explained belatedly, "Gramps is a mystery addict."

"I'll say I'm a mystery addict," Gramps Wiggins said. He stepped back from the table, swung open the doors of a locker, showed shelves packed with books, and magazines. "Here you are. Best mystery stories published during the last ten years, and clippings from the *True Detective* magazines about crimes I happen to know somethin' about. Makes it interestin'. Read about a crime in a paper, then after a while, an article will come out in one of these *True Detective* magazines. I clip it out an' fasten 'em all together. Lots o' times I'll sit up nights with newspaper accounts of a crime, tryin' to work out a solution. You'd be s'prised how often I hit it, too. Well, well, so we've got a murder, have we?"

"Two murders," Duryea said, somewhat lamely, fully conscious of the implications of the plural pronoun.

"Well, now," Gramps Wiggins announced, "I guess Milred's marryin' a district attorney ain't goin' to be so bad after all. I'm stayin' right here an' helpin' you solve 'em, son. You can count on me."

"Thanks," Duryea said dryly, "but I won't need to bother you, Gramps. I have the sheriff, you see."

"Sheriff!" the old man exclaimed. "Sheriff! Sheriff, hell! You've got *me!*"

Milred looked across at her husband. "Drink your coffee, dear," she said, "and then let Gramps fill your cup again. You'll probably need it."

CHAPTER 4

TED SHALE's suitcase yielded a pair of slacks and a sport shirt. He donned these. The coat of his single-breasted business suit had not been in the water, and he put it on.

His wet trousers, shirt, tie, and underwear he immersed in a bathtub filled with lukewarm water, manipulating the garments until the salty water had been rinsed from them. Then he drained the bathtub and hung the garments out to dry above the tub. The monotonous *drip-drip-drip* which fell on the porcelain furnished a mournful cadence which kept pace with his thoughts. The sales manager of the Freelander Pasteboard Products Company would hardly approve of having his salesman marooned in a Santa Delbarra hotel.

The telephone rang.

Ted picked up the receiver. A feminine voice said, "Mr. Shale?"

"Yes."

"Dressed to receive visitors?"

"Who is this?"

"Miss Moline."

"How about you?"

"Thanks to borrowed plumage, I'm all fixed up. As it happens, Miss Harpler and I seem to have identical measurements."

"Where are you?"

"At the yacht club. I presume your hotel would object to feminine callers in your room, but I know a nice cocktail lounge. You looked awfully cold when I last saw you. I'd like to get something that would counteract the effects of that chill. After all, you know, you saved my life and . . ."

"Yes, yes, go on," Ted interrupted, laughing.

"Suppose I drive by in about ten minutes?"

"I'll be waiting at the curb," Ted promised.

"Be seeing you," she said and hung up.

Ted slipped on his coat once more, adjusted the collar of his sport shirt, gave himself a somewhat dubious glance in the mirror, combed back his hair, and went down to the lobby.

Ted had made no explanations when he had entered the hotel in his wet clothes, and the clerk looked at him curiously. "Everything all right, Mr. Shale?"

"Quite."

"I thought perhaps you had . . . that is . . ."

"No, I hadn't." Ted smiled and walked on past the clerk to loiter around the entrance of the hotel, watching the cars that purred past. At that, he nearly missed her. He had hardly been prepared for the cream-colored sport coupe which slid out of the traffic lane and paused for a moment, its motor whispering a song of controlled power—a whisper which could quite evidently become a deep-throated roar of speed.

She was in slacks, a silk sport blouse and a chic red jacket with wide lapels. She had combed her wet hair back from her forehead, and tied it with a ribbon in the back. The effect was to make her look younger, less sophisticated.

She saw him, waved, then leaned across the front seat to open the wide door as Ted jumped to the running board and stepped in. As he swung the door shut, he had the satisfaction of noticing the curious hotel clerk staring with surprised incredulity. One would hardly expect salesmen who came in soaking wet to be picked up by attractive young women driving five-thousand-dollar automobiles.

"Did you get chilled?" she asked.

"No. The only mortality seems to have been suffered by my wardrobe. How about you?"

"I'm fine. Joan Harpler furnished a drink. It tasted so good I thought something should be done about you—and I wanted to talk with you."

"Talk ahead."

"Well, really I meant I wanted to be talked to. I'm jittery. That hit me a terrific wallop. You see, I knew both of those men. Don't let me get talking about that—please don't. And if I start crying, slap me. Will you promise?"

He shook his head.

She frowned. "I hope I haven't made a mistake in you. When I was screaming, you told me to shut up. I didn't do it because I just couldn't. Well, you slapped me, and it did me a lot of good. It's the first time . . ."

"Let's not talk about it. I'm sorry."

"Sorry! That's why I came to you, because of that slap. Will you hit me again if I start crying?"

"No."

She frowned across at him.

"I'm sorry, but it takes a major emergency to give me the necessary incentive."

"Oh, well, perhaps you're just being polite. After all, my jaw's still sore where you hit me. And please let's have no misunderstanding, Mr. Shale. The check is on me."

"Oh, but . . ."

"But me no buts," she interrupted. "And in case your masculine vanity makes you feel it's undignified to have women paying the check, I'm entrusting you with this."

She passed her hand over to Ted's. A warm, folded bit of paper was left in his hand as her fingers were withdrawn.

"Now, wait a minute," Ted protested. "After all, I'm not . . ."

She interrupted, "It's plain business. I need an escort, and you need a drink."

"I'm not a professional escort."

"Get your hair down, Rover," she said. "Don't start fighting."

Ted said, "I'm not fighting, just trying to keep a little self-respect. I could use a drink, but I'm not keen on going places

22

with a million dollars' worth of class in tow, and not being able to pay the freight."

"Now listen, I'm in a spot. . . . Someone, I think it's the Chinese, claim that if one person interferes to save the life of another, he's obligated thereafter to the one whose life he saved, on the theory that if he had let Fate takes its course, it would have all been over. Well, I'm calling on you to fulfill your obligation. I'm in a mess. And I'm pretty much broken up. Now then, will you, or won't you?"

"Okay, I will," Ted surrendered. "But my clothes . . ."

"Oh, forget that. We'll go to a really swank place. The more freakish you look there, the better service they give you. They'll think you must be a Hollywood director. What have you been doing, and how come you're representing this pasteboard company?"

"I'm selling paper cups because I thought I saw a chance to go in business for myself. I hocked everything I had to make a go of it."

"And?" she asked.

"And with keen business sagacity, an acumen which is doubtless destined some day to make me a millionaire, the business I selected to go into was—guess?"

"What?"

"Aluminum kitchenware."

"Oh-oh!"

"And so," Ted went on, "after I'd finally built up a good will that was a real asset, what with the factory notifying me that no more supplies would be available, and even refusing to fill some of the orders on which I'd already counted the commission, I found myself 'temporarily embarrassed.' "

"And then?"

"I got a job with the Freelander Pasteboard Products Company. . . . Say, why am I wallowing in all these details, anyway? Ordinarily, I never bare my soul to a girl until after the second drink."

"Under those circumstances," she announced, swinging her car up a graveled driveway, "let's not waste any time with the preliminaries incident to the first."

She surrendered the car to a young man in livery who spoke to her, Ted thought, as though he knew her. She took Ted's arm and said, "You'll find this place rather nice." Ted felt quite certain that the headwaiter knew her well enough to call her by name, but that there was something in the warning glance she gave him which prevented him from doing so. Ted also realized that, as the escort of this young woman, he was being treated with great deference.

When they were seated in a little private alcove with its own window overlooking the sweep of a crescent beach, the white, serrated lines of incoming surf, and the tranquil turquoise of the ocean, she said suddenly, "You can't turn back the hands of the clock. You've got to keep facing forward as you go through life, and take things as they come."

Ted said, "That's what makes life hard—and interesting."

The waiter brought them a wine list.

"They have some very fine brandy here," she said. "A double brandy would do us both good. How about it?"

Ted nodded. The waiter deferentially withdrew.

"I have the feeling that *you're* something of a soldier of fortune," she said.

"I like to plunge," he admitted.

"Perhaps you'd like to do something for me."

"Perhaps."

She was thoughtfully silent for a brief space. The waiter brought their drinks. She touched her glass to his, said, "Here's to . . ." and then her voice suddenly choked. Ted said, "Forget it. It's over. Keep facing forward." She blinked back tears. They sipped the brandy. Abruptly, she said, "I think the best way to get anywhere with you is to come directly to the point."

He nodded.

"What were you doing on the beach this morning?"

"Getting exercise and fresh air."

"How long had you been there before—before I fell overboard?"

"Oh, perhaps an hour."

"Surely you hadn't been walking up and down that same stretch of sand for an hour?"

"I'd been in the general vicinity."

"Near the yacht club?"

"Yes."

"Where you could have seen anyone go aboard the *Gypsy Queen?*"

"Yes."

24

"Look, let's be frank with each other. You're representing a paper company. Addison Stearne has a chain of hotels. He told me he was going to put in a large order for some supplies. Was your trip to Santa Delbarra in any way connected with that business?"

"Yes."

"Had you seen Stearne?"

"No."

"You were on the beach waiting for him?"

"Well—yes."

"You were watching for him to come ashore?"

"Yes."

She frowned down at the brandy glass. "Yet you didn't see *me* go aboard? What I'm getting at," she went on with a rush of hurried words after a brief pause, "is that there must have been *some* period when you had your attention distracted, or when you weren't in a position to watch the yacht."

"Well, yes," he admitted, "about fifteen or twenty minutes before I noticed you on the yacht, I became interested in a shell. I examined it closely for two or three minutes."

"And during that time, you weren't watching. That is, you weren't where you could see anyone who happened to get aboard the yacht."

"I guess that's right."

"That was fifteen or twenty minutes before you saw me?"

"Yes."

She nodded her head with quick emphasis. "That would make it just about right. In fact, I think I remember seeing you. You were crouched over—or kneeling or sitting down, holding something in your hand, and . . ."

"I was kneeling, looking down at the shell. I didn't pick it up because there seemed to be something in it."

"But you were holding your hand near it?"

"Probably."

"Yes. I remember seeing you—just in a general way. That was when I was casting off the skiff and going out to the yacht."

He asked suddenly, "What is it that you want me to do for you?"

"I want to know who goes aboard the *Gypsy Queen* during the next three or four days."

25

"Just during the days?"

"No. All of the time."

"That all?"

"Yes."

He laughed and said, "I'm afraid I'd have to be twins, standing out on that beach . . ."

"Oh, but you wouldn't have to. While I was aboard the *Albatross*—Miss Harpler's yacht, you know—I made arrangements with her to co-operate. She said she'd be glad to until I could make other arrangements. She said you could come on board her yacht and watch from there."

"You told her that I was going to do it?" Shale asked.

"Well, not exactly. I told her I wanted to have someone watch the yacht, that I was particularly interested in finding out who went aboard, and how long they stayed. I think she was the one who mentioned that you might be available."

"I'm afraid you've failed to take into consideration the fact that I'm working on a job. The sales manager of the Freelander Pasteboard . . ."

"He wants you to get the order for that hotel business, doesn't he?"

"Yes."

"Well, this would be working on it."

"I don't get you."

"You see, I'm going to have something to say about how the estate is managed. I can't give you all the details, but I'll have some voice in the business of the estate—directly or indirectly. Your company doesn't care where the order comes from. These hotels are going to keep right on using paper, you know."

He said cautiously, "If the sales manager could be convinced that you were . . ."

"Anyhow, the district attorney told you to wait here. You can't leave. If you do this for me, I'll do all I can to get you a whopping big paper order. Is it a bargain?"

Shale thought it over. "The district attorney told me to stay on at the Balboa Hotel. He'd hardly understand it if I went out to live on the yacht."

"That'll be all right. You can call the hotel for messages, ring the desk clerk four or five times a day."

"Suppose I don't know the persons who get on and off the yacht? What do I do then? Try to follow them?"

"No. Get a good description, the time they went aboard, the time they left, and whether they brought anything out with them. I'll give you a pair of very fine night binoculars. Use them. Try to be able to identify those people when you see them again."

"When does this start?" asked Ted.

"As soon as you've finished your drink."

Shale said, "It's a bargain."

"That's splendid. Please don't go back to your hotel. Just get in the car, and we'll drive down to the *Albatross*."

"Why don't you want me to return to the hotel?"

"Because if you do, someone's going to trace you to the yacht."

"I left some clothes in my room. I wanted to have them pressed as soon as they were dry."

"That's all right. You can telephone the hotel. The valet will go up and get your things. I'll telephone for you while you're paying the check. Where are they?"

"Hanging over the bathtub."

"No, no," she said as he made to rise, "stay right where you are. Get the check from the waiter and pay it. Then we won't lose any time."

She entered the telephone booth and pulled the door shut behind her. The waiter, hovering about, brought the check at Ted's signal. Shale took from his pocket the folded bank note Nita Moline had given him. It was a fifty-dollar bill.

CHAPTER 5

GEORGE V. HAZLIT, who for years had been Addison Stearne's lawyer, made it a point to cultivate an air of judicial dignity. With it, he was able to impress nearly all of his clients and many of his fellow members at the bar. He frequently served on committees of the Bar Association, impressing upon one and all that he was only too glad to donate his time for the betterment of the profession. These activities clothed him with an aura of professional respectability which was one of Hazlit's most valuable assets. Things which an ordinary attorney might do at his peril could be carried off by such a prominent and influential member of the bar with impunity. The few persons who ever saw evidences of irregularities either dismissed their conclusions as being unworthy of belief, or else felt that they were not acquainted with the entire circumstances.

Neldon Tucker, the junior partner, was a quick-witted opportunist. His greatest asset was his voice. Nature had given him vocal cords which enabled him to put just the right amount of irony, of sarcasm, or of amazed incredulity into his voice—just enough so that the jury and courtroom spectators would consider it the spontaneous and unconscious reflex of a genuine emotion. Other attorneys over-acted. Neldon Tucker never even seemed to be acting.

Tucker breezed through the courtrooms, handling trial after trial with the rapidity of an omnivorous legal machine. He didn't win all of his cases, but he won most of them. Those he didn't win, he didn't worry about. If he had paused to take stock of himself, he would have realized that he usually went into court only about half prepared, trusting to his ingenuity, his versatility, and his acting to make up for the lack of preparation.

George Hazlit, ensconced in his private office, frowned as he dialed the telephone. For more than an hour now, he had been fruitlessly spinning the dial of that telephone at frequent intervals. His face still wore its carefully cultivated expression of calm judicial impassivity, but there was a gathering frown on his forehead.

Outside, dusk settled on the street. Hazlit switched on the lights, dialed Exbrook 95621. After a few minutes, there came to his ears the faint sounds which indicated that the phone at the other end of the line was ringing steadily. If his party just happened to be returning home, fumbling perhaps with the doorkey, it would take some little time to reach the phone. So Hazlit waited for a good thirty seconds before dropping the receiver back into its cradle. Then he pushed back his chair, got up, and walked over to stare out into the gathering darkness. The office buildings in the downtown business section showed dark and gloomy. On a Sunday night there were hardly any lights showing in offices. There was, of course, plenty of traffic. It had been a fine day, and city dwellers had taken advantage of it. A steady stream of motorists flowed by beneath Hazlit's window. Surely Neldon Tucker would be headed for home by this time, and Parker Gibbs, who did detective work for the firm, would certainly be in soon. His wife had said she expected him any minute.

Hazlit had left word at the apartment house where Ethel Dunn, his secretary, lived, that she was to call him just as soon as she got in. There was, therefore, nothing for Hazlit to do except wait—and that was hardest of all. He could feel his nerves cracking under the strain. So much to do, and he couldn't even get started—just because Addison Stearne had seen fit to die on a Sunday.

Abruptly the phone rang. He snatched the receiver from the hook, but his eagerness automatically masked itself behind the dignity of his voice. "Good evening," he proclaimed. "This is Mr. Hazlit speaking."

It was Ethel Dunn. "You wanted me?" she asked, and there was just the trace of sullen defiance in her voice. Hazlit realized that what they were paying her was hardly commensurate with the long years she'd been with the firm. There had been only one raise during the entire period. He'd have to do something about that. No use in having a secretary who was dissatisfied. It might be dangerous. Into the telephone he said gravely, "Yes, Miss Dunn. A matter of the greatest importance makes it necessary for me to get in touch with Neldon Tucker. His residence doesn't answer. I wonder if you know anything about his plans for the week end."

"No. I haven't any idea where he is."

"You don't know where he intended . . ."

"No."

"Just a minute," Hazlit said hastily, sensing she was in a hurry, probably dashing out on some date, and thinking only of a quick shower and change. "This is a matter of the *greatest* importance. Think carefully, Ethel. See if you can't recall something he may have said."

Her answer came back so quickly that he knew his admonition to think had been entirely wasted. "I don't know a thing."

"Do you know the names of any of his most intimate friends?"

"You might try the Mainwarings."

29

"What's the first name?"

"I don't know. They live out on Buena Vista somewhere close to where Mr. Tucker lives. Those are the only ones I can think of. Good . . ."

"You haven't heard him speak of going anywhere, of any dates or plans?"

"No. I'm quite positive. Good-by."

Hazlit dropped the receiver into place, looked up the Mainwarings in the telephone book, dialed their number, and was rather surprised when he heard someone answer. He had been making so many fruitless calls this afternoon, it seemed odd when a voice actually responded.

"This is George V. Hazlit," he said impressively. "I'm trying to locate my junior partner, Neldon Tucker, and `. . ."

"Why, yes, he's here," the woman said.

Hazlit couldn't keep gratified surprise from his voice. "He's there?"

"Yes. Just a moment, I'll call him."

Hazlit, holding the telephone, could hear the sound of steps, then Tucker's voice. He knew as soon as he heard Tucker say, "Hello, George," that he'd been drinking.

"I'm up at the office, Neldon. There's a matter of the greatest importance. You'll have to come right away."

"Oh, I say," Tucker protested, "they're going to have dinner in about fifteen minutes. We're just having cocktails and . . ."

"Right away," Hazlit interpolated. "It's a large fee, a very large fee, which may slip through our fingers. It may amount to a cool hundred thousand."

"My car's outside. I'll be right up," Tucker promised. "I'll . . ."

"Neldon."

"Yes?"

"You've been drinking. We can't afford to take any chances. Don't drive. Take a taxi."

Hazlit hung up, walked over to the window once more, and stood looking down at the restless traffic. He looked at his watch. It should take Tucker about five minutes to get a cab, then it would take twenty-five minutes to get to the office. That would make half an hour.

It was as though Hazlit's luck had turned all at once. The

telephone rang again. This time it was Parker Gibbs. Speaking with his characteristic rapidity, Gibbs said, "The wife tells me you've been calling."

"Can you come up here right away?"

"How soon is right away?"

"Within half an hour."

"Make it forty-five minutes," Gibbs said. "I've just got back from deep-sea fishing, and I'm a mess. Going to be a big job?"

"I think so, yes. I'll explain the details when you get here."

"Okay, I'll make it as soon as I can," Gibbs said and hung up.

Hazlit walked over to his big easy chair, stretched out his legs, and lit a cigar. He was finishing the last of the cigar when he heard Tucker's key in the lock.

Tucker was still flushed with drink, but he had himself well under control. He was, Hazlit reflected, drinking a bit too much lately—and getting a little careless about his appearance. Hazlit decided to speak to Tucker about it at a more propitious moment.

"Hello, George, what's the rumpus?"

Hazlit said, "Close the door."

When Neldon had closed and locked the door, Hazlit beckoned him closer. He said in a low voice, "Addison Stearne's dead."

Tucker raised his eyebrows. "When?"

"Apparently, last night sometime. The body was discovered this morning. He was murdered."

"Murdered!"

"Yes."

"Where?"

"Up at Santa Delbarra. He and C. Arthur Right. It was a double murder."

"Any clues?"

"I don't think so."

"Any idea what it was all about?"

Hazlit said, "I don't know. We'll leave that to the authorities. You remember I drew a will for Stearne about two months ago. Under the terms of that will, he left most of his property to C. Arthur Right with some specific bequests for a Miss Nita Moline."

Tucker said, "I wasn't familiar with the will. You handled Stearne's business. I only knew you'd drawn a will."

Hazlit said, "It provided, among other things, that if C. Arthur Right should die first, all the property was to go to Nita Moline."

"Rather prophetic, wasn't it?" Tucker asked.

Hazlit said, "I've put similar provisions in a good many wills. I advise clients that the persons who are so close to them as to be objects of their bounty may well be riding in an automobile with the testators and be in an accident. One will survive the other only by a few hours."

"I see. Where does that leave us in this case?"

"From all I can learn so far," Hazlit said, "there's no evidence to show which one of the men died first. We've simply got to handle that estate. We're out of luck if Stearne died first. Right's wife, Pearl Right, hates the very ground I walk on. I told Right I thought she'd bear watching. He mentioned to me that every time he went out on a trip, he could never get her on the phone when he called. I suggested he hire detectives to shadow her. The damn fool told her what I'd said. And, as if that weren't bad enough, I've never met Miss Moline."

Tucker showed that he understood by giving a low-pitched whistle.

"I have Miss Moline's address," Hazlit went on. "It's the Maplehurst Apartments. She isn't in. She left there very early this morning, and the young man at the desk said he understood she was joining some friends on a yachting party."

"Oh-oh!" Tucker muttered. "How'd you get the tip-off on the deaths, George?"

"I happened to tune in on a news broadcast about an hour ago. This is a situation I hadn't anticipated. I had—well, I'd purposely refrained from cultivating Miss Moline. I thought it was better that way."

"You mean you expected a heart-balm suit?"

"Yes. Stearne suggested once that we should handle a matter on which she wanted legal advice. I discouraged him without telling him why. I'm afraid she may have gone to some other lawyer. If that's the case . . ." Hazlit broke off and shrugged his shoulders.

"How about Gibbs?"

"I've finally located him. He's been deep-sea fishing. He's cleaning up and should be here at any moment. There's another matter we have to consider."

"What's that?"

"Stearne had an option on some oil property. Under the terms of the agreement, yesterday was the last day in which he could take up that option."

"Did he do it?"

"I don't know."

"Who owns the property?"

"Two men, doing business under the firm name of Elwell & Fielding. They have this property leased, and Stearne had an option to take over the leases. He was to pay one hundred thousand dollars."

"Cash?"

"No. He'd obligate himself to pay the cash by the acceptance. Then he had thirty days in which to make the actual payment."

"That expired yesterday?"

"According to the copy in our files, yesterday was absolutely the last day."

"You don't know whether he took it up or not?"

"I know he intended to. There'd been some activity on adjoining property, and Stearne had become convinced they'd struck good showings and were covering up to freeze him out. He thinks another agreement had been reached, subject to Stearne not accepting his option."

"Then Elwell & Fielding were trying to manipulate things so the option would expire?"

"Yes."

Tucker knitted his brows. "If Stearne was murdered Saturday, there may be a tough legal proposition on that option."

Hazlit said, "There must be *some* legal loophole. Stearne had until midnight to make his acceptance. Sunday is a legal holiday. So is Saturday afternoon, but the option specifically waived any right to delays or extensions because of holidays. Saturday at midnight was the deadline. Perhaps that provision about waiving extensions because of holidays would be void as against public policy."

"Suppose this Moline woman has a lawyer of her own?"

"There isn't time for her to consult anyone else. *We're* ready to protect her interests."

Tucker said, "I'll get the papers ready. How about Ethel Dunn?"

Hazlit said, "She seemed sullen when I talked with her. I think she's got a date."

Tucker said, "I'll call her. She'll come for *me.*"

Tucker crossed the private office, jerked open the door to the law library, and switched on the lights.

A few moments later, Hazlit heard steps in the corridor, the gentle tapping of knuckles on the door of his private office. He crossed over, opened the door, and said, "Come in, Gibbs."

Parker Gibbs was a short, stocky man with a bony, determined face. His skin was bronzed from outdoor activities. A casual observer would have said he was a building contractor or farmer.

He walked across to a chair, his short legs moving with quick competency. He sat down and looked at Hazlit, waiting, saying nothing.

Hazlit said, "Addison Stearne, who owns *Gypsy Queen II*, was murdered in Santa Delbarra sometime yesterday. A younger man by the name of C. Arthur Right was murdered at the same time."

Gibbs pulled a notebook from his pocket, whipped out a pencil, made a quickly scribbled notation, and looked up, waiting.

Hazlit said, "If Stearne died first, most of the estate went to Arthur Right. When Arthur Right died, that half of the estate would have gone to his heirs, in this case, his wife. She hates me. If Arthur Right died first, all of Stearne's estate went to a woman named Nita Moline."

Gibbs nodded.

"Nita Moline resides at six-o-nine Maplehurst Apartments. She's out, went out this morning early, driving her car. It's a big, cream-colored sports coupe, license number 8P3036. The assumption is she went to Santa Delbarra to join the *Gypsy Queen*. She hasn't been heard from since. At the time of his death, Stearne had some property matters under negotiation. To protect the estate, some action must be taken tomorrow morning. My partner, Mr. Tucker, is going to work all night tonight getting papers ready for Miss Moline to sign. We want you to find her and have her in our office by eight o'clock tomorrow morning."

Gibbs made another note.

"After that," Hazlit said, "find some evidence that will show C. Arthur Right died before Addison Stearne."

"How long before?" Gibbs asked.

"It doesn't make any difference. An interval of one second would be enough."

"Suppose there isn't any evidence?"

Hazlit said, "If you had been listening carefully, you would have noted that I said I wanted you to find some evidence indicating Right died first."

"Come on out in the open," Gibbs said. "I want to know how far to go."

Hazlit frowned irritably. "Let me express it this way. In every business relationship, results are what count. When a person employs me to handle a lawsuit, I know he comes to me because he expects me to win that lawsuit. He doesn't care what methods I use. He doesn't care how many hours I work. He doesn't care what I say to the witnesses. He comes to me because he wants results. Of course," he added unctuously, "we want you to be entirely ethical."

Gibbs pushed back his chair. "Okay, I just wanted to know. I'm to see that there's evidence that Right died first?"

"Our client would be benefited by such proof."

CHAPTER 6

NITA MOLINE parked her car at the waterfront. The incoming tide had narrowed the sand between wall and ocean until there was no longer any strip of hard beach on which a person could walk comfortably. A cement walk skirting the edge of the sand connected with the float at the yacht club. Ted and Miss Moline walked rapidly along this cement ribbon.

A rope had been stretched across the entrance to the yacht club, and an officer, standing guard, promptly challenged Shale. "Member of the club?"

Shale said, "We're visiting a friend on one of the yachts. She's a member."

"What's the yacht?"

"The *Albatross*."

The officer pulled a typewritten list from his pocket, consulted it, and asked, "What's the name of your friend?"

"Miss Harpler," Nita Moline interposed. "Joan Harpler. She's expecting us."

The officer checked the name of the owner of the yacht on his list, said, "Okay, go ahead," and untied one end of the rope. Ted stood to one side, and Miss Moline preceded him through the opening.

They walked out on the landing float. A faint breeze was blowing from the sea now, and the ends of Miss Moline's hair blew about her neck as they stood waiting.

Nita Moline said confidently, "Her dinghy's tied up to the stern of the *Albatross*. She'll catch our signal in a minute." Taking a white handkerchief from her purse, Miss Moline waved it up and down. After a few moments, a figure detached itself from the cabin of the *Albatross*, and waved. She unfastened the painter of the dinghy, brought it up on the lee side, jumped in, and rowed over to the float.

Nita Moline said easily, "Ted Shale's going to stand watch for me. Okay by you?"

For a moment, Ted thought she hesitated perceptibly, then she said, quite easily and naturally, "Of course, I'll be glad to have him aboard—if it will help."

"How about letting me run the ferry?" Ted asked.

She surrendered the oars. "After the way you handled that skiff this morning, I'm much inclined to say yes."

Ted rowed the dinghy out to the yacht, gave a quick pull on his left oar at just the right moment, and then snapped it inboard through the oarlock so that it was out of the way as the dinghy swung broadside and came to rest a scant three inches from the side of the *Albatross*.

Joan Harpler jumped aboard with a lithe leap, her rubber-soled shoes padding on the deck as gently as the paws of a leaping cat. Nita Moline tossed her the painter, and Ted grabbed the rail of the yacht to fend off the dinghy. When the girls were both aboard, he relieved Joan Harpler of the rope, hauled the dinghy astern, and made it fast.

Miss Harpler led the way to the cabin. Up at the front was a raised platform where the person navigating the yacht could stand with his hands on the wheel, a semi-circle of wide windows giving full visibility. A shelf built in just below these windows furnished a place for charts and reference books. Ted noticed a pair of binoculars lying on the shelf. The objective lenses were particularly large. A leather strap was fastened to the glasses so that they could be suspended from the neck and held in a position of instant readiness.

Miss Harpler was completely free from self-consciousness. She had that easy informality of manner which so frequently characterizes persons who have spent much time in the close confines of a yacht.

"Well," she said, "make yourselves at home," and to Ted, "Hope you didn't get too chilled getting back to the hotel."

"Oh, I'm tough," Shale said.

"I certainly felt sorry for you when I saw you walking down the beach with your wet clothes clinging to you. I wished I'd had something aboard that would have fitted you, but there wasn't a thing."

Ted said, "I did feel rather conspicuous, but the real pay-off was when the clerk in the hotel saw me come in."

"What's doing over on the *Gypsy Queen?*" Miss Moline asked.

"Oh, lots of comings and goings, but all of them apparently are official. Men with cameras, men with bags—and just men.—I understood you didn't want descriptions of men who came aboard while the officers were there. Is that right?"

"That's right. When the officers leave, they'll lock up. I want to know everyone who goes aboard after that. Haven't been putting you to too much trouble, have I?"

"Not a bit. I've rather enjoyed it. It's probably what I'd have been doing anyway."

Miss Moline said, "We'll spell you now. Would you mind taking over, Mr. Shale?"

Ted nodded, ensconced himself in the chair behind the steering wheel. He picked up the binoculars and examined them curiously.

Miss Moline's voice underwent a subtle change. She was now very definitely in the position of an employer giving instructions. "Just keep an eye on things," she said crisply.

"Don't pay too much attention to what is happening until you see them lock up and leave. . . . Who's aboard now, Miss Harpler?"

"The sheriff is still there. The district attorney left shortly after we did, and hasn't been back. A man in police uniform has been out two or three times. I guess, altogether, there are half a dozen people aboard."

Miss Moline said to Ted, "Just sit back and take it easy. Keep an eye on things." She made an almost imperceptible gesture to Joan Harpler, and the two young women opened the door in the rear of the cabin, descended to the open cockpit, then down another companionway to a lower cabin.

Left to himself, Ted adjusted the binoculars to sharp focus, swinging them around casually, getting familiar with their balance and feel.

He realized they would be an excellent night glass. The lenses penetrated into dark shadows, furnishing sufficient illumination to show details which were entirely invisible to the naked eye. Turning them on the *Gypsy Queen*, he found he could see through the windows of the upper cabin, and occasionally even get a glimpse of motion through the portholes of the lower cabin. Watching closely, he saw a man moving about with a brush and a can of powder, in search of fingerprints. As Ted watched, the man evidently found one, for he disappeared from view and a moment later returned with a camera which he held up against the section of wall he had just dusted with powder.

For perhaps half an hour, Ted sat there keeping watch, then he heard the sound of steps on the companionway, and a moment later, the two young women joined him.

"Well?" Miss Moline asked.

"Nothing new," Ted said. "They're looking for fingerprints."

She said, "There's really nothing much to do now. I'll take over, and you can go below."

"Your stateroom's forward on the port side," Miss Harpler said. "You'll find it rather comfortable in there, just stretch out and see if you can get a little sleep. I'll call you later on. Make yourself at home, and if you want anything, simply shout."

"This is very comfortable," Ted said. "I don't feel particularly sleepy. . . ."

"You will before you've finished. You're going to have a long watch tonight," Miss Moline interposed. "See if you can get at least a few winks."

Ted, curious about the yacht, surrendered the binoculars, and went below. He found much more room than he had expected. There was a galley, a main cabin, a lavatory, and where the lines of the yacht pinched forward toward the bow, was a narrow passageway. On each side of this passageway was a door. Ted tentatively tried the door on the starboard side. It was locked. The one on the port side opened to disclose a small but comfortable stateroom, containing a built-in dresser and a wide bunk. On this bunk was a neatly folded blanket and a pillow.

Before settling himself in this stateroom, Ted moved around in the yacht, giving it a casual survey. Astern, under the cockpit, was housed the engine, a high-speed affair which took up but little room. The galley was neatly arranged. Seats in the main cabin could be turned into bunks, and a swinging table was so placed that it could be lowered from the wall.

Ted didn't feel that it would be possible for him to sleep, but he knew that the night would be a long, weary vigil. He entered the stateroom, took off shoes and coat, stretched himself on the bunk and pulled up the blanket. He closed his eyes and lay there, listening to the lazy lap of the little wind wavelets against the side of the hull. It was, he reflected, rather a large yacht for a young woman to be handling alone. She seemed so perfectly poised, so thoroughly at ease that one took her capability for granted, but even so—and that Moline girl was playing some sort of a game. She must have some suspicions which she hadn't communicated to the authorities. It had, of course, been quite a jolt to her. She wasn't the sort to give way to tears in public, but Ted felt certain she'd done some crying. There had been a swollen appearance around her eyelids, and her nose had been red, despite the powder. She hadn't attempted to make any explanation to him as to her relationship to the persons aboard the *Gypsy Queen*. . . . Certainly was restful aboard these yachts! The little splashing wavelets sounding against the hull made a man feel drowsy. . . . The yacht probably represented a bunch of money. Well, it was nice that some people had it. . . . Last night he'd hardly thought he'd be stretched out in a stateroom of a trim yacht. . . . Last night seemed far away—far away—last night—

Ted Shale wakened suddenly, realizing he had been asleep for some time. He knew that it was late afternoon by the angle at which the sun streamed through the small portholes above him, and made vivid golden splotches against the polished woodwork on the other side of the stateroom.

Something seemed to be wrong, but for the moment, Ted Shale's sleep-drugged senses couldn't appreciate just what it was. At length he associated it in his mind with the presence of some strange sound. There was no longer any lazy slapping of wavelets against the sides of the boat. Instead there was a hissing noise, also a peculiar vibration which he couldn't understand.

Trying to analyze his impressions and eliminate the confusion in his mind, Ted lay for a moment motionless on the bunk. Then, for the first time, he noticed the peculiar motion of the round patches of sunlight which came through the portholes. They marched up the wall with slow deliberation, then, pausing to hang suspended for a moment, started creeping slowly downward.

Ted Shale shook his head to clear his senses, and abruptly the drugged stupor which was the aftermath of his unaccustomed and heavy sleep in the middle of the afternoon left his senses.

He realized that the yacht was under way, that he was listening to the rapid purr of a powerful high-speed motor, that the hissing noise was made by the calm water of a tranquil sea sliding past the bow. A light swell was making the splotches of sunlight move sedately up and down the woodwork on the opposite side of the stateroom.

Ted jumped from the bunk, and wrenched at the knob of the stateroom door.

The door was locked.

CHAPTER 7

THE little Monterey-type cottage sat back a few feet from the sidewalk. From the windows could be seen the blue crescent of Catalina Island's bay. Behind it, the hills rose to the jagged crest of a mountain skyline.

The house was quite evidently furnished to be rented by the day, week, or month. The rugs were of a coarse weave which furnished a durable protection for the floor yet enabled sand from shoes and bare feet to sift through, rather than remain imbedded in the texture of the rugs themselves.

Much of the furniture was built in, enameled white, with an orange trim. The painting had evidently been done by an amateur—probably the slender woman, with the network of crow's-feet about her eyes, who owned the cottage.

Pearl Right and her brother, Warren Hilbers, sat side by side on the wicker settee in the front room. It was that hour which comes just after sunset when fading daylight merges into darkness. Every living thing seemed hushed and relaxed. The windless ocean was calm and tranquil. People, strolling quietly along the wide boulevard which skirted the bay, were for the most part content to walk silently. When they conversed, it was in low tones.

Enough light came through the window which faced the bay to show that Pearl Right had carried the beauty of the twenties into her early thirties. Her eyes were of the dark, brilliant type associated with a highly emotional temperament. Her nose was short, indicating a certain emotional instability; while the way she carried her head, the manner in which she pointed her chin, indicated independence and a love of freedom.

Her brother was her junior by three and a half years, yet seemed to have a more balanced responsibility of outlook. His high forehead, wavy black hair, long, clean-cut nose, and deep-set eyes indicated that he could carry thought to the point of brooding. His mouth was a bit too sensitive, but his voice when he spoke had a peculiarly deep resonance which created the impression of controlled power. That voice held vibrations as vaguely disturbing as those generated by the lower notes of a pipe organ. He said, "I don't see why you changed your mind."

Pearl Right spoke with the rapidity of one who is accustomed to talking as she thinks, spilling her thoughts haphazardly, rather than trying to shape them into finished ideas. "I'm tired of the whole mess. I don't care enough. I don't care if I never see him again. It's so much with me, and then I'm through. He can do whatever he wants. That mysterious cruise, that hypnotic spell Addison Stearne casts over him, have done their work on me. Last week I cared—a lot. Yesterday, I was mad. Today—I don't care. I don't change my mind. My mind changes me."

"But why did you want me to fix things so that . . ." He broke off as a boy on a bicycle dismounted in front of the little cottage. In silence, they watched the rider kick a support into place under his bicycle, march up the short stretch of cement walk, and knock.

The man and woman exchanged glances, then Warren Hilbers went to the door. "What is it?"

"I'm from the telephone company. There's a long distance call for the woman who is registered in this cottage."

"You have her name?" Hilbers asked.

"No, just the house number."

Warren Hilbers hesitated perceptibly, then pushed his hand down into his pocket, took out a quarter, gave it to the boy, and said, "Thank you."

"She'll come to the telephone office?" the boy asked.

Again the man hesitated.

Behind him, Pearl Right said, "Yes, I'll be right over."

The boy went back to his wheel and pedaled away. Brother and sister regarded each other with a puzzled frown. "There's only one person who would know you're here," Warren Hilbers said. "What are you going to do if he should tell you that what you said made him use that gun? You'd be responsible—in a way."

Pearl Right said rapidly, "I don't think it's Arthur. Come on, let's find out."

It was only two blocks to the telephone office. An operator

indicated a booth, said, "If you'll be seated, I'll have your party within a few minutes," and then within less than sixty seconds, rang the bell on the telephone. Pearl picked up the receiver. Nita Moline said, "Pearl, do you know who this is?"

Pearl Right hesitated a moment, said, "I'm not sure. It . . ."

She realized then that the woman at the other end of the line had been waiting only to make certain of her identity by hearing her voice. Once reassured on that point, the message came quickly. "Pearl, I'm at Santa Delbarra. Something terrible has happened. Get back to the mainland just as quickly as you can. . . . When you left Saturday, did you leave any message at your house—something perhaps addressed to Arthur?"

Pearl Right said, "I don't know what you're talking about. I can't understand why you're calling. I . . ."

"Pearl, snap out of it! Did you leave a message addressed to Arthur?"

"Well, I . . . Yes, I . . ."

"Get home and destroy it. And don't ever tell anyone I called you. Remember I'm doing this for you—and it's a lot more than you'd do for me."

The receiver clicked at the other end of the line.

Pearl Right dropped the receiver into its cradle, waited for a moment, scowling at the telephone, then pushed open the door of the booth and walked out. Warren was waiting for her half a block down the street. "What was it?" he asked.

"Nita Moline. I've got to get home at once."

"Why?"

"I left a note for Arthur to find. I didn't intend to ever go back. Something's happened. I must get back and destroy that note before it's found."

He studied her from his deep-set, thoughtful eyes. He asked, "What has happened?"

"She wouldn't tell me. She just said 'something terrible' and hung up."

"Pearl—could Arthur have repeated what you said to Stearne, and—"

"I don't care what he said," Pearl Right interrupted. "And don't you ever dare intimate that I'm responsible. Warren, you've got to trust me, and help me. I want to get back and destroy that note."

"You know where I stand, Pearl. Only I wish Nita had told you definitely. When do we start?"

"Now."

"Okay. The speedboat's ready."

CHAPTER 8

PARKER GIBBS had a passion for doing a neat job in a workmanlike manner. Had he been a manufacturer, he would naturally have gravitated into the field of precision instruments. Had he been an artist, he would have drawn with fine lines, etching in all of the little details. There would have been no trace of the impressionistic in his technique.

Gibbs drove his car to Santa Delbarra, where it took him two hours to find out approximately all that the authorities knew about the murders. A little judicious bribery even secured for him a set of the photographs the sheriff's office had taken. Those photos showed Stearne lying on his back, Right sprawled at his feet—and Right's shoulders were lying over Stearne's legs.

Gibbs studied the photographs with a magnifying glass, memorizing each detail. The position of the bodies indicated that Stearne had been shot first. Right, in falling, had slumped over Stearne's legs. There was, Gibbs noticed, a typewriter on a little stand near Stearne's body. He wondered if perhaps Stearne had been trying to type something when the bullet had struck him. Or perhaps Stearne had just finished typing something. Details of the typewriter were obscure. Flashlights had been used for the photographs, and the shadow of a desk had in each instance fallen on the typewriter, but Gibbs was able to see it was a portable of the same make as the one he used in making out his reports.

Having found out all the authorities knew, Gibbs started a search for Nita Moline.

It was no trick at all to learn that Joan Harpler had given Miss Moline dry clothes, and to get a description of those clothes.

Gibbs had a description of the car and its license number. A check-up on the public garages in Santa Delbarra revealed that the car was not stored in any of them. Calls to the hotels disclosed that no woman was registered under the name of Nita Moline. Gibbs retired to an all-night restaurant where he gave the matter considerable thought. He was, he realized, getting precisely nowhere, and, as Mr. Hazlit had pointed out, a man in his profession was paid to secure results. His next step was to ascertain if Miss Moline had registered in one of the hotels under another name.

Realizing that he had at least an all-night job on his hands, and feeling the need of some place where he could establish a headquarters, Gibbs decided to get a room in one of the commercial hotels. Appraising the situation with the eye of a hard-bitten traveler, he picked the Balboa as the hotel most suited to his needs.

He registered, had his baggage taken up to his room, and casually leaned up against the desk.

"Something else I can do for you?" the clerk asked.

"I don't know," Gibbs said. "I'm trying to locate a party—an attractive girl with golden blond hair, dressed in a blouse, a red sport coat with wide lapels, white sailor slacks, driving a big cream-colored sport coupe, license number 8P3036. She may be registered here in the hotel, or . . ."

"No, she isn't registered," the clerk interrupted. "I haven't seen her since around eleven o'clock this morning."

Gibbs was careful not to show too much anxiety in following up his lead. "You on duty at eleven o'clock this morning?" he asked.

"This is my long shift," the clerk explained. "I come on at ten and stay until one o'clock the following morning. I get these long shifts twice a month, and then . . ."

"Then tomorrow you go on day duty?"

The clerk smiled and shook his head. "No, tomorrow I go on at night."

"I see. So you haven't seen this party since this morning?"

"That's right."

"And she isn't registered here?"

"No."

"Just visiting someone in the hotel?"

"No. She stopped to pick up a chap who's staying here in the hotel, a Theodore Shale, in room three-sixteen. Something queer about Shale—but I guess I shouldn't talk about that."

45

"Why not?"

"Well, for one thing, we're not supposed to talk about guests."

"Oh, bosh," Gibbs said. "After all, you're among friends. Shale, wasn't he the one who did the rescue act this morning?"

The clerk's eyes lit with interest. "I hadn't heard about it. What was it?"

Gibbs was purposely vague. "I don't know. He jumped overboard after some woman who fell off a yacht."

"That's the one all right," the clerk said. "He came in soaking wet, and he didn't offer a single word of explanation."

"So this woman went up to Shale's room?"

"No, not up to his room. He came down to wait for her. They went away together."

"Don't know where they went, do you?"

"No. Shale hasn't returned."

"He should be back by this time, if he's going to get any good out of his room."

The clerk grinned. "If that baby had stopped by for me in that buzzbuggy, I wouldn't be back either."

"I think I've met this man, Shale," Gibbs said. "He's blondish, isn't he, with stooped shoulders and . . ."

"Not this one. He's dark, wavy black hair, and a good pair of shoulders, athletic-looking fellow. He evidently only has the one suit of clothes. He put on some slacks and a sport shirt with his business coat, telephoned back about noon to have the trousers sent out to be pressed."

Gibbs said, "Guess that isn't the Shale I knew. What's he doing, do you know?"

"Yes. He got a commercial rate. Wait a minute. I have his card somewhere. Let me take a look. Oh, yes, here it is. Freelander Pasteboard Products Company."

Gibbs said, "No. This fellow I knew was in the insurance business. Well, guess I'll go out and take a little stroll. I have trouble sleeping. Some nights I can't get to sleep before three or four o'clock in the morning."

"I know just how you feel," the clerk said. "When I change shifts, I have a lot of trouble sleeping for a day or two."

Gibbs strolled out through the lobby, stood on the curb, hesitating as though trying to decide whether to turn up the street or down, then turned to the left, and sauntered toward the place where his car was parked.

Gibbs had something definite to work on now. He knew that the district attorney had ordered Ted Shale to remain in Santa Delbarra. It was hardly possible that he would violate the district attorney's instructions and run the risk of being incarcerated. He was, moreover, evidently with Nita Moline. This meant that Gibbs had a problem which was greatly simplified. In place of looking for a young woman who might be anywhere, Gibbs could now look for a couple, strikingly dressed, and either in Santa Delbarra or at some place reasonably close.

There were three night spots in Santa Delbarra. Gibbs covered them all without result. He learned there were some four or five road houses which, being beyond the city limits, made a practice of staying open until three and four o'clock in the morning. It would, he estimated, take him approximately an hour and a half to cover these road houses.

The methodical part of Gibbs' mind suggested that this was the proper thing to do, but his instinct as a detective made him feel vaguely uneasy at the prospect. If it should prove to be a blind lead, an hour and a half would have been wasted, and that time was doubly precious.

Gibbs sat back behind the steering wheel of his automobile, closed his eyes, and took inventory of the situation. It was obvious that Nita Moline had not as yet registered at any hotel, at least under her own name; that Ted Shale, who was already registered and who had been ordered by the district attorney to remain available, had not returned to his hotel room.

Gibbs felt certain the two were together, that since their meeting had been fortuitous, the possibilities of a longer and more intimate friendship could be eliminated. They must be in some public place—and yet Miss Moline's clothes . . .

Suddenly Gibbs asked himself how he knew that she was still in the same clothes. His investigation earlier in the evening had unearthed the information that the young woman who had owned the *Albatross* had offered to loan Miss Moline dry clothes. It was well within the bounds of possibility that by this time Miss Moline had her own clothes back. Gibbs hadn't asked for a description of those clothes, and he bitterly regretted the oversight. It would be rather difficult to get the young woman who owned the *Albatross* up out of bed at this time, but then, as Hazlit had so aptly told him, he was being paid to get results.

Gibbs started his automobile, drove rapidly to the waterfront, skirted around to the parking space by the yacht club. He left his car and started walking toward the clubhouse and float.

A dark figure detached itself from the shadows. Rays from the distant street lights glinted on brass buttons. "What's the idea, buddy?" the man asked.

"Looking for a yacht."

"Member of the club?"

"Yes."

"Let's see your membership card."

Gibbs promptly reached in his pocket, pulled out his wallet, started fumbling with cards. "Got a flashlight?" he asked.

"Oh, I guess it's okay," the policeman said. "Just trying to keep out sightseers. What's your yacht?"

"Right at present I'm with Miss Harpler on the *Albatross*."

"The *Albatross*, eh?"

"That's right."

"She ain't there."

Gibbs raised his eyebrows.

The officer indicated the stretch of black water where the ghostly forms of yachts loomed gray and indistinct, like the wraiths of incoming fog. "Pulled out," he said. "Understand she pulled out all of a sudden like. There was a young woman who was supposed to go on that yacht and got left behind. She made quite a commotion about it."

"Perhaps that was the woman I want. Could you describe her?"

"Girl with blond hair and a red sport jacket. Had on some kind of white pants. I didn't see her myself. I wasn't on duty, but the man I relieved told me about her, told me to keep an eye open for her. She seemed awful anxious to catch up with that yacht."

"Any idea where I could locate her?" Gibbs asked eagerly.

"No, I wouldn't know."

"How about the man you relieved? What's his name?"

"Now, don't go bothering him," the officer said. "He's had

a hard day, and he's entitled to his sleep. That's the thing that makes it so tough on a cop—having to put in his days working, and then answering questions on his time off. By the time you make a pinch, make out a report, and then have to tell some more stuff to the city attorney or the D.A. and then go to court and get on the witness stand and have questions yelled at you by a bunch of lawyers, you almost feel as though it ain't worth while makin' a pinch."

"I'll try not to disturb him," Gibbs said. "What time did you relieve him?"

"Ten o'clock tonight."

"Did he tell you what time it was when she showed up?"

"Yes, shortly after he went on duty. It was just a little before sundown—oh, maybe an hour."

"How long had the yacht been gone then?"

"I don't know. It pulled out this afternoon sometime." The officer lowered his voice. "But I'll tell you something. It's been my experience that guys on yachts are all nutty. I've seen 'em do some mighty queer things. They'll sit up all night, and then hole up all day, just sittin' out there, tied to those mooring buoys. Why the devil don't they go out and get some fishing or something?"

"Perhaps they need the sleep more," Gibbs said, smiling.

"I reckon they do, but I can't see the idea of keepin' a yacht to get drunk in when you can do it just as easy ashore."

"As easily, but not as comfortably," Gibbs pointed out.

"Guess you mean as completely, don't you?" The cop grinned.

Gibbs laughed loudly at the sally, said, "Well, so long," and turned back toward his car, his mind already turning over the problem of what moves a young woman would make who was trying to locate a yacht.

At first, Gibbs thought a speedboat was his clue. Then he realized that there was a lot of ocean to search, and the search would automatically be finished with the coming of darkness. If the young woman had any intelligence, and she certainly had, she'd rent a plane. Were there any hydroplanes for rent in Santa Delbarra?

The answer was surprisingly easy. A caretaker at the municipal airport supplied Gibbs with a telephone number. The person who had that number, when he had recovered from

a slight irritation at having been called at that hour of the
night over a simple matter of information, disclosed that a
young woman who answered the description Gibbs gave had
chartered his hydroplane that afternoon. It had, he explained,
been within half an hour of sundown by the time he had the
plane up in the air. She hadn't wanted to go any place in
particular, simply cruise around. He thought she was doing it
for a thrill. They'd gone out over the ocean, headed down
along the coast two or three miles out to sea, then made a
circle back up the coast. She'd watched the sunset, seemed to
get quite a thrill out of it, didn't want to come back. He'd insisted on getting back before dark. . . . Yes, they'd gone
down low over the ocean once. . . . Yes, there'd been a yacht
below them. He hadn't noticed it much. It was headed toward
Santa Delbarra, he'd noticed that. . . . There were usually
yachts out off the coast, particularly on a Sunday. . . . She'd
asked him to drop down at that particular point. . . . No,
he didn't know where she'd gone after they'd landed. She'd
paid him, and driven away. . . . Yes, that was right, a big
cream-colored sport coupe. . . . The young man with her?
. . . Why no, there hadn't been anyone with her. . . . No,
no one had waited in the car. He was certain of that.

Gibbs thanked him, made what apologies and explanations
he could for the lateness of the call, and drove back to the
waterfront. The yacht in which Miss Moline had taken such
an interest had been headed back toward Santa Delbarra. That
was a clue. Gibbs parked his car and settled himself to a wait,
calming his nerves with frequent cigarettes.

He became conscious of the beam of a searchlight playing
on the water, then saw red and green running lights, noticed
a yacht feeling its way in to a mooring. He saw a white-clad
figure run along the deck, lean over the bow with a flashlight.
A looped cable and float were located by the beam of the
flashlight. A boat hook dragged the loop up to the deck. A
moment later, an electric winch sounded briefly, then the running lights were switched out.

Gibbs started toward the place where the officer was standing guard at the entrance to the yacht club, then thought better of it and decided to wait and see if anyone came ashore
from the yacht.

Five minutes later, he saw the headlights of an automobile

swirl around the corner. The speed of the car elicited a screaming protest from the tires. Gibbs watched the car swing into a parking place beside his own, and when Nita Moline, still garbed in the white slacks, blouse, and red sport coat, placed a rubber-soled tennis shoe on the pavement, Gibbs raised his hat and said, "I've been looking for you, Miss Moline."

He saw her stiffen into the rigid immobility of a surprised dismay. "What—What do *you* want?"

"A friend of mine wants to see you."

"Well, isn't that nice!"

"This friend is a lawyer."

"Well, what's the idea?"

Gibbs said, "Addison Stearne was a rich man, or did you know it?"

"Well, what of it?"

"You inherited his property."

"What makes you think so?"

"I happen to know."

"How?"

"Because that's my business."

She laughed.

"You don't seem the least surprised," he said.

She said, "I'm never surprised at a line anyone hands me.— The fact that I never believe them may have something to do with it."

"Suppose I could prove it?"

"It would be interesting."

Gibbs said, "Let's quit beating around the bush. Addison Stearne left a will. Arthur Right was named in that will as executor. He was given the bulk of the estate—but the will provided that if Arthur Right died *before* Stearne, the bulk of the property was to go to you."

There was a long silence during which Nita Moline stood looking down at the vague outline of her white tennis shoes.

"I've got a lawyer," she said. "I don't need another one."

"There's only one lawyer who can do you any good now. That's George V. Hazlit of Hazlit & Tucker. I know."

"He was Addison's lawyer."

"That's right."

"He hates me. He thought I was trying to stick Addison for

· 51 ·

something. Addison wanted me to go to him. . . . Say, why should I tell you all this?"

"I know all about it," Gibbs said. "You're not telling me anything. I'm telling you." He lowered his voice. "If Right died first, you get the property. If he didn't, you don't get it. See what that means? If Right's wife manages to get in the saddle, she'll take possession of everything, and by the time she gets done, you'll be on the outside looking in. If we can get you in the saddle, you can keep her out."

"I'll talk to my lawyer about it. I know him. I don't know this man Hazlit."

"Don't be silly," Gibbs said impatiently. "You haven't time to do any swapping of horses. Hazlit is working all night so he'll have papers ready to file first thing tomorrow morning. If *your* lawyer was old man Blackstone himself, he couldn't do you any good now. The only thing he could do would be to try and keep you away from Hazlit so he'd be the one to hog the fee. Now, do you want that dough, or are you going to throw it into the ocean just so some lawyer can hand you a line?"

She said, "I like you when you get mad. You talk straight then. All right, I'll go see this man Hazlit in the morning."

"Now," Gibbs said.

"Why now?"

"You've got to give him some information so he can . . ."

"Listen, I have an appointment."

"With that yacht that just came in?"

"How did you know?"

Gibbs said, "Because I know all about how you've been trying to find it. You located it from the hydroplane, didn't you? When you saw it was headed back toward Santa Delbarra, you knew you were too late, didn't you?"

He saw from the expression on her face that she was surprised, and a little frightened.

Gibbs said, "You've been playing things pretty much on your own. It might be a good plan to let Hazlit give you some advice before you stick your neck out any farther."

"I'm not sticking my neck out."

"That's what you think."

"My clothes are aboard that yacht."

"Leave them there."

"Why?"

"Because," Gibbs said, taking a shot in the dark, "wherever that yacht went, it went for a reason. That reason may have had something to do with the cruise Addison Stearne intended to start on this afternoon, or it may have had something to do with Addison Stearne's murder. If you connect yourself with the yacht, you may connect yourself with something you won't like. If you'll take my advice, you'll slide over behind the wheel of that automobile, I'll climb in with you, and we'll start for Los Angeles right now."

She studied his face for a moment, surveying the bony, aquiline nose, the high cheekbones, the straight, firm mouth, and the strong jaw. "All right," she said abruptly, "you've won an argument. You're in a hotel here in town?"

"Yes."

"Which one?"

"The Balboa Hotel."

"You're a detective?"

"Yes."

"Hazlit hired you?"

"I'm not at liberty to talk about my clients."

"Are you going to try to follow me?"

"I'm going to Los Angeles with you."

"That's all you want?"

"Yes."

She said, "I'll make you a proposition. Get in your car, go to the Hotel Balboa, and stay in your room. I'll give you a ring at three o'clock in the morning. That will put us in Los Angeles in time to sign the papers."

He shook his head.

"It's that or nothing."

"You might forget your appointment."

"I'll give you my word."

He hesitated.

She said, "Don't think you can work a rush act with me. You've told me enough now so I'm going to see a lawyer. If you trust me and meet me at the hotel at three o'clock, I'll go to Los Angeles with you and see Hazlit. Otherwise I'll call my own lawyer, and Hazlit can go jump in the lake."

"How do I know you'll keep your promise?" Gibbs asked.

She looked at him, her eyes steady. "You don't."

"It's a bargain," he said.

"If you try to follow me," she warned, "all bets are off."

Gibbs had played the game too long not to be a good judge of human nature—and a good gambler. He considered the two alternatives, then made one last effort to get what he wanted. "Let me stay with you," he said. "I may be able to help you. You'll need a witness in case someone tries to claim you said something or did something that . . ."

"No," she interrupted. "When I play the game, I go all the way. I don't quibble, and I don't welsh. Go to the hotel, and I'll meet you there at three o'clock. Stay here and interfere with me, or even ask one more question, and Hazlit will never see me. What's it going to be?"

Gibbs climbed in his car, turned on the ignition, and drove away without a word. She waved at him when he was half a block down the street, the approving friendly gesture of a graceful, up-flung arm.

Gibbs went directly to the Balboa Hotel, and dragged out the portable typewriter. He was going to make a report which he could submit to his client, a report which would show the diligent persistence with which he had tried to locate Nita Moline, the manner in which the proposition had been put up to him, the choice he had had to make. He felt certain she'd be back at three o'clock, but in the event she wasn't, he was going to have it all down in black and white, so Hazlit would have to hear all of his side of the story before forming an opinion.

He'd just had the typewriter overhauled. A new platen and a new ribbon had been installed. Gibbs opened his suitcase, took out paper and carbon paper. He tapped the keys gently to make sure the carriage was freed from the locking position it assumed when the cover was placed on the typewriter. He struck the letter J. It tapped lightly against the new platen and left an imprint.

Gibbs fed in the paper, held his hands poised over the keyboard, then suddenly he stopped as an idea struck him.

He whipped the paper back out of the machine, regarded the new platen thoughtfully. He tried a tentative experiment, depressing the keys slowly one at a time. He tapped out: *"Arthur is dead. Theygotme and dd I cant"*

Gibbs looked at what he had done. In some ways it was

crude, but it might stand up. That would be up to the lawyers. He wasn't under any misapprehension as to what shape the yacht would be in when Nita Moline finally was permitted to take possession. Every square inch of it would have been combed in the search for clues—anything which he could do would have to be done before that time—would have to be done immediately.

Gibbs made another of his quick decisions. He put the carriage into its locking position, and snapped the case on the portable typewriter. He pushed back his chair, got to his feet, looked at his watch.

It was twenty minutes past twelve.

CHAPTER 9

JACK ELWELL, moving with the paunchy dignity of a middle-aged man who eats, drinks, and smokes too much, fitted a latchkey to a door on the frosted glass of which appeared the legend ELWELL & FIELDING, OIL INVESTMENTS.

He hung up his hat and coat, and looked at his watch. It was seven-fifteen. The morning sun, streaming in through the eastern windows, glinted in dazzling reflection from the top of a massive mahogany desk. Elwell crossed to the window, lowered the venetian blinds, and adjusted them so they shut out the glare. He unfolded a newspaper and settled back in his chair. He tried to lose himself in the sporting section, but his mind wasn't on what he was reading. Whenever there was the faintest noise in the corridor, Elwell raised his head from the paper to listen attentively.

At seven-thirty-two the phone rang. Elwell said, "Hello," and the voice of Ned Fielding came over the wire. "Just wanted to make sure you were there, Jack."

"Uh huh."

"Anything come in?"

"No. The mail isn't here yet."

Fielding said, "Well, the lawyer says we aren't safe until after the morning mail's been delivered. If he put an acceptance in the mail Saturday, it sticks us. I don't think there's any

chance he did. I've made an appointment with this other outfit for lunch."

Elwell said, "Old Stearne is just that sort of an egg. He'll
play with you as a cat plays with a mouse. He's got lawyers,
and he knows exactly what he can do and what he can't do.
You coming up here?"

"I'll be there in fifteen or twenty minutes. I'm just grabbing
a cup of coffee at a restaurant now."

"You were supposed to be here at quarter past seven," Elwell said.

"I know. I slept a little late—that is, my alarm clock didn't
go off. I made a mistake in setting it, Jack. I had to see the
lawyer last night. We had a long conference. I got in pretty
late, and when I wound the clock . . ."

"Nuts," Elwell interrupted. "Cut out the excuses, finish your
coffee and get up here."

He hung up the telephone, read a few minutes longer on
the sporting page, then turned to the first page, and glanced
at the headlines. Abruptly he jerked to startled attention,
sucked in a quick breath, and held it for several seconds. He
reached for the telephone, and tried to dial a number. He was
so nervous that his first two attempts were failures, then on
the third try, he heard Fielding's voice on the line.

"Hello, Ned. . . ."

"Oh, all right, all right!" Fielding interrupted irritably. "If
you want to be a damn snoop and play detective, go ahead. I
was stalling! I'd just woke up when I telephoned you. So what?
I was crocked last night, and . . ."

"Shut up," Elwell yelled into the telephone. "Listen to me.
Go out and get a paper. Don't stop to shave, don't do anything, just grab a newspaper."

"What's in the newspaper?"

"All over the front page. Someone bumped the old man
off. He was killed on his yacht at Santa Delbarra. They found
the bodies yesterday. C. Arthur Right was on the yacht with
him, and got his. The police haven't any clue. They don't
know who did it. It was done Saturday, but they don't even
know what time it was done. Get that?"

Fielding gave a low whistle, said, "Suppose he died before
midnight?"

"I don't know. That's up to the lawyers, but dead men sign no options. That's a cinch."

"He might have mailed one before . . ."

"Get dressed, grab a paper, and get up here. Make it snappy."

"Okay, Jack, I'll be right up."

Ned Fielding slammed down the telephone. Elwell dropped the receiver back into place, but kept his hand on the telephone, too engrossed to even change his position as he read the details of the murder.

When he had finished, he dialed a number, and when he received no answer, looked at his watch, dropped the receiver back into place, took a cigar from his pocket, and was clipping off the end when he heard steps in the corridor. The events of the last few minutes had distracted his attention from the significance of those steps, and it wasn't until he heard the sound of mail being shoved through the letter slot in the door that he pushed back his chair, got up, and walked quietly over to stand where he could see the mail, yet far enough back so his silhouette would not be thrown against the frosted glass.

When the postman had moved away Elwell grabbed up the mail, and carried it over to the secretary's desk. He riffled rapidly through the envelopes, looking quickly at the imprints in the upper left-hand corners. A slow smile appeared on his lips, and then, as he came to the envelope next to the bottom of the pile, the corners of his mouth turned sharply down. He stood for the space of four or five seconds staring at the envelope which bore the imprint, ADDISON STEARNE. The envelope was postmarked "Santa Delbarra, California," and had been mailed at four-fifty-five P.M. on Saturday, the tenth. It had not been sent by registered mail.

Elwell turned it over and over in his fingers before he finally slipped a knife from his pocket, carefully and methodically slit down the side of the envelope, and shook out a folded piece of paper.

Instinctively Elwell looked at his watch to mark the time. It was exactly twelve minutes before eight o'clock.

He unfolded the letter, and read an epistle which was so entirely typical of Addison Stearne that there could be no question of its authenticity.

The letter was addressed to Elwell & Fielding and read:

GENTLEMEN:

With reference to the option on the Ventura Oil Properties dated the tenth ultimo and under the terms of which I was to have up to and including midnight of the tenth instant to register an acceptance, please be advised that I have deferred action because of well-authenticated rumors which have come to my ears that favorable oil indications had been found in holes which were being put down on an adjoining property. I heard that the owners of this property had approached you and, at first, being in ignorance of my outstanding option, had offered you an amount vastly in excess of the purchase price specified in that option, that you decided to accept this new offer if you could trick me into letting my option expire. You took the drilling company into your confidence and found them only too glad to co-operate. For this reason, work virtually ceased upon the adjoining property. The owner thereof gave the widest publicity to a statement that there had been no favorable indications.

I have, of course, given no credence to any such wild rumor. I merely mention it to show to what extravagant lengths garbled gossip will go, and to explain why my acceptance has been delayed. Had there been any truth in the report, you can well imagine how much satisfaction I would have derived from sitting on the sidelines and watching your machinations; but, since there is no foundation for this entirely unwarranted rumor, there is no need to comment upon this.

However, that there may be no doubt, you are hereby notified that the undersigned elects to exercise the option given him by you under date of the tenth ultimo, and will proceed with the purchase of the said properties in accordance with the terms in said option contained. The undersigned is ready, able, and willing to pay the purchase price at the time and in the manner specified, and will expect full and faithful performance on your part of the terms of said agreement.

Trusting that this will not greatly interfere with any of your plans, and assuring you that had it not been for a slight uneasiness caused by those false rumors, this acceptance would have been communicated to you at an earlier date, I remain,

Sincerely yours,
ADDISON STEARNE.

Elwell threw the letter down on the desk, and clenched his fist. His face darkened with purplish anger. He said slowly and with emphasis, "The damned bastard!"

After a few moments, he picked up the letter again and held it out in front of him at arm's length. His eyes narrowed as he looked at the envelope, stared speculatively at the door, once more consulted his watch. For a few moments he was lost in thought, then he hastily folded the letter, pushed it back in the envelope, shoved letter and envelope in his pocket, picked up the balance of the mail, walked over to the door, and arranged the letters in a pile at the bottom of the letter chute. He stepped back to inspect the general effect, shook his head, and tried rearranging the pile. Midway in this, he was struck with another idea. He scooped up all the letters, jerked open the door of the office, stepped outside, and pushed the letters in a bundle through the letter drop, leaving them jammed in the brass mail slot, held in place by the pressure of the bundle.

Having done this, he walked rapidly down the hallway to the men's lavatory where he once more took the letter from his pocket. Striking a match, he held it to one corner and watched the flame lick up around the edges of the paper. When it had all burnt away, he flushed the ashes, and the small corner he had been holding between thumb and forefinger. Then he walked down to the elevator, and frowned when the elevator operator said, "You're early this morning, Mr. Elwell."

"Thought perhaps my partner would be in," Elwell said in a low voice.

Riding down in the elevator, he tried to think of something else to say which would make his appearance at the office seem more casual, less of an event to be remembered in case there should be an inquiry; but realized that anything he might say would only impress upon the mind of the operator the fact that he had been there. He left the elevator quietly, walked across the lobby, moved a few feet down the sidewalk, and stood carefully scanning the stream of pedestrians which poured along the street.

After he had waited for nearly ten minutes, he saw Ned Fielding, a newspaper under his arm, hurrying toward the building. Elwell stepped out, swung into step alongside his partner, and grasped his arm.

Fielding jumped with a convulsive start, frowned, and said, "Good God, Jack, don't ever do *that!* I thought it was a pinch."

"Come on," Elwell said, puffing at his cigar. "Snap out of it. Keep moving."

"Don't you want to go to the office?"

"No."

"How about our lawyer?"

"Stay away from him."

"What's the idea?"

"We can't talk here."

Elwell piloted his companion into the relative seclusion of a side street. "It came," he said.

"What did?"

"The letter."

"An acceptance?"

"Uh huh. He's been wise to the play the whole time. He was just stringing us along and letting us kid ourselves."

"Damn him," Fielding said, his voice vibrant with intense feeling.

"Okay," Elwell said in a low voice, "use your bean. We never received the letter, see?"

Fielding blinked at him.

"Get the sketch?" Elwell asked. "I pulled out of the office and stuck the mail back through the door. The stenographer will come in at eight-thirty. She'll pick up the mail, and open it. We'll give her plenty of chance to read it all through and get familiar with it. We'll come in about nine o'clock, just as though nothing had happened. We'll ask her what's in the mail and ask her if there was any letter from Addison Stearne. When she says there wasn't any letter, we'll grin at each other and shake hands as though we're highly pleased. We'll call up these other people right then and tell 'em it's a deal. I'll have a newspaper under my arm. After I hang up the telephone,

I'll open the newspaper, and we'll start talking about the news. Then you'll give a yell and point to the headlines. In that way, we'll find out for the first time that Addison Stearne is dead. The stenographer will be a witness to the whole thing. Get me?"

"Martha Gayman ain't exactly dumb," Fielding pointed out. "We'll have to play it just right so she won't think it's an act. She . . ."

"Bosh!" Elwell interrupted. "She's got sense enough to do filing and take dictation. Aside from that, she's just a dumb cluck. Every time I look at her, she reminds me of a cow with a full stomach. But she's honest, and if we can convince her, she'll make a swell witness."

Fielding squinted his eyes. "It's okay, Jack, but if they should ever prove we had that letter . . ."

"How they going to prove it?" Elwell demanded. "That letter's gone. There isn't even a chance they could recover a cinder the size of a pinhead."

"That letter was typewritten?" Field asked.

"Uh huh."

"He'll have kept a copy."

"What do we care? It doesn't cut any ice with us. He could have written a dozen letters. He can't hold us unless the letter *was put in the mail.* He may have written the letter and intended to put it in the mail, but he never did; see? We never got it. Our secretary can swear to that. She got into the office first and opened the mail."

Fielding said, "Wait a minute, Jack. Let me think this over. It . . ."

"It's been done now," Elwell said. "There's nothing to think over. Don't be so damn conservative. You've got to take a chance once in a while. There's two hundred and fifty thousand involved in the deal."

"That's what makes it so dangerous," Fielding said. "Keep quiet for a minute. Let me think . . . That letter was postmarked from Santa Delbarra?"

"Yes."

"He went up there on his yacht. He didn't have any secretary with him. He must have written it himself. Probably had a typewriter along. Did you notice down in the lower left-hand corner if there were any marks that showed whether it had been dictated or not?"

Elwell frowned. "No," he said, "I didn't. Hell, I never thought of that."

"*You* wouldn't!"

"Well, what difference does it make?"

"It might make a lot."

Elwell shook his head doggedly. "We never got any letter," he said. "That's all that counts, as far as we're concerned. Stearne never mailed it."

Fielding said, "That's okay, but the thing to do is to find out if he had a typewriter aboard the yacht. In other words, was the letter written up there, or was it dictated at his office before he left. Get the idea? If he didn't have a typewriter on the boat and the letter was dictated at his office, he was carrying it in his pocket, intending to mail it. He was killed before he had a chance to mail it. The letter disappeared and . . ."

Elwell interrupted to say impatiently, "You try to cross too damn many bridges before you come to them. We didn't get any letter. That's all."

Fielding said, "Well, while I'm crossing bridges, I'll give you another one to think about. Where were you Saturday afternoon and night—in case the district attorney at Santa Delbarra should ask you?"

CHAPTER 10

NITA MOLINE deftly guided the big cream-colored coupe through the streets of Los Angeles and finally into a parking place, slid across the seat, opened the right-hand door, and thrust out a trim pearl-gray suède shoe. There followed a quick glimpse of stocking. Her suit was gray, a few shades darker than the shoes. Her body looked trimly tailored, freshly supple, but her face gave evidence of the strain to which she had been subjected.

She moved briskly up the walk which led to the stucco Spanish-type bungalow and rang the bell.

The maid answered the door, said, "Good morning, Miss

Moline," and stood aside for her to come in. "Mrs. Right said she just couldn't see anyone. I'm sorry."

"Where is she?"

"In her bedroom. She . . ."

Nita Moline swept past the maid, saying, "I'm sorry. This is too important to be put off."

The maid followed for a few steps, protesting, then kept silent until Nita Moline opened the door of the bedroom. Then she said, "I'm sorry, Mrs. Right. She . . ."

Pearl Right still had the remains of a breakfast on the tray by the window. She said, "Never mind, Edna," to the maid, and when the door had closed, said to Nita Moline, "Had breakfast?"

"Hours ago."

"Well?"

"I wanted you to know that I've instructed my attorney to get me put in charge of Addison Stearne's estate."

"My lawyer phoned a few minutes ago and told me the application had been filed," Pearl Right said in a voice that held no expression.

"Are you going to contest?"

"I don't know."

"It would be better if you didn't."

Mrs. Right regarded her visitor thoughtfully. She wore a blue velvet housecoat and light blue mules with white puffs at the tops. Her face was as fully made up as though for the street. Her cheeks had been carefully rouged, and her hair combed. There was even mascara on her eyelashes. There was the red imprint of lipstick on the side of the coffee cup just below the rim, but she had renewed the color of her lips.

"Well?" Miss Moline asked.

"I suppose you think you have something on me. You're trying to tell me I'll have to behave or else. Is that it?"

Nita Moline said impatiently, "Snap out of it, Pearl. I want to talk with you."

"Go ahead and talk."

"Addison Stearne provided in his will that the bulk of his property would go to Arthur. But if Arthur died first, then everything except a few thousand went to me. Did you know that?"

"Not exactly, but I'd supposed it would be something like

that. He hated me. Of course, he'd try to keep me from having the benefit of any of his money."

"It was a crazy thing to do," Nita Moline said. "There's a good chance for a lawsuit."

"Why?"

"Trying to determine which died first. As I understand it, from the position in which the bodies were found, Addison *may* have died before Arthur."

"That means I get the money?" Pearl Right asked, regarding Nita Moline with steady eyes.

"That means you get the money."

"And that's why you're here?"

"In a way, yes."

There was a sudden sharp suspicion in Pearl Right's eyes. "You wouldn't be here unless you thought Addison Stearne had died first. You're here trying to . . ."

"Don't be silly, Pearl. I'm here trying to talk sense. It's quite possible the question of who died first will never be solved. Personally, I see no reason for you and me throwing a lot of money to the birdies."

"Meaning I should step aside and give you everything?"

"No. Meaning that we'll act sensibly. I'll take charge of the estate for the purpose of getting it all together, finding out just what property there is, and carrying on with Addison's business. I won't touch a penny of the money, except to see that business is carried on. By that time, we'll know who died first—if we can ever get definite proof."

Pearl Right said, "Arthur probably left a will disinheriting me. It would be the same in any event so far as I'm concerned. If Arthur died first, you'd get the money. If he didn't, we'd both be out."

"Do you know if he left a will?"

"No."

"Didn't he leave some insurance?"

"Oh, I suppose so."

"You're the beneficiary of any policies, aren't you?"

"I guess so. I suppose you know the relationship between us?"

Nita Moline hesitated a moment, then said, "I don't know as that needs to enter into it, Pearl. This is just a business matter."

Pearl Right said bitterly, "Addison Stearne broke us up. If he hadn't been killed, I'd have sued him for alienation of affections."

"For how much?"

"Two hundred thousand dollars. The papers were all ready."

"Why did you want to do that, Pearl?"

"You know why."

Nita Moline shook her head.

Pearl Right said, with growing feeling, "Well, you *should* know why. You were the one that was back of it all. How did you know that I'd left a letter for Arthur?"

"I'd rather not go into that."

Pearl Right regarded her visitor curiously. "You're a queer one," she said. "If I weren't too numbed to feel any emotion, I'd hate you. As it is, I'm trying to get you classified. I suppose that telephone call to me at Catalina was selfish."

"Why?" Nita Moline asked.

"Because you didn't want the letter I'd left for Arthur published."

"*I* didn't!" Nita Moline exclaimed in surprise.

"Yes."

"Why not?"

"Because you were mentioned in it."

"What are you talking about?"

Pearl Right said, "Are you going to try to tell me you didn't know what Arthur and Addison Stearne were hatching up on that yachting trip?"

"I haven't the faintest idea."

Increasing bitterness came into Mrs. Right's voice. "Oh, no, you haven't the faintest idea. The subject's getting pretty close to home now, isn't it?"

"What do you mean?"

"You know what I mean. Addison Stearne wanted to get rid of you. He was afraid you might sue him for breach of promise, unless he eased you out of the picture very tactfully. He'd known for a long time Arthur was crazy about you. And Arthur was so simple, he'd never suspect that you and Addison were . . ."

Nita Moline jumped to her feet. "Pearl, don't you say that! That's a lie! That's . . ."

"Oh, no, it isn't. Addison always hated me. He tried to turn

Arthur against me. Well, he finally succeeded. And he managed to dangle you in front of Arthur's eyes and keep talking about you until Arthur fell in love with you."

"Pearl, you're crazy."

She said sneeringly, "I suppose you want me to believe that you didn't know."

"He . . . Why, I'd only seen him a few times."

"On yachting trips."

"He'd been on some trips with Addison when I'd been along."

Pearl Right said, almost musingly, "Addison poisoned Arthur's mind against me. But Arthur didn't realize he was in love with you until Thursday—not that it makes a great deal of difference. He's dead now. He told me Friday night that we were all finished. He was in love with you. He said if I didn't go to Reno and get a divorce, he would."

Nita Moline said, "Pearl, please believe me. I never knew anything of that. Honestly I didn't."

"Bosh! You knew what would be in the letter I'd left for him when I walked out Saturday. You knew the officers would come here. You didn't want them to find that letter. You didn't want your name dragged into it—and speaking of keeping your name out of the mess, suppose you tell me what *actually* happened up there at Santa Delbarra?"

"What do you mean, Pearl?"

"You know what I mean. How long were you aboard that yacht before you gave the alarm?"

"Why, just a few minutes. I . . . ."

"Long enough to get rid of the gun and perhaps the note."

"What do you mean?"

She said, "Arthur would have left a note. He's like that."

"I don't know what you're talking about."

"Oh, yes, you do. Addison wanted Arthur to meet him in Santa Delbarra. That was when Addison was going to see that Arthur had a chance to tell you of his infatuation.—Your friend, Addison, talked too much. I knew that some day Arthur would kill him. I even tried to get to Addison's office last week to warn him, but he wouldn't see me."

"Pearl, what are you talking about?"

"You know what I'm talking about. Arthur was absolutely crazy about you. He told me so Friday. And I was afraid

Addison would let something slip about your relationship. Arthur had begun to suspect. Something I . . . Well, Arthur killed him, and then committed suicide. He'd have left a note. You came aboard the yacht and found the bodies. You tossed the gun overboard so it would look like murder, and heaven knows what you did with the note—not that I blame you. I'd probably have done the same thing under similar circumstances, but we may as well understand each other."

Nita Moline, white faced, said, "And what do you think was my relationship with Addison Stearne?"

"You're asking for it," Pearl Right said.

"I'm asking for it."

"You were a cast-off mistress."

"Pearl, do you actually believe that?"

"Of course I believe it."

Nita Moline, standing with her hands clenched into tight little fists, said, "There's no reason on earth why I should, but, just so you'll get something straight for once in your life, I'm going to tell you. Addison was in love with my mother. He tried to marry her, wanted desperately to marry her. She turned him down and married my father. My father left her. Mother died. Two years ago, Father was killed in an auto accident. Addison Stearne read about it, and started a search for Mother. He found out then she was dead. His investigators found me. I looked very much as my mother had when she was my age. Addison wanted me to treat him as a father. There were things about him which attracted me to him, and there were other things which repelled me. I know just how my mother felt. The cold-blooded efficiency of the man, his habit of reducing everything to dollars and cents, his cynical belief that every man had his price—oh, well, what's the use?"

"What's the use?" Pearl Right echoed mockingly. "It's a nice explanation to make—*after* Addison's death. I suppose you lay awake all night thinking it up."

Nita Moline said, "I should have known better than to have come here. I only thought we might be able to save the washing of a lot of dirty linen, and get things settled fairly and amicably instead of having them tied up in lawsuits." She started for the door.

"Wait a minute," Pearl Right said. "I haven't answered *your* question yet."

"What question?"

"About what I'm going to do in contesting your appointment."

"I don't care a fig what you do."

Pearl said, "You're peculiar. You won't face facts."

"As it happens, your statements aren't true."

"Oh, yes, they are. Arthur had a crazy streak in him. He'd begun to get suspicious of your relationship with Addison. He left here Saturday carrying his revolver. I tried to warn Addison. He wouldn't see me. That was his hard luck."

"Arthur was carrying a revolver?"

"Of course he was, a thirty-eight caliber Colt. Don't act so surprised. You know what happened. He killed Addison, and then shot himself. But Arthur would have left a note. He'd have had to explain just why he did it. That was Arthur all over, always going into details to justify himself, not caring what it might mean to others."

Nita Moline's eyes suddenly narrowed. "Wait a minute," she said. "Arthur told you on Friday he was in love with me?"

"Yes."

"That he was going to leave you?"

"He said one or the other of us would have to get a divorce."

"And then he started carrying a gun?"

"Yes."

"For Addison Stearne?"

"Of course."

Nita Moline said positively, "That's because when he told you he was in love with me, you taunted him with the fact that I was Addison Stearne's cast-off mistress, didn't you, Pearl?"

Pearl Right avoided her eyes.

"Didn't you?"

"What if I did?"

"You . . . You . . ."

"Oh, don't be so self-righteous," Mrs. Right said. "Arthur would have left a statement justifying his act. You know what happened as well as I do. You destroyed that note, and tossed the gun overboard. You made it look like a double murder so you could keep *your* name out of it, and, by making it look like a double murder, you had a chance to show Arthur died first. If it had been murder and suicide, Arthur would have inherited . . ."

"That shows all you know about it," Nita Moline interrupted heatedly. "If Arthur had killed him, neither Arthur nor his heirs could ever have taken a penny of Addison's money, regardless of what was in the will. That's the law."

Pearl Right smiled. "Well, well," she said, "you *did* give yourself away, didn't you, dearie? You've already asked your lawyer about that."

Nita Moline said angrily, "That was just *one* of the questions I asked my lawyers."

"Oh, yes," Pearl said, "leave it to you! It would be just *one* of the questions. You'd keep the lawyer from suspecting by asking a hundred questions which didn't have anything to do with what you really wanted to know."

Nita Moline snapped, "You put that thought into Arthur's head. You taunted him with falling for a cast-off mistress. Why, if he had killed Addison, you'd be a murderess."

Mrs. Right said, "And so you thought up this explanation of Addison Stearne's fatherly interest. You had all night to do it. And you came to me to get me to keep my mouth shut. . . . Well, why not? After all, Arthur was finished with me. I don't blame you for that. I blame Addison. . . . And we can be sensible. Nita, come back here."

But Nita Moline, stalking angrily to the door, walked out, slamming the door shut behind her.

CHAPTER 11

PARKER GIBBS sat in the room which he had reserved as an office at his house. He was pounding away on a portable typewriter. Mrs. Gibbs was running the vacuum cleaner in the living room. She paused from time to time, shutting off the motor of the vacuum cleaner, listening to the clack of the typewriter as though the tapping of the keys might convey some information of what her husband was writing.

After a while she pulled the plug in the cleaner and opened the door of her husband's study. He paused in his writing to look up at her. His eyes were dark ringed and slightly blood-shot. "What is it?"

"Go to bed."

"Can't. I've got to make this report, then I've got to get back to Santa Delbarra."

"What are you going back there for?"

"I left my car up there."

"That woman isn't going back with you?"

"No, dear, of course not."

"Where was she when you found her?"

"In an auto."

"When?"

"I don't know just when. It was pretty late, around mid-night."

"Where were you?"

"Down by the beach."

"She wasn't in a hotel when you found her?"

"What makes you think that?"

"It was time for her to be in bed."

"Oh, it wasn't that late."

"You wouldn't lie to me?"

"Why, no, hon. Why should I lie?"

"Because men are made that way."

He laughed.

"It's all right for you to laugh. You're running around the country, having heaven-knows-what adventures. Why did you have to come down in *her* car?"

"Because I had to see she got here."

"She certainly likes to show her legs."

"Aw, hon, that's just the way they take pictures for the newspapers. They dug that old picture out of their files. It shows her when she was coming back from an ocean trip. All ship reporters get pictures of women showing their legs."

"Well, she certainly showed hers! She was glad to co-oper-ate . . . What time did you leave Santa Delbarra?"

"About quarter after three."

"I thought you said you found her at midnight."

"I did, but she wouldn't leave until three."

"What were you two doing between twelve and . . ."

"She wasn't with me. I was alone in the hotel."

"Where was she?"

70

"I don't know."

"You're sure she isn't going back with you?"

"No, of course not."

"How do I know she isn't? After she's spent half the night . . ."

"Good heavens, hon, she looks on me as an old, old man. These girls in the early twenties think a man of forty is a doddering old relic."

"Some of them do, but the girls that are on the make go for anything that wears pants. And where do you get the idea she's in the early twenties? She looks thirty to me."

"You can't tell from a newspaper picture. She . . ."

"Oh, so you think she's more beautiful than the picture then, do you?"

Gibbs said, "To tell you the truth, hon, I was awfully sleepy. I didn't pay much attention to her. I slid down against the back of the seat and slept most of the way in. She wanted to drive."

"What did you two talk about?"

"We didn't talk. Now I've got to get out of here and catch that train back to Santa Delbarra. Don't be foolish. After all, I'm working for a living."

His wife stood in the doorway, looking after him dubiously as he walked down to the corner where he waited for a streetcar. Gibbs turned to wave to her. She didn't return his wave, simply went back into the house.

Gibbs sighed, conscious that she was standing behind the lace curtains of the living-room window, looking at him. She was driving him crazy. He'd almost put his foot in it by saying Nita Moline was in the early twenties. She was getting worse all the time, wanting to know where he'd been, what he'd been doing, what time he did this, what time he did that. Of course, she was lonesome, staying there by herself. She'd trapped him into telling her about that gap in time after he met Nita Moline and before he started for Los Angeles. He hadn't intended to let her know anything about the interval between midnight and three o'clock. She'd have more questions to ask him by the time he got back. And she'd have long hours to brood. The more you tried to humor her and kid her along, the worse she got. Gibbs was a man who hated friction. If he had anything to say, he said it and got it off his chest. That nagging left him all churned up inside. He couldn't put up with it much longer. And he didn't want her asking too many questions about what had transpired between midnight and three o'clock. It would be dangerous to have her start brooding over that. No telling what she'd do, once she got one of those jealous ideas in her head.

CHAPTER 12

JACK ELWELL and Ned Fielding returned to their office shortly after two-thirty. The aroma of fragrant cigars trailed along behind them. Elwell's waistcoat was stretched taut. His face held a placid expression of well-fed satisfaction. Ned Fielding seemed thoughtful, but he couldn't keep the triumph out of his eyes. Younger than Elwell, broad shouldered, and not as yet putting on weight, he wore his double-breasted suit with an air of distinction. He lacked Elwell's quick decision, was definitely more cautious, but he knew how to use his magnetic personality. That, and his even, regular profile were responsible for the names of many feminine investors which appeared on the books of Elwell & Fielding.

Martha Gayman looked up as they came in.

"Any telephone calls?" Elwell asked.

"Mr. Hazlit of Hazlit & Tucker wants you to call."

Elwell grinned at his partner. "Anything else?"

"No, sir, that's all. Shall I get Mr. Hazlit?"

"Not right away," Elwell said. "He's going to be disagreeable. I'll finish my cigar first."

"What shall I say if he calls again?"

"Tell him we're still out."

"Yes, sir."

She looked up at them with wide bluish-green eyes in which there was not the slightest trace of expression. She seemed like some human automaton who, as Elwell had said, knew just enough to do the filing, to take down what was said in shorthand, and pound it out afterwards on the typewriter. She was not bad-looking, yet her features were too heavy to be beautiful. Her attempt to keep up her personal appearance was hampered by poor judgment and a limited budget. She did her hair herself. In place of buying a few clothes of better quality at the end of the season, she tried to keep abreast of the very latest styles. Her limited salary necessitated clothes which were cheap copies of the things she should have been wearing.

Elwell regarded her as an office fixture, very much the same as the typewriter, the adding machine, or the office safe. She was, of course, animate, but, so far as Elwell was concerned, hardly human.

Fielding never discussed her with his partner—not after that night when Fielding had had some dictation to do before catching a train, and had asked her to stay down and help him get caught up. They had gone to dinner together, and had returned to the office. Fielding's train had left at midnight.

Elwell led the way into the private office, closed the door carefully behind him, took from his pocket the signed typewritten document and dropped it on his desk. Then he said slowly and impressively, "Two . . . hundred . . . and . . . fifty . . . thousand . . . dollars . . . net . . . profit!"

The two men reached across the desk and shook hands.

"Suppose Hazlit finds out about that letter having gone out on Saturday?" Fielding asked in a low voice which was hardly above a whisper.

Elwell said, "What the hell do we care? We never received any letter. If it had been mailed on Saturday, we would have received it this morning." He closed one eye and said, rather loudly, "I know damn well there wasn't any letter in the mail because I made it a point to ask Martha about it."

There was a pad of paper on the desk. Fielding pulled it toward him and scribbled a message to his partner. It read, "Be careful what you say. There's a lot involved in this deal, and they may have a dictograph planted somewhere in the office."

Elwell read the message, nodded. Fielding struck a match to the corner of the paper, waited until it had burnt off all of the part which had any writing on it before he dropped the remaining corner into the ash tray.

Elwell said, "Hazlit will want to talk with Martha. I think it's best that he should. We'd better talk with her before he does. Just explain to her that she isn't to get rattled or confused because someone asks questions, but simply to keep her head and tell the truth."

Fielding nodded.

"Want to get her in here now?" Elwell asked.

Fielding said, "I think you'd better do that yourself, Jack. Two of us talking with her might confuse her."

Elwell flashed his partner a quick glance, said, "Okay, Ned."

"I'm going out and get a haircut," Fielding said. "You talk with her."

Elwell said, "It won't take long. Thank heavens all she has to do is tell the truth. She's too dumb to lie. That's going to be a big help."

"She isn't so dumb," Fielding said. "She does good work. You don't ever catch any errors in her letters."

"Oh, she's all right in a way," Elwell said. "Sometimes she gets on my nerves, looking at me with that ox-like expression on her face. Now that we've put this deal across, we can get better offices—really fix them up, and get a secretary that really amounts to something. Martha's a good enough stenographer, but we need a real secretary. I don't know about you, Ned, but it irritates me to have a stupid woman around."

"She isn't stupid," Fielding said. "She's just average."

"To men like you and me," Elwell pointed out, "being average is being stupid. Well, I'll get her in here, and explain things to her. Gosh, Ned, think of it. Thirty days ago we were thinking we'd be sitting on easy street if Addison Stearne only took up that option and we unloaded for a hundred thousand. Now, we're getting two hundred and fifty thousand above the price we paid."

Fielding nodded. "How long will it be in escrow, Jack?"

"Not over four or five days. The title's all searched. It's just a question of getting the papers ready, and putting the money up. That syndicate said they'd have the papers down here sometime this afternoon. In the meantime, this little old agreement right here protects us. They obligate themselves to put the dough in escrow as soon as we put in the papers."

Fielding said, "Well, I'm on my way. You won't want me here when you talk with Hazlit on the telephone?"

"Gosh, no, what is there to tell *him?* He'll simply ask if we didn't get a letter, and I'll tell him no. He'll perhaps try to

74

run a bluff and say that he happens to know his client dictated and signed one, and intended to mail it. That's their hard luck. Stearne intended to wait until the last minute just to keep us on the anxious seat—and got murdered before he had a chance to drop it in the mailbox. I suppose old Hazlit's been breaking his neck, running around and getting a special administrator appointed, and now he thinks he's going to run some sort of a bluff."

Fielding put on his hat. "Be seeing you in about half or three-quarters of an hour, Jack."

"Take care of yourself. Now listen, Ned, don't start drinking."

"Of course not."

Elwell's eyes grew suddenly hard. "Listen, Ned, I'm not kidding on that. There's too much involved for you to fall off the waterwagon and start making careless comments."

"I never get to a point where I don't know what I'm saying."

"That's what you think. Until we actually have the money on this thing, you don't do any drinking whatever. You're on the wagon. Afterwards, we'll go out and get pie-eyed together —take a drive up to one of the resorts."

Fielding hesitated, then said, "If you put it that way, Jack."

"I'm putting it that way. That's final."

Fielding gave a little gesture of aquiescence, said, "Okay, big boy," and walked out of the door of the private office into the corridor.

Elwell stepped to the door which led to the outer office, smiled benignly at Martha Gayman, and said, "Come in, Martha. No, you don't need to bring your book. I just want to talk with you."

She entered the office and stood looking at him.

Elwell said, "Sit down, Martha. I want to talk with you."

He noticed as she walked that she really did have a good figure. She sat down in the chair which Elwell had indicated, a chair reserved for clients. She had pretty legs, Elwell saw. She didn't cross them, simply sat there with her knees clamped tightly together, the hem of her skirt just at the edge of the kneecap.

"Rather an important business deal has been consummated this afternoon," Elwell said. "It's too complicated for me to try to explain it to you. You wouldn't understand it if I did.

It wouldn't have been possible for the deal to have been made if a certain letter had been in the mail this morning—a letter from a man named Addison Stearne."

She nodded, the mechanical nod of one who feels that something is expected of her and that a nod in the affirmative will come closest to satisfying the expectations of the other person.

Elwell frowned slightly. "Now, don't take this as merely routine, Martha," he said. "Try to follow me closely so you will understand me. Mr. Hazlit is the attorney for Addison Stearne. Addison Stearne is dead. He was murdered sometime Saturday afternoon. It is quite possible that Mr. Stearne *intended* to mail us a letter sometime on Saturday, but the point is he *didn't* mail that letter. That is, there was no such letter in the mail this morning. You opened all the mail, didn't you?"

"Yes, Mr. Elwell."

"And if there had been a letter from Addison Stearne, you would have noticed it?"

"Yes, I think I would."

"Not *think*," Elwell said, frowning slightly. "You're employed here to take care of the office. As part of your duties, you have to open the mail. You read the letters in order to see whether they're important, how they should be filed, and whether they should go to Ned or to me. That's right, isn't it?"

She nodded.

"And you would have noticed if there had been any letter from Mr. Addison Stearne this morning?"

Again she nodded.

"That's all you need to remember," Elwell said. "Don't bother that pretty head of yours with anything else, my dear. Just remember those simple facts, and in case Mr. Hazlit or any other lawyer should talk with you, should try to browbeat you, or ask you a lot of questions, don't let him rattle you. Just tell the simple truth."

She said, "Yes, Mr. Elwell."

"You think you can remember that?"

She nodded.

"And remember not to say that you don't *think* there was any letter from Mr. Stearne. You remember positively that

76

there was no letter from Mr. Stearne—and you can say that very positively, can't you, my dear?"

She nodded again.

Elwell reached for the telephone. "That's all, Martha," he said. "When you go out, get me Mr. Hazlit on the line."

She didn't make any move, however, to rise from the chair; but continued to regard Elwell with that placid expression which he found so irritating, an expression of respectful attention.

"That's all," Elwell said again.

She said, "Mr. Elwell, there's something I want to ask you about?"

He frowned. "I'm rather busy this afternoon, Martha."

"It's very important to me."

"Well, what is it?"

"Do you remember about six weeks ago when Mr. Fielding was working on these Ventura leases? He had to take a midnight train to Salt Lake City to see a man."

"Well?"

"He had a lot of correspondence to get out, and he asked me if I'd mind coming up to the office with him that night. We worked until almost eleven o'clock."

Elwell showed his annoyance. "My dear," he said, "if you're trying to ask us for a raise, come out and say so. We try to be fair with you, but business is pretty bad these days, and the government fixes it so that if you do make anything, you are robbed in income taxes. Then there's the social security tax and . . ."

"Yes, I understand, Mr. Elwell. I wasn't going to ask for a raise."

"Well, what is it then?"

"That night Mr. Fielding was—most attentive. He—he—he made love to me."

Elwell's frown became a scowl. "Martha," he said, "I'm not in the least interested in your private affairs. You're certainly over . . . How old *are* you, Martha?"

"Twenty-five."

"Well, my God, I can't act as chaperon to . . ."

"And he's been very cool to me lately," Martha went on. "For a while, after he came back, he was very nice, very attentive, and very considerate, and then lately he seems to have cooled off."

"Well, I can't . . ."

"And I thought you could speak to him, Mr. Elwell, and perhaps do something to make him do . . . well, the right thing."

Elwell dropped the telephone and stared at her as though he hadn't ever seen her before. *"The right thing,"* he said, surveying the expressionless countenance.

She nodded her head. "Yes," she said. "The right thing."

"My God, girl, what do you mean?"

"I thought he was in love with me. I thought he wanted to marry me."

"Did he say so?"

"Well, not in so many words, but . . ."

Elwell raised his voice. "Well, let me assure you that he *won't* say so. Ned Fielding has a career ahead of him. He's not going to waste it by tying himself to some dumb little stenographer. I'm sorry, Martha, but you asked for this. And let me give you a little advice. Don't ever in the future forget yourself enough to intrude upon your employer with a lot of silly personal problems. In the first place, if Ned Fielding made a pass at you . . . Hang it, you're certainly not dumb enough to think . . . You've got a good figure. You're twenty-five years old. You've been around. Why, hang it . . ."

When Elwell had sputtered himself into silence, Martha Gayman said quietly, "You see, I have a very sensitive disposition, Mr. Elwell. The reason Ned—Mr. Fielding's—indifference hurts so much is because I'm inclined to notice *little* things. Things that perhaps no one else would notice always catch my attention. I've always been that way."

Elwell was speechless with exasperation.

"Like this morning," she went on smoothly. "The way I noticed that you'd been in the office, had waited for the mailman, then pushed the mail back into the slot again. Lots of girls wouldn't have noticed that, but you see, little things mean so much to me that—I always have . . ."

Elwell snapped to straight-backed attention, leaning across the desk, staring at the girl who sat regarding him with such a wistful expression, with eyes that were wide and round and —damn it, yes, utterly ox-like.

"What the devil are you talking about?" Elwell asked, and even to his own ears his voice sounded frightened.

"Little things that most people wouldn't notice," she said. "For instance, you hadn't been in your private office. You came up here and waited in the outer office. That means you must have been waiting for something—like the mailman."

"I don't know what you're talking about," Elwell said.

She went on as though he hadn't said anything. "You always read the sporting section of the paper first. It had been folded so that the sporting section was turned around, then you'd looked back at the headlines and had seen that about Addison Stearne. You'd dropped the paper on the floor then. You see, the janitor cleans out the ash trays, and polishes them as well, on Saturday. Your cigar ashes were in the ash tray and also the band from the cigar—that particular brand that you smoke, Mr. Elwell. You have them mailed to you from Florida, and your initials are on the band. Remember when you had me write the letters to the man who advertised that he made custom-built cigars?"

Elwell started to say something, then kept silent.

"And," she said, "even the mailman has his little peculiarities. He has a certain particular method of sorting the mail for the offices in the building. You probably wouldn't have noticed it, Mr. Elwell, because you don't get the mail out of the mail chute, but I have done it morning after morning, so I've noticed the mailman's system. The addresses are always facing up, and all the envelopes are stacked so that the addresses are straight up. Moreover, he puts the small envelopes on top, and the larger envelopes on the bottom. Well, this morning that was just reversed. The larger envelopes were on the top, and the smaller envelopes on the bottom, and the addresses weren't the way the postman has them. Some of the addresses were up on the envelopes, and some of them were down. I'm just mentioning it, Mr. Elwell, to show you how sensitive I am and how I notice little things, and how Mr. Fielding's conduct to a girl that's as sensitive as I am makes so much more difference than—well, than if I were the kind who didn't notice little things."

Elwell said very slowly in a voice which sounded strangely unlike himself, "Just what do you want?"

She said innocently enough, "I thought perhaps that something had happened and Mr. Fielding felt I didn't like him any more. Perhaps I've hurt his feelings and—well, you know how it is with lovers. You read about it in books and magazines. A person's pride gets hurt, and he won't come to the person he loves the way he would to someone else, and ask forgiveness and . . ."

"All right, just what do you want?"

"I thought perhaps you could speak to Mr. Fielding and tell him that I'm not at all angry with him, that I feel just like I did—like I always have. And you know, Mr. Elwell, of course, I wouldn't want you to intimate that if he'd ask me to marry him, it would make me very, very happy, because I always think it's better for a man to be a little in suspense when he proposes, don't you? In that way, it's sort of the high spot in his life. He remembers it always then."

Elwell studied her face. "By God," he said, "Fielding will always remember it, all right."

"There's a lot involved in this business deal, Mr. Elwell, the one that you said Mr. Hazlit might talk to me about?"

"Yes."

She said, "Don't you think it might be better for you to talk to Mr. Fielding before I talked with Hazlit? You see, I've been frightfully upset about this, and I'd hate to have something on my mind that would make me, perhaps, say the wrong thing."

Elwell reached for his hat. "You're quite right," he said. "I'll talk with Ned before you talk with Hazlit. If Hazlit rings up again, tell him I haven't been in, and that I may not get in again this afternoon."

"Where did Mr. Fielding go?"

"Down to get a haircut."

"I think he has his hair cut at the barbershop right here in the building," she said. "You'll find him down there, and—and—"

"What now?" Elwell asked, his voice rasping.

"Nothing," she said. "Only I haven't any engagement for this evening—in case Mr. Fielding should ask you. Well, Mr. Elwell, I'm sorry I bothered you with a lot of my private affairs, but it's been on my mind a lot lately. I feel *so* much better now. I feel that I can really concentrate on my work. I've got some filing to do. I hope I didn't presume on your kindness, Mr. Elwell."

He said nothing, but sat rigidly straight-backed at his desk, regarding the door through which she had left the office as though that door might hold the key to some secret. His cigar had gone out, and when he started to light it again, he saw that he had chewed the end of it into a ragged, soggy mass. With an exclamation of annoyance, he dashed it into the cuspidor, got up, and walked through the exit doorway into the corridor.

CHAPTER 13

FRANK DURYEA arrived home Monday night to find his wife, a mischievous twinkle in her eye, walking about the house with an exaggerated limp.

"What now?" he asked.

She regarded him solemnly. "It's the right one."

"Right what?"

"Leg, to you."

"What about it?"

"It's half gone."

He thought for a minute before getting the idea from the expression in her eyes. Dropping into a chair and assuming his most professional manner, he said, "Let me take a look. We may have an action for damages."

She lifted her skirt, slid her right leg across his knees, and Duryea examined it gravely, running the tips of his fingers up the sheer silk of her stocking.

"Well?" she asked.

"It's *very* bad," he admitted solemnly.

"That's what I feared," she whispered. "From looking at it, can you tell what caused it?"

"Yes. It's been talked off."

She nodded. "And I was so proud of it. Tell me, will it grow back?"

"That depends on a variety of factors. When did you first notice that it was disappearing?"

"This morning shortly after you left for the office. Oh, Frank, I'm *so* afraid you'll have the same trouble!"

He asked, "Was there more than one subject of conversation to whittle it down, or was it all . . ."

"No. It was all about the one thing. What can you do, Doctor?"

"Well, first we'll have to get at the cause."

"That isn't going to be easy, I'm afraid."

"Don't forget I have great powers. I might have him arrested as a vagrant."

"He'll get out again. He says no one has ever been able to keep a Wiggins in."

Duryea laughed. "Perhaps a thirty-day recess might help a lot. What are you doing?"

"Cooking dinner, my love. Remember, the maid's having *two* days off this week."

"Oh, yes. . . . Where's the source of your leg trouble?"

"Out in his trailer right at present. He's been a busy little man all day. You know something, Frank?"

"What?"

"According to rumor, Gramps Wiggins is the very, very, very black sheep of the family. Wine, women, and song; and anything he lacks along musical lines, he's made up in the other two."

"Well?"

She said, "I thought a quart of whiskey and a bottle of cocktails might get him completely blotto in case you don't feel like talking a lot of shop. Then we could go see that movie. I've even gone so far as to purchase the requisite liquid refreshments from my housekeeping allowance. I've budgeted 'em under 'Medical Necessities.' "

"Well," Duryea said gravely, "we might get Gramps in here and try some of the medicine. If he doesn't pass out, we might take him to the movies with us."

She said, "Not Gramps. He's picked out a mystery movie he thinks you should see. He's absolutely and utterly steeped in mystery. He makes dark, cryptic remarks and grim forecasts. I'll bet he's sleeping with a gun under his pillow."

"Is he getting on your nerves, babe?"

"Heavens, no," she said, laughing. "*I* don't mind him, but you married me and not my family."

He asked, "Where is that bottle of cocktails?"

She produced it, and Duryea drew the cork. "Let's get him in for a toast to crime," he said.

Gramps Wiggins' voice, shrill and high-pitched, sounded from the doorway. "Don't need to call me when you're pullin' the cork on a bottle, son. Some sort of a psychic sense brings me 'round right at what they call the psychological moment. Of course, I ain't absolutely perfect. Here an' there in the last sixty-eight years I reckon I've missed an occasional drink, but it's been few and far between."

Duryea poured out the cocktails into a shaker filled with cracked ice, then into three glasses. They touched rims. "Here's to crime," Duryea said.

Gramps Wiggins' eyes danced. "Bigger an' better crimes!" He pulled a blackened pipe from his pocket, pushed tobacco down in it, lit a match, and filled the kitchen with a thick, pungent smoke. "Son," he said, "about those murders . . ."

"Have a refill on that cocktail," Milred said quickly.

"Don't care if I do."

Duryea poured the cocktail, and Gramps Wiggins tossed it off with a quick, all-but-casual gesture. "Now, son, about them murders . . ."

"Gramps," Milred interrupted, "you could help put some of the things on the table."

"Okay, what do I do?"

"Split open those baked potatoes, put a couple of squares of butter in each one. Sprinkle on some paprika, and get the pad on the table for the steak platter. This steak is going to be sizzling when it comes out of the broiler."

"Okay," Gramps said. "Where are the potatoes?"

"Coming right up," she said, opening the oven door, and bringing out a pan, which held three large baked potatoes. "Use these pot-lifters, Gramps, and you won't burn your fingers. Just push the ends in so you break them a little, and . . ."

Gramps said indignantly, "Think I don't know how to bust an' butter a potato?"

He picked up the pot-lifters, grasped the potatoes by the ends, pushed them together, and, as cracks opened in the top, inserted squares of butter. "Now, son," he said, "about these here murders . . ."

Milred looked at her husband. "I surrender. I've done every darn thing I can."

Frank laughed. "Go ahead, Gramps. *What* about the murders?"

"Been scoutin' around a little bit," Gramps Wiggins said with that close-lipped, nervous, high-pitched voice which was so characteristic of him. "Been doin' quite a little scoutin', talkin' around with different people. S'prizin' how much you can learn just by sittin' around an' visitin' with people."

Duryea, sipping his cocktail, said, "I guess that's right."

Milred said, "Lots of elbow room, please. Here comes the steak." She opened the door of the broiler, slid out a three-inch loin steak done to a delicious brown. "Gramps, pick up that hot platter on top of the stove. Hold it with the pot-lifters down here where I can slide the steak on it. . . . There, that's fine. . . . Now, let's have that butter."

Gramps Wiggins looked at the steak with the eye of a connoisseur. "Chop just a little bit of garlic into some olive oil and pour it on while she's cooking," he said. "Gives it a nice flavor. Then there's a way of packing it in moist salt. The salt bakes into a crust, an' you break it right off when the steak's done. That way you seal in the juices an' . . ."

Milred said, "Yes, I know. There are lots of different ways of cooking steaks, but I like my way the best."

"What's your way?" Gramps asked.

"It's a secret."

Wiggins helped with the steak, then turned back to Duryea, casually picking up his empty cocktail glass from the kitchen table as he did so. He held the glass in his right hand, making little gestures with it. "Well, let's get back to them there murders. Like I said, you learn a lot talkin' with . . ."

"Gramps' glass is empty," Milred said. "Remember, it's out of household money and budgeted as medicine."

Duryea refilled all three glasses.

Milred held up the glass and announced, "I don't know what this is going to do to me."

"This!" Gramps Wiggins exclaimed in surprise. "Why, this is just sort of a tonic. You can't drink enough of this to get any effect. Dry Martini, ain't it? Thought so. Ain't no particular strength to 'em, just a good flavor. Well, son, like I was sayin' about these here murders . . ."

Milred said, "Come on, let's get dinner on the table. You men go in and sit down."

Wiggins tossed off his third cocktail, said, "Like I was sayin',
I just poked around a little bit today, foolin' around down
there on the beach, talkin' with people, askin' questions. Well,
I met a family, name o' Tucker—mighty nice people—out here
from the interior, spendin' four or five days, stayin' out at
an auto camp. Awful nice chap, Tucker. Works in the oil
wells, but he an' old John Barleycorn go to the mat once in
a while in a big wrestlin' match. The companies don't like
that. They've sorta laid him off, an' the finance company was
lookin' for his automobile. So he decided to take his wife an'
go on a little vacation. Registered under an assumed name on
that account, but he's all right, awfully nice fellow."

Milred said parenthetically to her husband, "Whenever
Gramps gives anyone the endorsement of being a mighty fine
chap, you can rest assured he's either been in jail, is hiding
from the sheriff, or is a confirmed drinker. Perhaps it's all
three."

Wiggins looked sternly at her over the tops of his steel-
rimmed glasses. "Now, don't go puttin' on airs, Milred. You're
a mighty nice girl, sort o' took after the Wiggins' side of the
family. Mighty good thing you did, too. Your father resem-
bled his mother a lot, only he was a lot more pantywaist than
his mother ever thought o' bein'. You're a Wiggins. Don't go
spoilin' it now. Havin' a little trouble ain't nothin' to hold up
against a man. Now this here Tucker . . ."

Frank Duryea picked up the carving set, started slicing the
steak.

"Got some coffee made?" Gramps Wiggins asked Milred.
She nodded.

"I'll go get a bottle o' that brandy," Wiggins said, jumping
up. "Goes mighty nice in coffee. A little of it straight ain't
goin' to hurt you none either. It sort o' stimulates your stomach an' makes it handle food faster. Since I been drinkin' that
brandy, never have had even a touch o' stomach trouble.
Don't have no trouble digestin' anything."

Milred said, "You don't digest it, Gramps. You just pickle
it."

"Mebbe so. Mebbe so. I'll go get a bottle anyhow. Got a
lot of it in the trailer." He pushed back his chair and his short
legs fairly twinkled as he bustled through the kitchen and out
to the trailer.

Milred said, "It's even worse than I thought it was going to be. He's all loaded for you. I hope you're not going to mind it too much, Frank."

He laughed and reached across the table to take her hand. "I think I'm going to like it."

"Well, just remember you can't depend on anything he says —I mean, on the people he has for witnesses. Gramps has a genius for picking up people who are just a little off-color."

Duryea said, "After all, Milred, I'm going to have to prosecute someone on these murders. It isn't going to hurt any to talk it over a little."

"*Talk* it over!" she exclaimed. "You won't get a word in edgewise. You're being awfully nice to him, Frank—and to me."

"I think he's swell—and I'm learning a lot about you. So you're a Wiggins?"

She smiled. "A dissolute wanton," she said. "I come by it honestly."

Gramps Wiggins came bustling back with two bottles of brandy. "This here one is only about half full," he said. "Thought I'd better bring another one along, just in case."

He passed his coffee cup over to Milred. "Just about half a cup, sister," he said.

She held the cup under the faucet of the electric coffee percolator, drew off about two-thirds of a cup. Gramps Wiggins promptly filled the other third with brandy, stirred it up, tasted it, and smacked his lips. "Better try some o' this, son," he said.

"Later," Duryea said.

Gramps Wiggins cut off a slice of steak, pushed it in his mouth, scooped up baked potato, broke off a piece of bread, and shoved it in after the potato. Then, ignoring the amount of food in his mouth, started talking, his words all but indistinguishable. "Now that there Tucker . . ."

Milred said, "Gramps, why don't you chew your food?"

He looked at her indignantly. "I am chewing my food."

"You're talking."

"Well, I gotta open my mouth, ain't I, to get my teeth in position? And I close it to bring my teeth down on the food. I also gotta open it an' close it to talk, so I just combine the two operations. Can't tell whether I talk to chew, or whether I chew to talk. . . .

"Well, gettin' back to this here Tucker. Nice chap. Everett Tucker his name is. Wife's name Marjorie. I got their address an' all about 'em. Ain't got no children now. Had a boy that was purty wild, got killed in an auto accident. Well, what I was gonna say, son, was how about this here Moline girl that fell overboard from that yacht? When did she go aboard the yacht?"

"She says about ten or fifteen minutes before young Shale picked her up in the boat. She was aboard the yacht just long enough to discover the bodies."

"Uh huh. Anyone *see* her goin' aboard the yacht?"

"Apparently not. Shale, it seems, was about the only one who was in a position to notice her, and he happened to be examining a seashell as she walked past. He says that was just about ten or fifteen minutes before he picked her up out of the water. That's the only time she *could* have gone aboard without his seeing her."

"That ain't no way to prove anything."

"Why not?"

"How long had this here Shale boy been on the beach?"

"Nearly three-quarters of an hour."

"Well," Wiggins said, "Tucker had been there at least for a half an hour. He thinks probably three-quarters of an hour, but he's sure of half an hour because after he'd been on the beach a few minutes, he looked at his watch. He remembers what time it was."

"What did he see?" Duryea asked.

"That's just the point," Gramps said. "He didn't see a gol-darn thing. Now, if that girl had walked along the beach an' out on that yacht club float, an' rowed over to this here *Gypsy Queen*, Tucker would have seen her."

"He might not have remembered her," Duryea said. "That quite frequently happens. Unless a witness realizes something is important, he'll see some routine happening and then forget entirely that . . ."

"Not Tucker," Wiggins interrupted positively. "He ain't one not to have seen a good-lookin' gal. He was lookin' at them yachts, talkin' to his wife about how he was out of a job and havin' trouble with the finance company, an' here were a lot o' people rollin' in wealth an' leisure, with yachts to sail around in, just for their own pleasure."

Milred said, "It probably didn't occur to him that if he'd applied himself and quit drinking, he might have stood a chance of getting up to the top of the heap himself."

Gramps said, "Oh, sure. People who own yachts don't drink. They just apply themselves industriously to work. They don't . . ."

"Well, I haven't sympathy with a man who hasn't gumption enough to make something of himself, and then starts crabbing because other people have made more of a success."

Duryea, his eyes alert with interest, said, "You have his name and address, Gramps?"

"Sure. He's stayin' here at an auto camp. Like I told you, he's stayin' under another name. Tucker, that's his real name. That's the name you'd have to use in a subpoena if you was goin' to bring him into court."

"What does his wife say?"

"The same thing."

"I'll want to talk with them."

"Wait a minute. You ain't heard anythin' yet. Now, Tucker was sittin' on the beach Saturday afternoon. Purty much of a crowd there Saturday. There wasn't a breath stirrin', but it was purty nice weather. This here *Gypsy Queen* was tied up right there at the same place Saturday afternoon. Tucker noticed her because she's the biggest yacht in the harbor. He seen a girl go aboard. She went out to the end of the float and waved, and a man rowed out from the *Gypsy Queen* to pick her up. That girl had on a plaid skirt and a red coat. Young and good lookin'. Tucker looked at these pictures of the Moline gal in the newspaper an' thinks maybe this was the same one."

"What time Saturday?"

"Oh, it was along about mebbe three o'clock."

"How long did she stay?"

"Until around four. She had some letters in her hand when she came off the yacht. She dropped 'em in the mailbox there at the end of the streetcar line. Tucker watched her."

Duryea said, "I'm supposed to interview the witnesses again tonight. Do you suppose you could get Mr. and Mrs. Tucker up to my office?"

"Reckon I could," Gramps Wiggins said. "They'd do anythin' for me. . . . How about a little more coffee, Milred? Just a speck, just about half a cup."

Duryea said, "My appointment with the sheriff is at seven-thirty, Gramps. If you're going along, don't you think it'd be better to go easy on that stuff?"

"What, this?" Gramps asked in surprise, indicating the brandy.

Duryea nodded.

"Why, shucks, son, that stuff never hurt nobody—taken in reasonable quantities. I never was one to abuse it."

Milred said, "So we don't get to see that movie?"

"Why not? We can make the second show."

Gramps said, "There's a mystery picture that they say's a humdinger. We'll all go to see it. Now that there Moline girl certainly is class. Seen her pictures in the paper. Certainly looks like a million dollars' worth of curves."

Milred said, "You keep an eye on my husband, Gramps. After all, you know, we wouldn't want to have a scandal in the Wiggins' family."

"That's right," Gramps agreed. "There ain't ever been a Wiggins that applied for a divorce."

Milred showed her surprise. "Why, I thought you and Grandmother were divorced."

"Yep. That's right, but she was the one that got it. That's the way with the Wiggins' strain. If there's goin' to be any divorcin' done, the other side is the one that has the grounds. That's mighty good steak, Milred. Couldn't a' done it no better if I'd put wet salt all around it, an'—an' how's for just a leetle more coffee? We might's well get this here brandy bottle empty."

CHAPTER 14

THE desk light was arranged so that the chair on the opposite side of Frank Duryea's desk was bathed in brilliance. The district attorney and the sheriff were in a less brilliantly illuminated area. Slightly to one side, where he could distinctly hear everything that was said, but would not be conspicuous, the court stenographer opened his books and tried out his pens.

"All ready?" Duryea asked.

Lassen said, "All ready to go, I guess."

Duryea raised his eyes to the shadowy figure of the sheriff's deputy who guarded the door to the outer office.

"Let's have Miss Moline in first," he said.

She was dressed now in her smooth-fitting gray outfit. Her hair, freed of the salt water, had the full rich glint of amber in the sunlight. She entered the room, promptly crossed over to the chair indicated by the district attorney, sat down and said briskly, "This is going to be more comfortable than our last interview."

Duryea smiled perfunctorily, and then plunged into the interrogation. "Now, it's very important that we have these questions answered correctly. So take your time, don't get excited, and be certain that you're answering the questions the way you want to answer them."

She nodded.

"How long have you known Addison Stearne?"

"About a year."

"C. Arthur Right?"

"About the same length of time."

"What was the relationship between you and Mr. Stearne?"

"What do you mean by that?"

"I'm sorry if I seem to pry into your personal affairs, but it's necessary. Was there a love interest on his part—or on yours?"

"No. The man was old enough to be my father."

Duryea smiled and said, "I think we can reserve the platitudes, Miss Moline. He was in the late fifties. He was wealthy, and he was attractive. Did he ever talk about matrimony with you?"

"Never."

"I understand you've been appointed a special administratrix with the will annexed?"

"Yes."

"And under the terms of that will, the bulk of the property goes to you?"

"Yes."

90

"Men like Addison Stearne don't leave wills in favor of young women unless there's a reason."

"Obviously."

"Very well, perhaps we can spare you some embarrassing quesions if you tell me what that reason was."

"Does that have anything to do with the murder?"

"It may. I want to know all the details of your relationship."

"It's none of your business."

"It may be that you're right. Again, you may be wrong," Duryea said quietly, "but I am the one who is going to be the judge."

"Why, you have absolutely no right to pry into my private affairs."

"Let me ask it this way. Did your money in any way come from Addison Stearne? Was he giving you any income, directly or indirectly?"

"That has absolutely nothing to do with the case."

Duryea said, "As nearly as we can ascertain, Miss Moline, eighteen months ago you were working in a millinery store. You were working for a small salary, and living within that salary. You had, to all appearances, no other source of income."

She flushed indignantly, started to say something, then caught back the words, and sat looking at the district attorney, her face hot and angry.

"Then suddenly you made the woman who owned the store an offer to buy her out. She fixed her price. You put up the money in cash. You expanded. You advertised, increased your stock, added to your employees, and about eight months later sold out at a very handsome profit. Since that time, you haven't worked. You have bought and sold property. You have, I believe, invested in some stocks and bonds. Everything you've touched has turned to money. It's at least a fair inference, Miss Moline, that the excellent business judgment which enabled you to make a neat profit on every transaction was furnished by brains that were—if not more shrewd, at least more experienced in business affairs than your own."

She still remained silent, her eyes glinting with angry lights, her chin held high.

"At just about the time you started on this meteoric rise to prosperity, you began to associate with Addison Stearne.

The origin of that association seems to be rather obscure; apparently it was an association which ripened rapidly into intimacy. Am I correct?"

She said, "Your intrusion in my private affairs is an insolent usurpation of high-handed power."

Duryea said patiently, "Here in this office we become realists. We see life as it is. We don't theorize. We know that when a man of mature years interests himself in a young and beautiful woman, when this young woman makes no attempt to rebuff his interest, and almost immediately begins to show signs of prosperity, we feel that the relationship is apt to be somewhat more than platonic."

She hesitated for a moment, then pushed back her chair. "I don't have to stay here and listen to this."

A deputy moved over to guard the door.

"I'm afraid that you do," Duryea said.

"Well, I don't. I have some rights."

Duryea said patiently, "Perhaps we can go at it in another way. Let me show you why this inquiry is important."

"I've been waiting for that," she said, still standing.

"When did you go aboard the *Gypsy Queen?* What time Sunday morning?"

"I've told you, it was ten or fifteen minutes before I ran out to the deck and fell overboard."

"How long were you aboard the yacht?"

"Just a few minutes—just long enough to find the bodies."

Duryea said, "I've been unable to find anyone who saw you going aboard the yacht on Sunday morning."

She remained scornfully silent.

"But," Duryea went on, "I have a witness who saw a young woman boarding the yacht Saturday afternoon."

She suddenly ceased breathing, standing there motionless for several seconds. Then, slowly, she started breathing once more.

"Well?" Duryea asked.

She said, "If you have a witness, bring him in."

"Were you in Santa Delbarra Saturday afternoon?"

"Don't be silly!"

"Were you?"

"Listen, you've tried to bully me and browbeat me. You've made nasty insinuations. I suppose you have a right to ask any question you want, but I also have a right to answer only the questions I deem fair."

"You're avoiding the question."

"I'm doing better than that. I'm ignoring it."

Duryea turned to the deputy who stood guard at the door. "Carter, ask Mr. Shale to step in, if you will, please, and at the same time you can ask Mr. and Mrs. Tucker to look in here."

The guard said, "Mr. Wiggins—the old man—says he wants to come in when the Tuckers come in."

Duryea smiled. "All right, let him."

The guard opened the door, said, "Shale and the Tuckers. Okay, Wiggins, you can come."

The four filed into the room. Nita Moline turned to survey them. She had a flicker of a smile for Shale. The others she regarded coldly. She resumed her seat, waiting scornfully.

Duryea looked at Tucker and raised his eyebrows. Tucker, a tall, dispirited man whose shoulders and face sagged listlessly as though tired of holding up their own weight, apparently failed to get the signal. Mrs. Tucker whispered something to Gramps Wiggins. Gramps in turn nudged Tucker and passed on the whisper.

Tucker slowly shook his head.

Gramps said in his quick, high-pitched voice, "Better talk with us a little later. Okay for us to wait here?"

"No," Duryea said with a smile. "Wait outside," and then as he saw the look on Gramps' face, relented and said, "You may sit down over there by the sheriff, Mr. Wiggins. Mr. and Mrs. Tucker can wait outside. Shale, if you'll come over here and draw up that chair by the corner of the desk, I want to ask you a few questions."

Shale silently complied with his request.

"You are employed as a salesman?" Duryea asked of Shale.

"That's right."

"You didn't know C. Arthur Right or Addison Stearne?"

"I'd never met either of them."

"You were on the beach Sunday morning?"

"Yes."

"Do you know when Miss Moline boarded the yacht?"

"I didn't actually *see* her go aboard the yacht, but I know when she must have boarded it."

"When?"

"At just about fifteen minutes before I picked her up in the skiff."

"You first saw her when she came to the rail of the yacht?"

"That's right."

"How long did she stay there at the rail?"

"A minute or two."

"And then?"

"She fell overboard."

"How long did it take you to get to her?"

"I don't know. I wasn't thinking about the passing of time at that particular moment. I was simply trying to get there."

"Can you make any estimate?"

"Well, let's see. I had to run about fifteen or twenty yards, then I had to get a boat untied and row out. Oh, three minutes perhaps."

"During that time she was struggling in the water?"

"I don't think she was struggling. She went under either once or twice. I think she was coming up for about the third time when I arrived with the skiff."

"Now what makes you say she boarded the yacht about fifteen minutes before you first saw her?"

"I didn't say fifteen minutes before I first saw her," Shale said cautiously. "I said about fifteen minutes before I got her out of the water. It was probably about eleven or twelve minutes before I first saw her—that is, if you want to be absolutely accurate."

"Well, what makes you fix the time when she must have boarded the yacht?"

"Because that was the only time she could have boarded the yacht without my seeing her."

"Explain that, please."

"Just about fifteen minutes before I picked her up out of the water, I became very much interested in a peculiar shell."

"You seem to be rather positive that it was exactly fifteen minutes before you picked Miss Moline out of the water."

"Well, of course, I didn't time it. I'm only giving an estimate."

"You were staying at the Balboa Hotel?"

"Yes."

"And returned there after I had finished questioning you aboard the yacht?"

"Yes."

"And Miss Moline got in touch with you there?"

"Yes."

"Then what?"

"We went out and had a drink."

"And you went aboard the *Albatross?*"

"Yes."

"At her suggestion?"

"Well, yes, in a way."

"Had you ever met Miss Harpler before?"

"Not before that day, no, sir."

"Was there some particular reason you went aboard the *Albatross?*"

"Miss Moline suggested it."

Duryea said dryly, "You don't have to answer any of these questions, you know. And if you do answer them, you don't have to tell the truth. But telling an untruth might well lead to complications. Now, Mr. Shale, was there any particular reason why you went aboard the *Albatross?*"

Nita Moline said, "He did so at my request."

"I'm asking Shale," Duryea said.

Shale said, "I have nothing to add to what Miss Moline has said. If you want to know anything about what I did *after* I left the *Gypsy Queen,* you'll have to ask her."

Duryea thought that over for a few minutes, then asked, "Why do you adopt that attitude, Shale?"

"Because I don't believe that what I did after that has anything whatever to do with the murders."

"The *Albatross* put to sea around two or three o'clock in the afternoon, didn't it?"

"I wouldn't know."

"Weren't you aboard at the time?"

"I was asleep."

"When did you wake up?"

"When we were out at sea somewhere."

"What did you do?"

"I tried to get out of the stateroom."

"Did you?"

"No, sir, not right then. The door was locked. I raised quite a commotion, however, and eventually Miss Harpler came down to let me out."

"What did she say?"

"Said that she felt that some of the officers aboard the *Gypsy Queen* thought we were taking too great an interest in the *Albatross,* so she decided to embark upon a little cruise just to make things seem casual."

Nita Moline started to say something, then checked herself. "What time was it when you woke up?" Duryea asked Shale.

"Shortly before sundown."

Duryea said, "I guess that's all for the present. I'm satisfied that subsequent to the discovery of the bodies, something happened, and that you people are trying to keep what that something was from coming to my attention. Until I get more co-operation from you on that point, you will be subject to certain inconveniences."

He waited for one of them to speak, but neither one said anything. They exchanged a quick, brief glance, then avoided each other's eyes—and his.

Gramps Wiggins hitched forward in his chair. "One question I'd kinda like to ask," he said.

Duryea frowned.

"Now listen," Gramps Wiggins interpolated, "this is important, son."

"What is it?" Duryea asked, his tone unconsciously curt.

"I'd like to have Shale tell us whether Miss Moline didn't ask *him* about what time he *wasn't* looking at the yacht before she told him when she came aboard."

Shale frowned at Gramps Wiggins, then smiled, turned back to Duryea, and said, "I can answer that very easily, Mr. Duryea. She did nothing of the . . ." Abruptly he stopped. A puzzled frown came over his face. He looked quickly at Nita Moline, then away again.

Gramps Wiggins got up out of the chair and walked around to where he could look down at Shale. "Didn't she come up to the hotel, take you out and buy you a drink?" he shrilled, his voice high-pitched with excitement. "And ask you how it happened you didn't see her when she went aboard the yacht? Didn't she ask you if there wasn't some time when you weren't lookin'? Didn't she pump you first?"

Shale said to Duryea, "Who is this person?"

Duryea said, "He's not a member of my official family. You're under no obligation to answer the question *if you don't want to.*"

Shale said, "I think I've said everything I need to."

"And that yacht, the *Albatross*," Gramps Wiggins went on, shaking a finger at the witness. "Didn't she go out and have a meeting with another yacht some place, sort of a rendezvous?"

"I don't know," Shale said. "I was asleep. By the time I was permitted on deck again, the yacht was headed back toward Santa Delbarra."

"Humph," Gramps Wiggins snorted.

Duryea said, "That's all, unless there's some statement you wish to make. If there is, I'll be glad to hear it."

Wordlessly, they scraped back chairs and left the office.

When they had gone, Gramps Wiggins said, "That wasn't the young woman Tucker seen goin' aboard the yacht Saturday. But he didn't see her on the beach Sunday either. He seen her come out on the deck o' that yacht an' pitch herself overboard."

"She says she fainted," Duryea said.

"That's what she says. Tucker says she pitched herself overboard."

"Why did you ask him about the *Albatross* having a rendezvous with some other ship?" Duryea asked.

"I keep wonderin' about this trip the *Gypsy Queen* was scheduled to make that Sunday afternoon," Gramps Wiggins said, pulling a moist black plug of chewing tobacco from his pocket and whittling off a small piece. "Stearne let the crew all go until three o'clock, then she was goin' to take a cruise. That's a funny time to go cruisin'. Well, the *Gypsy Queen* didn't go, an' the *Albatross* did. Now then, seems like the *Albatross* just went out to sea for a while, an' then came back. Why'd she do that?"

Duryea said, "You've got me there, Gramps."

"She was tryin' to keep the *Gypsy Queen's* rendezvous. Where's that Harpler girl?"

Sheriff Lassen said, "I let the Harpler girl go. She don't know anything at all, except she saw young Shale start to run for a boat. She began lookin' around, and saw a few ripples in the water, then got a glimpse of some blond hair, so in she went."

"How about this here yachtin' trip she went on Sunday?" Gramps asked.

The sheriff regarded him with a jaundiced eye. "It was her yacht, wasn't it? What are you tryin' to do, anyway?" Duryea interposed hastily, "We can reach her any time we need her, Sheriff. I confess that I didn't consider her as a particularly important witness, and saw no reason for holding her here."

He pushed back his chair, stretched, yawned, said, "Well, I guess that's about all for tonight." He nodded to the deputy at the door. "That'll be all, Carter. Tell 'em all they can go home. I won't need you any more tonight."

Carter opened the door into the entrance office, said, "Everybody can go now." The sheriff arose and sauntered out, without saying good night.

"You have Tucker's address?" Duryea asked Gramps Wiggins.

"Uh huh."

"Well, keep in touch with him. We'll let things simmer along for a while, and . . ."

Sam Carter, the deputy sheriff, re-entered the office. "Man out there by the name of Hazlit says he wants to see you, and that it's important."

Duryea frowned and shook his head. "I'm investigating this murder case now, and . . ."

"Says he's a lawyer."

"That's different," Duryea said. "Show him in. You don't mind waiting a minute, do you, Gramps?"

"Nope. Want me to wait outside?"

Duryea smiled at the man's anxiety to be allowed to remain. "I'm afraid Mr. Hazlit will want to talk with me in private," he said. "If he's an attorney . . ."

Carter opened the door, and Hazlit came bustling into the office accompanied by Nita Moline.

Miss Moline said, "Mr. Duryea, this is my lawyer, Mr. Hazlit."

"Oh," Duryea said, shaking hands. "I'm glad to meet you, Mr. Hazlit. I didn't know Miss Moline had a lawyer waiting."

"I wasn't waiting," Hazlit said. "I just got here—just this minute got here."

"If I'd known you were coming, I'd have waited to question Miss Moline . . ."

"Oh, it isn't that. As far as that's concerned, I've told her to go ahead and tell the truth. Answer all the questions you want to ask. She has nothing to conceal."

Nita Moline said indignantly, "I didn't know the scope his questions were going to take. He's even insinuated that . . ."

"Just a minute, my dear. Just a minute," Hazlit said, holding up a warning hand. He turned to Duryea, and, with his voice at its unctuously agreeable best, said, "I have something which I think is a clue, something which could be investigated."

"What is it?" Duryea asked, sitting down.

Gramps Wiggins, realizing that the interview was going to proceed without any objection to his presence, tiptoed over to the darkest corner of the office and lowered himself quietly into a chair.

Hazlit said, "I am Miss Moline's attorney largely because of my familiarity with the affairs of Mr. Stearne. I handled all of his legal business during his lifetime. One of the important matters was an option which was to have expired at midnight Saturday, an option which apparently Mr. Stearne hadn't taken up, although it seemed most advantageous from a business standpoint that he do so. I had Miss Moline appointed special administratrix with the will annexed this morning, so that she could file an application asking for an extension of time on this option, and she duly signed an acceptance of the option late this afternoon. I suppose, of course, there'll be litigation over it. However, I'm only mentioning that to give you the general picture."

"I see. You mentioned that you had a clue?"

"Yes. It now appears that Mr. Stearne exercised that option."

"Well?" Duryea asked.

Hazlit took an envelope from his pocket, handling it almost reverently. "I have here," he said, "an envelope addressed to Mr. Addison Stearne at his Los Angeles office. This envelope was mailed at four-thirty-five P.M. Saturday from Santa Delbarra."

"Yes?" Duryea asked.

"In it," Hazlit said, "is a carbon copy of a letter to Elwell &

99

Fielding, exercising the option, and in a large measure explaining why the acceptance had not been made before. On the second sheet of this carbon copy appears, in the handwriting of Mr. Stearne, a notation to the effect that he had mailed the original letter himself from Santa Delbarra before five o'clock Saturday afternoon, by depositing it in the post office at Santa Delbarra."

Duryea said, "Let's see that letter."

He took the carbon copy in his hands, studied it for several minutes. "Was this letter written in his office prior to the time of his departure?" he asked.

"I don't think so. If it had been, the carbon copy would have been left in the office, and he'd have taken the original with him to mail."

Duryea said, "I notice that it's dated at Santa Delbarra."

"Yes."

"Did he have a typewriter on his yacht?"

"Yes. He had a portable typewriter. Occasionally, he used it—although C. Arthur Right, who had at one time been his secretary, quite frequently did typing for him. Elwell & Fielding assure me absolutely that they have received no such letter in the mail. I think, Mr. Duryea, that's a plain, deliberate lie. They were advised of Mr. Stearne's death and thought they could capitalize on it by claiming that this letter had never been received. What I want you to do . . . er . . . that is, what would seem to be indicated," and Hazlit paused long enough to take a deep breath, before saying slowly and solemnly, "is bring those two crooks in front of your grand jury. If Stearne mailed that letter, it is a matter of importance in helping you fix the time he met his death. It might well be important in connection with a motivation."

Duryea smiled. "In other words, you're going to engage in a lawsuit with these men. You'd like very much to have me blaze a trail for you to follow—and perhaps pull a chestnut or two out of the fire."

Hazlit said with dignity, "I am not trying to lead you to believe that I might not derive some advantage from the investigation, but I am approaching you simply as a district attorney."

Old Gramps Wiggins, who had advanced on tiptoe to peer over the district attorney's shoulder, suddenly reached out and tapped the letter. "Lookut here," he said. "Down in that lefthand corner those initials, 'A.S.—A.R.' Betcha 'A.R.' is the stenographer who took the letters. Betcha she's the girl Tucker saw leavin' the yacht Saturday afternoon with the envelopes she placed in a mailbox. Betcha, by gum, she's some stenographer livin' right here in Santa Delbarra."

Hazlit said sternly, "The notation in Mr. Stearne's handwriting is that *he mailed the letter himself* from the United States post office."

"Don't care what it says," Gramps Wiggins shrilled. "That's what happened. We got a witness that saw the girl leavin' the boat. She mailed the copy. Stearne mailed the original."

He looked eagerly at Duryea.

Duryea smiled encouragingly. "That's a very logical deduction."

Hazlit said, "Well, Counselor, I have called this matter to your attention because I felt it was my duty to co-operate with you in every way."

"An excellent attitude," Duryea said, "and perhaps you'll be able to impress it upon your client."

Gramps Wiggins started for the door. "You take Milred to that there movie," he shrilled. "I don't want to see that romantic tripe, anyway. I got some things to do."

CHAPTER 15

DURYEA found Milred dressed and ready for the movie. "Where," she asked, "is Gramps?"

Duryea said, "He started out to do some detective work, and I didn't have the heart to stop him. It's the sort of wild-goose chase that will keep him out of mischief."

"What's the goose?"

"He's looking for a public stenographer whose initials are 'A.R.' He's inclined to favor Alice, Alberta, or Ailene."

"Where do the initials 'A.R.' enter into the case?"

"Addison Stearne sent a letter to his office on Saturday—or rather the carbon copy of a letter. Down in the lower left-hand corner were the initials of a stenographer, 'A.R.' There's some evidence that a young woman was aboard the yacht

Saturday. Gramps thinks she may have typed the letter."

"Well," Milred Duryea asked, "what's the joke? Am I dumb, or is it that I just don't see things?"

"Want to go to that movie?" he asked.

She said, "I'm all dressed up. My nose is powdered, my lipstick applied carefully, and I'm wearing a hat that looks like a cross between a last year's bird nest and a flower pot that's been stepped on by an elephant. If you think I'm going to stay home, Frank Duryea . . ."

"Okay, let's go places and do things."

"Okay, but what's the joke about the stenographer's initials?"

Duryea said, "It seems not to have occurred to Gramps yet that 'A.R.' are the initials of Arthur Right, and Right was formerly Stearne's secretary, and frequently did typing for him when they were on yachting trips."

She thought that over for a few seconds, then said, "Well, I hope you don't have to get Gramps out of jail."

"Why?"

"You forget he's a Wiggins."

"What's that got to do with it?"

"Turn him loose in this city," she said, "looking for public stenographers whose first names are Alice, Alberta, Ailene and Aphrodite—well, of course, he's slowed down a good bit, but still—Did you notice the way he was all slicked up?"

"Did I! He's a mighty spry-looking gent when he gets that blue serge suit out of moth balls."

"Why'd you let him go on a wild-goose chase like that, Frank?"

"Oh, just to give him his fling. It's a thrill to him. At that, he made a couple of deductions from the evidence that were pretty good. Come on, let's go."

They got as far as the front door. As Duryea switched on the porch light, an automobile came to a stop at the curb. A man and a woman got out, came toward them.

"Mr. Duryea?" the woman asked.

Duryea raised his hat, bowed.

Emotion constricted the woman's vocal cords so that her voice sounded harsh and high-pitched. "We simply *must* see you for a moment," she said. "We'll try not to detain you."

Duryea hesitated. "I have an appointment. I . . ."

"I'm Mrs. Right," she interrupted, "the widow of C. Arthur Right."

That simple statement carried enough weight to insure a granting of the woman's request. Duryea's glance at his wife was an implicit shrug of the shoulders. He opened the front door. Milred went in, switching on lights. Duryea followed his visitors into the living room.

"I'm sorry," Mrs. Right said, "that we interfered with your plans, but I've driven up from Los Angeles. I simply had to see you. I . . ."

The man said, quietly, competently, "If you'll just go ahead and tell him, Pearl."

Duryea looked inquiringly across at her escort. The man introduced himself. "Hilbers," he said.

"The first name?"

"Warren. I'm Mrs. Right's brother."

Duryea said to Mrs. Right, "I can appreciate what a shock this has been to you, Mrs. Right. However, I presume you didn't come here to listen to condolences."

"I did not. I came here to give you some evidence I think you should have."

"What is it?"

"I . . . well, you see . . ." She glanced at Milred. "I'm going to have to tell you something of the setup. Addison Stearne dominated my husband. Arthur thought that Addison Stearne was sort of a god."

Warren Hilbers said quietly, "Pearl, why don't you give him the information you want him to have, then let Mr. Duryea ask the questions? If you'll be brief, it is quite possible he can still make his appointment."

"You tell him, Warren."

Hilbers took a cigarette from his pocket. He lit a match, moved it back and forth until he had lit the cigarette. His eyes met those of the district attorney steadily. He said simply, "She thinks her husband killed Addison Stearne, and then committed suicide."

Duryea frowned. "But I understood Mrs. Right to say that he worshiped . . ."

Hilbers interrupted without seeming to do so. His voice had a certain timbre which made it cut across the thread of conversation as effectively as though he had shouted down the district attorney's comments. Yet he had not raised his voice from the ordinary conversational level. "There was another factor about which my sister dislikes to speak. She thinks that, in a way, she's responsible. I've tried to tell her one person is never responsible for the acts of another, but she's nervous and upset about it. She thinks the whole thing may have happened because of something she said. . . . Go ahead, Pearl, tell him the whole story."

"In order to say that which I have to tell you," Mrs. Right said, "it's necessary for me to try and be very fair to a woman whom I hate."

Duryea bowed his head slightly in acknowledgment of her statement, giving her a silent invitation to proceed.

"The relationship between Addison Stearne and Nita Moline," Mrs. Right said, "was rather peculiar. I thought it was founded on an intimacy. I realize now that there is some possibility the man regarded himself, in a way, as her father, and . . ."

"Go ahead, Pearl," Hilbers said as she hesitated.

"And," Mrs. Right went on, "that he actually was her father."

Duryea kept any expression whatever from showing on his face.

"Miss Moline is a very peculiar young woman. She is very poised, and she knows exactly what she wants. I don't know whether you're familiar with that type, Mr. Duryea, but it's a deadly combination in a woman. Men are fascinated by that calm poise. I think at first it arouses their interest because it challenges them."

Hilbers broke the thread of silence which followed her remark by saying in his peculiarly powerful voice, "Never mind the philosophy, Pearl. Mr. Duryea wants to know what happened. Your husband was desperately in love with Nita Moline. She didn't return his affection. Now go on, Pearl, and get it over with."

Mrs. Right said nervously, "Of course, that's one of the things a man doesn't consult his wife about—but I knew. Arthur had worshiped the ground Addison Stearne walked on. Everything that Addison did was all right in Arthur's eyes. Well, Addison kept throwing Nita Moline and Arthur together. Addison hated me. He wanted to break up our marriage. He was very, very successful. Arthur fell madly in love with Nita Moline.

"I don't know when Arthur first realized how far he'd succumbed to Stearne's influence. I don't know when I first realized it, but Arthur and I had been drifting apart. I'd told him dozens of times when Addison was trying to come between us, trying to split us up. At first, he laughed at the idea. Later on, he'd fly into a rage whenever I said anything against Addison Stearne. So finally we had a sort of tacit understanding that when he was going somewhere with Addison Stearne, he could just go right ahead, and I'd find something else to do. It was that which kept me from realizing until recently that Addison was throwing Arthur and Nita together as much as he possibly could. Then it dawned on me all at once."

"Tell him how you found out, Pearl," her brother said.

"My husband told me."

"When was this?" Duryea asked.

"Last Friday. He told me that we'd been drifting apart, that he thought it was foolish to continue trying to keep up the pretense, that he hadn't loved me for a long time, but that recently he'd fallen in love with someone else. I insisted that he tell me who it was, and then was when I learned for the first time.

"Well, naturally, I was angry and hurt. I don't think that it was because my heart was broken. I guess some of it was because my vanity was hurt, and I tried to hurt him. I knew him well enough to know the one thing I could say which *would* hurt him. Perhaps you know enough to understand how it is, Mr. Duryea. When people have been really intimate and have one of those bitter quarrels, they try to tear each other's emotions to shreds. They want to hurt. But I wouldn't have said it, if I hadn't *thought* it was the truth."

"What did you say?" Duryea asked.

"I made a remark about his being a convenient hitching post for Addison Stearne's cast-off mistress."

For a moment, there was silence in the room.

"Then what?" Duryea asked.

She said, "Good heavens, the man certainly should have had eyes in his head. But apparently the idea struck him for the first time, and it struck him like a blow. I never saw him like that. His face went absolutely white. I could see from the way he stared at me that at last the truth was dawning in his mind. There had been so many, many things that indicated it, and he had been so blind to them. When they were pointed out to him, and he saw them all at once, it was a terrible emotional shock."

Hilbers rushed to his sister's defense. "The point is," he explained to Duryea, "that Pearl was absolutely sincere, and heaven knows she had plenty of grounds to suspect that was the case. It wasn't until this morning that Pearl and Miss Moline had a talk, and Pearl learned for the first time that there was—well, that there might be another side to the story. Personally, I still don't believe it. I think it's simply an ingenious explanation that Nita Moline concocted after she knew there was no possibility she could be contradicted. I think it's something she and her lawyer had thought up, to dress up a nice case for her if someone contests the will. The point is that it's upset Pearl so very terribly.

"You know how it is when women fight. They claw at each other, and . . ." He broke off and glanced with quick apology at Milred.

"Don't mind me," Milred said with a grin. "I never bar any holds myself."

"Well," Hilbers said lamely, "Pearl and Miss Moline had one of those fights this morning. Then I came to the house and found Pearl in tears. She'd been thinking over what Miss Moline said, and had come to the conclusion that if there was any truth in it, she'd done something terrible in telling Arthur what she had. The more she continued to brood over it, the more she got the idea she'd been responsible for everything that happened. I've told her time and time again that the evidence shows it couldn't have been murder and suicide. As I understand it, it was very plainly a double murder. I don't think Miss Moline or her relationship to Addison Stearne entered into it at all. But Pearl has been driving herself frantic. This afternoon she had hysterics, and I decided to bring her up here, let her tell her story, and see if there's any chance her idea of what happened might be right. In that way, she'll know definitely. I think anything would be better than this suspense."

"I know it's right," Pearl said in a voice which somehow

carried conviction. "As soon as I made that statement to Arthur, he stood stunned for several seconds, then he turned without a word and walked upstairs. I heard him open and close the bureau drawer. For a while the significance of that didn't occur to me. Then he left the house without saying anything to me. I kept thinking back over our quarrel, and suddenly the significance of that bureau drawer occurred to me. I ran upstairs and opened the one where he kept his gun. The gun was gone."

"Then what did you do?" Duryea asked.

"Then I tried to get in touch with Addison Stearne, and Addison wouldn't see me. I know he was in his office, but he'd left word that I was never to be permitted to get in touch with him."

"Did you actually *see* him take the gun?" Duryea asked.

"No, of course not. But I heard him open and close that bureau drawer, and then the gun was gone."

"I keep telling her," Warren Hilbers said, "that she's torturing her imagination. Arthur could have taken that gun out of the drawer any time within a month and for a dozen different reasons. She's never even bothered to check up on it before. It may be in his car—in his office. He might have given it away."

"But the evidence doesn't indicate a murder and suicide," Duryea said.

"Of course it doesn't," Hilbers said. "Only now Pearl thinks . . ."

"Stop it, Warren," Mrs. Right interrupted. "There's been altogether too much of *that*. We're not going to say anything more."

Hilbers said cautiously, "I'll put it this way, Mr. Duryea. Pearl feels that Arthur would have left a note vindicating himself to the world, explaining the reason he did what he was doing, and, above all, explaining to Nita Moline.

"Now, then, *if* Pearl is right, and *if* it was a murder and suicide, the gun is missing. That note is missing. Personally, I'm absolutely convinced Pearl has worked herself into a state of hysteria. I can't believe that . . ."

"Oh, but it *was* murder and suicide," Pearl Right broke in. "I *know* it was. That much I'll swear to. I saw that look in

Arthur's eyes. Something happened to the evidence. It was removed."

"By evidence, you mean the gun?" Duryea asked.

"And the note. I know he would have left a note, probably on the typewriter, because it would have been long. He wouldn't have left one of those short, cryptic notes, saying, 'I had to do this,' or 'I did this because I found out something about the woman I loved.' Not Arthur. He'd have killed Addison Stearne, then sat down at the typewriter, and composed a long letter. It would have gone back to his first association with Addison Stearne, would have told of his love for Nita Moline, of his suspicions, that he couldn't go on facing life, knowing that the woman he loved had been the mistress of the man he had placed on a pedestal, and he'd probably have left . . . well . . ."

"Left what?" Duryea asked as she hesitated.

"Probably left a will disinheriting me," she admitted.

"And that will's disappeared?"

"Apparently."

"You haven't found any will in his papers?"

"No. That's another thing that shows what he had in mind. He'd drawn a will, placed it in a sealed envelope, and left it in the hands of his banker. The banker telephoned me about it. He seemed rather worried, because Friday afternoon Arthur called and got the envelope containing the will. He said he wanted to make a new one."

"Did that other will leave everything to you?" Duryea asked.

"I don't know. The banker said it was about six months old, so I presume it didn't. There's probably some provision made, but . . . well, you see it was about six months ago. . . . The banker told me the first will had been made about two years ago, then about six months ago Arthur said he wanted to change it. He withdrew the envelope, and about three days later substituted another one, then Friday afternoon he wanted to change the will again."

"The banker doesn't know what was in that other will?"

"No. It was in a sealed envelope."

Hilbers said, "I'm hoping you'll understand our position, Mr. Duryea. Pearl has had this preying on her mind. Even if she's correct in her idea of what happened, I can't see where she's at all to blame—and I can't think there's any possibility she's right. Let's suppose that Addison Stearne *was* Nita Moline's father or stood in the position of a father to her. That would account for his relationship with her. It would also account for the things he'd given her. Now then, it isn't as though Arthur walked up to Stearne, suddenly pulled a gun and shot him. Arthur went on the yacht with Stearne. They were together for at least several hours before the shooting took place. That means that even if Arthur *had* been carrying the gun and *had* intended to shoot Stearne, he would have given Stearne some opportunity to make explanations. Now that's logical, isn't it?"

"That is very logical," Duryea said.

"And if Stearne had been the girl's father, he only needed to say to Arthur, 'You're crazy, Arthur. I'm the girl's father,' or 'I look on her as my daughter,' and that would have settled the whole business."

"That's a very conclusive and logical point," Duryea admitted.

Pearl Right said, with a note of hysteria in her voice, "You're just trying to make me *feel* that it's all right."

Her brother said impatiently, "Don't be a fool, Pearl. We're talking facts and figures." He turned to Duryea parenthetically, "I've been all over this with her a dozen times, but she won't listen to *me*. I thought that perhaps you could reassure her. She knows that it's your duty to investigate what happened. You're certainly not going to overlook any possibilities, simply to reassure my sister, are you?"

Duryea smiled. "Absolutely not."

"That's what I've told her. Now let's get back to the evidence. If Nita Moline was Addison Stearne's mistress, and if Arthur accused Stearne of that, and Stearne admitted it and Arthur shot him, I can't see where Pearl is in any way responsible."

Duryea said cautiously, "You're right about one thing. If Stearne had any explanation to make, he must have had an opportunity to make it before Mr. Right shot him."

Warren Hilbers said, "As I see it, there are several possible explanations. One is that Miss Moline's connection with Addison Stearne had nothing to do with it, that it was a double murder. The other is that Arthur killed him and committed suicide. But *if* that happened, it is absolutely impossible that the relationship between Miss Moline and Addison Stearne could have been as innocent and platonic as she now pretends."

"And if that were the case," Duryea said, "you have some theory about what happened afterwards, Mr. Hilbers?"

"Yes," Hilbers said. "I think Miss Moline . . ."

"Warren, stop," Pearl interrupted. "There's been too much careless talk already."

Hilbers paid no attention to her, but kept on talking, his manner completely dominating the situation. "Under those circumstances, Arthur would have left a note, and, of course, the gun would have been very much in evidence. There is only one person who would have profited by removing the gun and destroying the note. That person is Miss Moline. In that event, she must have been on the yacht long enough to have switched things around to suit herself, destroying the evidence she didn't want found, and planting evidence she *did* want found.

"As I see it, if Miss Moline *had* been Addison Stearne's mistress and was breaking up Pearl's home, Pearl certainly had a right to say what she did to her husband. If it wasn't true, Addison Stearne certainly had every opportunity to set Arthur right. Personally, I think Pearl is torturing herself needlessly."

Duryea turned to Mrs. Right and asked, "You went to Catalina Saturday?"

"Yes. I tried to see Addison Stearne Friday night. I couldn't see him. I gave my brother a ring and told him I was very much disturbed, that I wanted to ask his advice about something."

"But you didn't tell me about missing the gun, Pearl."

"No. I didn't tell you about that until Sunday."

Hilbers said, "She told me about the quarrel and what she'd said. I suggested she let the thing work itself out. She'd tried to see Stearne, and that was all she could do. Of course, at that time, Mr. Duryea, we had no intimation there might be any other relationship between Stearne and Miss Moline than that which my sister had suspected."

"When did you go to Catalina?" Duryea asked.

Hilbers said, "We left about eight o'clock, wasn't it, Pearl?"

"Not that early. About eight-thirty. I left the house about seven-thirty. I don't think we actually started over in the speedboat until around eight-thirty."

Duryea asked, just as a matter of course, "You were together after that?"

"Yes," Hilbers said, and then added quickly, "Now wait a minute—if you want to be absolutely accurate. There were short periods when we weren't together—perhaps fifteen-minute or half-hour intervals."

"And I took a nap Saturday afternoon," Pearl Right said. "I was asleep for over an hour, perhaps an hour and a half."

Duryea smiled. "Oh, I wasn't trying to check up on you *that* closely. I just wanted to know generally."

Mrs. Right said, "We went over to Catalina. We cruised around a little bit, and then Warren got us a cottage."

"Do you remember where?"

"I'm afraid I don't know exactly . . ."

"It was Mrs. Raleigh's cottage," Hilbers interposed. "It's owned by a Mrs. Elvira Raleigh. I rent it occasionally when I'm over there with a yachting party. You know a speedboat is not like a cruiser, and even so, it's nice to have a place on shore where you can bathe in fresh water."

"When did you leave Catalina?"

"Sunday night. That's another thing that you should know about, Mr. Duryea. When Pearl left the house Saturday morning, she didn't intend to come back. She left a note for her husband. The note said that she had put up with his indifference, with his friendship for a man who had been deliberately trying to break up their home, that now Arthur had come to her with the suggestion she get a divorce so he could marry the cast-off mistress of that man, that she had decided to decline with thanks, that as far as she was concerned, Arthur could try and get a divorce right here in California, and that she would contest that divorce. Moreover, she intended to sue Addison Stearne for alienation of affections, and would file a suit Monday morning."

"Where did you leave that note?" Duryea asked Mrs. Right.

"Where Arthur couldn't fail to see it, right on the top of his dresser."

"Could the servants have seen it?"

"No. It was in an envelope."

"Was the envelope sealed?"

"No. I didn't seal it," Mrs. Right said, after thinking a moment.

Hilbers said, "Sunday evening, just as it was getting dark, a messenger came to the bungalow where we were staying over in Catalina. He said Pearl was wanted on the phone. Pearl went to the telephone. It was Nita Moline. She said that something terrible had happened, that Pearl must get home right away and that if Pearl had left any messages she wouldn't want to have made public, she had better get home and destroy them."

"How could *she* have learned about that message?" Duryea asked.

"That's what we want to know. As I see it, there's only one way. Arthur *must* have been at the house some time after seven-thirty Saturday morning. He must have read that message, must have put it back in the envelope, must have seen Nita Moline and told her what was in it."

"You found the message there when you returned?" Duryea asked Mrs. Right.

She nodded.

Hilbers said, "Nita Moline has been pretty shrewd. She wanted to keep from being smeared in the press. She knew that letter was there. She was afraid that if Pearl didn't show up, the officers would search the house and find it."

"Have you asked Miss Moline how she knew the message was there?" Duryea asked Mrs. Right.

"No. I don't think she was quite as definite as Warren makes it sound. She simply intimated that she knew I had left the house without intending to return and said something to the effect that if I'd left any message, it might be a good plan to go home and get it. Something like that. I can't remember the exact words."

Hilbers looked at his watch and smiled apologetically. "I'm sorry, Mr. Duryea, we've taken up a lot more of your time than I had intended, but I did want Pearl to get this off her mind, and I'd like to have you tell her that the evidence at least indicates that Addison Stearne had every opportunity to explain things to Arthur Right."

Duryea said to Mrs. Right, "That's absolutely correct. The evidence indicates that Arthur Right was on the yacht with

Mr. Stearne for some little time. He either sailed with him for the yacht harbor, or else he joined him here in Santa Delbarra some little time before the murder was committed. At least, that's the way the evidence looks now. If your husband had decided to kill Addison Stearne, it would certainly seem that Stearne had every opportunity to explain everything he *could* have explained. And, of course, if your assumption of murder and suicide is correct, the evidence has been tampered with. If that has been done," and Duryea's mouth suddenly became firm, "it's a crime in itself, and the person who would do it is entitled to no consideration whatever."

Hilbers flashed him a quick glance of gratitude.

Pearl Right said, almost tearfully, "Promise you'll do one thing, Mr. Duryea. Please, please, try to find out whether Addison Stearne *really* was her father or—well, you know, taking the position of a father—or . . . or . . ."

"Whether she was his mistress," Hilbers interposed.

She nodded.

Hilbers turned once more to Milred. "I hope," he said, "we're forgiven for intruding on your evening. It means so much to us. I realize how . . ."

She impulsively gave him her hand. "Don't apologize, Mr. Hilbers. I think you did just the right thing."

Duryea escorted them to the door. When they had left, he turned to his wife. "Well?" he asked.

She said, "I could sympathize with both of them, Frank. It's a terrible ordeal for her, and I think he's splendid. Do you suppose that she's right, and the evidence *was* tampered with?"

"There's a very good chance," Duryea admitted. "Let's pull a Gramps Wiggins."

"How?"

"Go down and look that yacht over, just a quiet checkup before we tell anyone about this."

"Given up the idea of the movie?"

"Yes. The second show will have started fifteen minutes ago. We'll see that picture show tomorrow night. It's on at the Mission Theater tonight, tomorrow, and Wednesday, then it goes to the El Cajon and stays there until the end of the week."

"Come on," Milred said. "What's holding us back? After all, I'm a Wiggins, you know—or has Gramps told you?"

CHAPTER 16

"WHAT's the sheriff doing?" Milred asked as Frank Duryea drove his car around the turn to the waterfront. "Leaving it all up to you?"

"Oh, he's going through the motions, picking up witnesses here and there, and uncovering clues. But he isn't furnishing any flashes of inspiration. He'll ride along. If the case naturally gets solved, he'll be in on it. If it doesn't, he'll find some way of squirming out from under. He's a good politician, and he takes the position that after he's unearthed the people who had contacts with the murdered men, it's up to me to take their statements and—well, you know how Lassen is."

"I know."

Duryea swung the car into the parking zone by the yacht club. "Any guards?" she asked.

"No. We took them off and locked the yacht. Miss Moline's been appointed special administratrix. She wants possession, and we'll probably surrender the keys to her tomorrow."

Duryea took his wife's arm, led her across a strip of roadway to the narrow macadamized walk which led to the yacht club. "I'll have to stop in at the club," he said, "and get permission to use one of the skiffs. They . . ."

She said, "Why do that? You'll just make the whole thing so conspicuous. Why not do it all under cover?"

"Are you suggesting that I, the district attorney of Santa Delbarra County, violate the law by stealing a skiff?"

"Uh huh."

"If we get caught, I'll prosecute you," he warned.

"Would the judge let me argue my own case to the jury?"

"Perhaps."

She smiled up at him and said, "I think I'd have you at a disadvantage. Shhhhhh, Frank. Let's tiptoe. There's someone in the yacht club."

Duryea looked through the big lighted windows. Half a dozen persons were gathered in a little group, sitting in reclining wicker chairs, drinking and chatting. The air was blue with tobacco smoke. "Bet they're discussing the murder," Mildred said.

"Why don't you bet on something that isn't a cinch?"

"Never give a sucker a break," she said. "Frank, I suppose I'm a frightful nuisance. You've had enough to put up with, with Gramps messing around, but I *want* to do this."

"It's okay, babe."

"You aren't mad—or bored at my tagging along?"

"No. I'm getting a kick out of it."

"What's wrong with this boat?" she asked, stopping in front of a skiff which was tied up to the float.

"No oars, no oarlocks," he pointed out.

"There's one up ahead," she said.

"Not so loud," he warned.

They walked quietly along the float to where the painter of a skiff had been wound around a cleat.

Duryea said, "We'll take a chance. Hop in."

She jumped into the skiff. Duryea untied the painter and pushed off. "What I don't know about handling a boat," he apologized, "would fill my whole law library."

She watched him with a critical eye. "You play a swell game of tennis, Frank."

"Uh huh."

"And you ride well."

"Uh huh."

"I know now why you played tennis and took me riding with you while you were courting me. You never did take me rowing."

"My father was a smart man, too," he admitted modestly.

"He must have been. Think of how history might have changed. Watch out, you're going to hit that other yacht. Pull on that—no, the other oar. The *other* one! My gosh, don't scare me like that again. . . . Is that the *Gypsy Queen?*"

He turned his head, said, "Uh huh. Thought I was headed for it."

"Why don't you get up in the bow so you can take the painter and jump aboard, and let me row?"

"Don't you like my rowing?"

"I'm crazy about it, but I would so like to get home before daylight. And it looks as though we'll never make it."

He laughed and moved up to the bow of the skiff. She slid

into the rower's seat, braced the heels of her shoes, picked up the oars, and swept them back in a long, clean stroke which sent the little skiff fairly boiling through the water.

"Been holding out on me, eh?"

"I won a race once—for women. That was in college. Now listen, landlubber, when I come up on the beam of that boat, grab that painter and jump aboard, and don't miss it."

"Aye, aye, sir."

"There should be a landing ladder on the thing somewhere."

"It's on the other side."

"Don't say 'other.' Say 'starboard.'"

"Starboard."

"That's better. Which side is port?"

"That's easy."

"I bet you don't know."

"Why, of course I do. It's the exact opposite of starboard."

"All right, which side is starboard?"

He laughed, then suddenly peered out over the bow of the boat and said, "It's the side the landing ladder is on on the *Gypsy Queen*. That's the right side. That means port is left."

She gave one last quick sweep of the oars, sent the skiff alongside the *Gypsy Queen II*. Duryea jumped up to the deck, started to tie the painter.

"Not there," she said. "From the stern. And I'd better watch the knot you tie, because it would be unhandy to swim back."

Duryea raised his hand in a salute. "Aye, aye."

She fastened the painter with a quick, deft twist of the rope.

"Where did you learn so much about seamanship?" he asked.

"Girl and woman," she said, "come this Michaelmas, I've sailed on yachts for nigh onto two weeks, stranger."

"I'll have to look into this. Aren't yachting parties pretty wild affairs?"

She said demurely, "You'll have to ask Gramps about that."

"One of these days, I'm going to become very, very suspicious of that Wiggins strain in your blood."

She sighed. "As though I didn't know that. Why do you think I've been keeping Gramps away from you all these years?"

"That is an idea," he admitted.

"You have a key to this padlock?"

"Supposed to have. I'd hate to think we'd made this voyage across the briny deep in vain." He fumbled through his pockets.

She said, "Don't tell me it's in your other pants."

He triumphantly produced a key and fitted it to the padlock which held the sliding doors at the entrance to the companionway in place. A few moments later they were in the pilothouse cabin. Duryea opened an unlocked door, and they descended into the lower cabin where the murders had taken place.

He said, "I hope this will get you over this idea of yours that crime is something romantic. The place stinks of death, and in case you're interested, that's dried blood on the carpet."

"Gosh, Frank," she said, "the . . . the darned thing really *does* fascinate me."

"What's fascinating about it?"

"I don't know. The idea of trying to deduce what's happened from little clues that have been left behind. Was there anything in the position of the bodies to support this murder and suicide theory?"

"It's a pretty fair inference that Stearne died first. A part of Right's body lay across Stearne's legs."

"Were they both killed with the same gun?"

"Apparently. I haven't a complete report from the post mortem yet. Dr. Graybar wanted to have some assistance. A friend of his has been called up from Los Angeles, a Dr. Petterman. He's something of an authority."

"Was this where the bodies were found?"

"Right there. You're standing just about where Addison Stearne's body lay."

She looked down at the bloodstained carpet, said, "How interesting. I suppose you wanted me to jump or give a little scream, didn't you?"

"I'm afraid you're a bloodthirsty wench."

"Jumping and squealing wouldn't bring him back to life," she said. "If it could do any good, it might be different. And you think he dictated that letter to Right, do you?"

"It's a possibility."

"And Mrs. Right feels her husband wrote a long statement on the typewriter, confessing what he'd done, and telling all the reasons? Was there a typewriter near the bodies, Frank?"

"I think there was. The photographs show it. It was moved when they . . . There it is, on that little taboret in the corner."

"Oh, yes. A portable. Did the sheriff examine it for fingerprints?"

"Oh, yes. He told me he went over everything he thought would be important. He would . . . Hey, wait a minute! There's something on that platen!"

Milred said, "There is . . . a string of letters? No, it's . . ."

"Let's take a look," Duryea said, dropping on his knees in front of the typewriter. "Don't touch it, Milred. Wait a minute. Wait a minute. What's this?"

She bent over his shoulder.

Duryea gave a low whistle.

Milred said indignantly, "How do you suppose Sheriff Lassen could possibly have overlooked *that?*"

"I don't know. Of course, he's no Sherlock Holmes. To tell you the truth, Millie, I probably should have done a little more looking around here, but I just can't stomach scenes of violence. I took over the examination of the witnesses, and left it up to the sheriff and Bill Wiegart to make an investigation of the cabin itself."

"That's a new platen on the typewriter," she pointed out. "And, of course, that could have been written at any time."

"Of course," he said, "only the yacht has either been guarded or locked ever since the discovery of the bodies."

"This Moline girl hasn't a key?"

"No. The sheriff bought the padlock. There were only two keys to it. The sheriff has one, and I have the other. I was supposed to keep mine in my office. I intended to put it in the safe. To tell you the truth, I forgot all about it until those people came."

"It's been in your pocket all day?"

"Uh huh. Well, let's call the sheriff."

She laughed. "Boy, oh, boy! Won't Gramps burn when he finds out what's happened?"

Bill Wiegart straightened from an examination of the typewriter with a magnifying glass. "Not a fingerprint on it anywhere," he said.

"Isn't that unusual?" Duryea asked.

"Well," Wiegart said cautiously, "I'd say it was. To tell you the truth, Mr. Duryea, I haven't had much experience with typewriters. I'm going to do a little checking up."

"You can't find a single fingerprint on any part of it?"

"No. It looks as though someone's gone over it with an oiled rag. Now, that might be all right. Just keeping the typewriter in condition. I suppose the salt air raises the devil with metal parts, and a good caretaker would keep it pretty well cleaned and oiled."

"How about the keyboard?" Milred asked.

"Well, you've got to bear in mind that a person banging his fingers down on a keyboard doesn't hold his fingers still. There's a certain twisting motion."

"Well," Duryea said, "let's concede that Stearne used it in writing some letters, that he either wrote them himself, or had them written by someone to whom he had dictated the correspondence. Then let us suppose he went over the typewriter with an oiled rag, cleaning it up preparatory to putting it away. What I can't understand is why there aren't fingerprints on it from that last message. If he crawled over to the typewriter and tapped out that message just as he was dying, he certainly should have left fingerprints."

"You'd think so," Wiegart said thoughtfully.

"You didn't go over this before for fingerprints?"

"No, I didn't. I don't believe I paid very much attention to the typewriter. Lassen said to concentrate on door-knobs, bits of the brass work around the ship's rail, catches on the windows, and places of that sort where you'd expect to find prints left by someone who'd broken in or who was escaping after a murder."

"Get anything?" Duryea asked.

"I got a few prints that don't tally with those of the two dead men. Of course, you can't tell. Some of them may be fairly old."

Sheriff Lassen, who had been prowling around the yacht, came down the companionway. "Find anything, Bill?"

"Not a sign."

"It may be a plant," Duryea said, "something to throw us off the trail. Or, more likely, something that would assist one of the claimants in the estate matter."

Lassen said, "Well, I guess that covers things. Huh?"

Duryea nodded.

"Then let's go," Lassen said.

Riding back down California Avenue, Milred, strangely subdued and thoughtful, said, "Frank, put yourself in the position of a dying man. Isn't it rather odd that he'd try to leave a message on a typewriter?"

"I've thought of that," Duryea said, "but the bullet struck against his spine. He was paralyzed from the waist down. He couldn't walk, but he could have reached the keyboard of the typewriter. The photographs show that."

"And he died while he was typing the message?"

"Not necessarily. He was dying when he typed it. The effort was probably too much for him. He thought he could rest and then finish it. When he started to type, he thought he had more strength than he did have. Thought he was going to be able to write a longer message. That frequently happens with persons who are suffering from internal hemorrhage. They don't realize the extent or gravity of their injuries. They concentrate on doing something and don't appreciate the fact that they're dying until their strength gives way entirely."

She made a little shivering gesture with her shoulders and said, "Well, I guess I haven't what it takes, after all. I never thought murder was quite as—as gruesome."

Duryea said, "Murder is a tear across the whole fabric of life. It isn't just the snapping of one thread. It leaves unmistakable clues if a person has the patience to unravel all of the threads. How about driving me to the office, hon, and then taking the car home? Sheriff Lassen will drive me home when we quit."

"What are you going to do?"

"The doctors are working. I may find out something from them."

"And we have a date for a movie tomorrow?"

"Absolutely."

She drove him to the courthouse. He kissed her, said, "Don't wait up for me. I may be late."

CHAPTER 17

MILRED was in the shower when Frank Duryea awoke. He had that peculiarly lifeless feeling which always enveloped him when he had worked too late at night. He knew that it was late; but lacked the energy to pick up his watch from the dresser. He knew he should be getting up, but postponed doing anything about it.

Milred emerged from the shower, fresh and glowing, a rose-colored robe thrown over her shoulders. She saw that he was awake, and said, " 'Lo, Sherlock."

" 'Lo, Watson."

"Sleep?"

"Uh huh. How about you?"

"Fine, after I once got quieted down. What time did you get in?"

"Nearly two."

"Good heavens, *what* were you doing?"

"Oh, a lot of gruesome things," he said with a little grimace of distaste. "Post mortems, trying to fix the time of death."

"Were you there?"

"I talked with the doctors, and they insisted on showing exhibits A and B. Doctors are a cold kettle of fish. Haven't ever seen a post mortem, have you, Millie?"

"No."

"Don't."

"What did you find out about the time of death?"

"You can't be positive," he said, "but apparently they died around five o'clock Saturday afternoon. Say between four and six. One thing's certain. They didn't eat dinner Saturday night."

Milred vanished into her dressing closet to emerge presently, pulling a housedress down over her head.

"What time is it?" Duryea asked lazily.

"Eight-thirty."

"Oh, my gosh!"

"What's the matter?"

He struggled up out of bed. "Have an appointment with

121

these oil lease men, Elwell & Fielding, for this morning."

The unmistakable sound of a spoon banging against the bottom of a frying pan came through the open window.

"That," she said, "will be Gramps calling us to breakfast. I heard him chasing the maid out of the kitchen. That's what woke me up."

Duryea grinned. "Boy, I could go for some of his scrambled eggs, and that special brand of coffee he makes. Go tell him to hold it for a minute, and I'll be there. Just going to jump into the shower, then come over and eat breakfast in my robe."

"You'll shock the neighbors."

"To hell with the neighbors."

She laughed. "After all, if they've stood Gramps this long— I'd better go keep him from beating a hole through that frying pan."

Duryea jumped into the shower, needled off with cold water, rubbed with a coarse towel, put on underwear, wrapped a heavy robe around him, and shuffled slippered feet to the trailer, where Gramps Wiggins was turning hotcakes by the simple expedient of tossing them up in the air and catching them in the frying pan as they came down. He had both burners on the gasoline stove going, and was working two frying pans, flipping the hotcakes over with his left hand as easily as with his right.

"Come on, sit down, and hop to it," he said. "This is the kinda grub that really sticks to your ribs. These here are sourdough hotcakes. Just sink your teeth into 'em—an' put on lots o' that maple syrup. Met a chap in a trailer camp in Florida last winter that has a grove o' sap trees on his place up in Vermont. He sends the syrup to me by mail. Hundred per cent pure, smooth as oil. Them there hotcakes ain't gonna hurt you, folks; eat all you want."

Duryea slid into the cushioned seat. Milred poured coffee into a big agateware cup.

"That brandy bottle's over there. . . ."

"Just about half a dose," Duryea said. "I have an appointment."

"Heard you uncovered some new evidence last night."

"Who told you?"

"It was up and down the street."

"News travels fast. Those hotcakes certainly melt in your mouth."

"Uh huh. Those sourdough hotcakes certainly are good. Put lots o' butter on 'em, son, an' then sop on a lot o' maple syrup."

"I'm following instructions."

"Find out anything more about the typewriter?" Milred asked.

"No. The photograph shows that the typewriter was where he could reach it. . . ." The district attorney speared his fork into the hotcakes, and paused with the dripping morsel half-way to his mouth. "The photographs show that typewriter certainly was in a peculiar position—as though it had just been used."

Gramps glanced at Milred, said, "I'd like to see one o' those pictures."

Duryea winked at Milred and said, "No, you wouldn't, Gramps. They're pretty gruesome."

Gramps snorted. "Say, I've seen things that would turn *your* blood into sour milk. I simply gotta see them pictures."

"Strange thing about that typewriter," Duryea went on. "The pictures were taken by flashlight. Of course, they didn't know the typewriter was going to be quite so important at the time. It doesn't show in any of the photos clearly enough for an enlargement to show whether that message actually was on there at the time the picture was taken. Of course, some-one *could* have done it later."

From the stove, Gramps Wiggins said, "You know, a good expert can take a look at typewriting and tell you what model typewriter, what year, an' all the rest of it."

"I know," Duryea said. "Be sure and give Milred the recipe for these hotcakes, Gramps. They're better than any I've ever tasted."

"More nourishment in 'em, an' better for you," Gramps announced. "Kind of a job keepin' the sourdough to work 'em up from every day. That there carbon copy of the letter Stearne is s'posed to have sent them oil men—you could check it with that typewriter."

The district attorney sipped coffee and brandy. "You've got something there," he said, winking at Milred.

"It's just sort o' checkin' up," Gramps said, "but you can't afford to overlook nothin'."

Duryea looked at his watch. "Find anything of that stenographer whose initials are 'A.R.,' Gramps?"

"Nope. Can't do much at night. I'll find her today."

Duryea said, "We have a diver coming up from Los Angeles around one o'clock. You might like to be there, Gramps."

The old man's eyes fairly sparkled. "Now *that's* right considerate of you, son. Watcha lookin' for—a gun?"

"Perhaps. Or we might find something else."

Gramps thought that over while he poured more batter into the pans. "Sometimes," he announced at length, "I'm right proud o' you, son. You got what it takes. Here, take a leetle more o' that tonic in your coffee."

Duryea had two more hotcakes, then dashed out of the trailer, his robe trailing along behind. He shaved, dressed, and drove to the office. When he had gone, Gramps sat down, poured a big cup of coffee, and brandy, said, "A mighty smart lad, Milred. When he's got more time, I'm goin' to give him a tip about that there case."

She smiled, her eyes indulgent. "I suppose you're waiting for me to ask you what it is?"

"Yep. I got a theory. I want to try it out on you."

"Well, try ahead."

"What was that mysterious cruise this here *Gypsy Queen* yacht was leavin' on at three o'clock?" Gramps asked, lowering his voice mysteriously. "An' why did that *Albatross* yacht pull out just in time to take over the job?"

"But it didn't."

"The heck it didn't! She pulled out the first part of the afternoon an' didn't get back until nearly midnight. This here Ted Shale was on it. He woke up about sunset. That was right around seven o'clock mebbe. The yacht was headin' back then . . . mebbe a five-hour run. . . . Well, where did it go? To keep an appointment those two dead men on the *Gypsy Queen* had made. That's where."

"But, Gramps, you haven't any evidence. You haven't anything to go on."

"Shucks, I got me a pay-off hunch. My fingers itch, that hunch is so hot. We gotta sell Frank on that idea."

"But a district attorney can't drag people in and question them and make insinuations unless he has some definite evidence."

"How's he goin' to get evidence if he don't question people?"

"Well—he has to build up a case—has to move slowly."

Gramps Wiggins said, "You go talk that picture out o' him. I want to look at it. Then we got work to do."

"We?"

"Uh huh. I need somebody to help me."

She laughed. "I'm afraid I'm not much of a detective."

"Why not?"

"I got just a little squeamish last night."

"Humph," Gramps said. "You're a Wiggins, ain't you?"

She laughed. "After last night, I'm not so sure."

"Don't go tellin' me you take after your grandmother's side o' the family. Your father did, but that don't mean so much. You've got the Wiggins look. First time I took a look at you when you was a baby, I says right away, 'She's a Wiggins, thank God.'" He broke off to chuckle. "Your grandmother didn't like that much, but we was divorced at the time, an' there weren't much she could do."

"What was the trouble between you and Grandmother?" Milred asked.

Gramps slid into the seat Duryea had vacated. "You better have some more o' these hotcakes, Millie."

"No, thanks. I had plenty. I feel as though I'm full right up to my neck."

"Can't let good food go to waste," Gramps said, pulling the platter of hotcakes over to him, spreading on plenty of butter, and emptying the syrup jug.

"Why did Grandmother get a divorce?"

"She had grounds."

"I suppose," she said, smiling, "you were just a plain heller."

He put down his knife and fork to look across the table at her. "You're gol-dern right. An' I'm still dynamite when I get to snortin'."

She laughed at him. "Just a naughty boy, trying to boast about how bad he was. The family gossip, as I got it, was that you were a model husband, that Grandmother was frightfully nervous, and got a lot of crazy notions about you, and filed suit for divorce, that when you read what she'd said in the suit, you came to the conclusion you'd been called a 'heller,' and you've been trying to live up to it ever since."

Gramps jumped to his feet, his lips quivering with indignation. "Ain't no such a damn thing! You got that from your father, didn't you? He took after his mother's side o' the family!"

Milred contented herself with a smile. Later on, however, while Gramps was doing what he called his "chores" in the trailer, she slipped into the house to call her husband. "Frank, I know how to handle Gramps," she said.

"How?"

"We can get rid of him whenever we want to. Just start telling him he's a conservative, model citizen, and that Grandmother was suffering from nerves when she divorced him. He can't take it."

Duryea said, "You lay off Gramps. He just gave me a darn good idea."

"What?"

"Checking the typewriting on the carbon copy of that letter to see if it really was written on the machine we found on the yacht."

She sighed. "And here I thought I was doing you a favor. Well, I've planted the seed now and Heaven knows what Gramps will do to show that he really is what he calls a 'heller.' "

CHAPTER 18

FRANK DURYEA nodded to the three people who entered his office. Jack Elwell took the initiative. He stretched out his hand, and said, "I'm Elwell. Mighty glad to know you. Only too glad to come up here and do anything we can. Stearne was a nice chap, and if we can do anything to help bring his murderer to justice, we want to do it. . . . Ain't that right, Ned?"

Fielding nodded.

"My partner, Mr. Fielding," Elwell introduced.

Duryea shook hands.

"My wife," Fielding said, turning to the young woman at his side.

Duryea bowed again, muttered, "Mrs. Fielding."

"They were married yesterday," Elwell explained, grinning. "Little romance in the office going on right under my nose. They flew to Yuma and got spliced. Now, what can we do for you?"

Duryea said, "You control some Ventura County oil leases. You'd given Stearne an option on them. He had until midnight Saturday to exercise that option. Is that right?"

"That's right. And he never exercised it."

"His special administratrix did?"

"That's a question for the lawyers. As far as we're concerned, we're in the clear. The option read that he didn't have any rights whatever in the property after Saturday. The option period wasn't to be extended by operation of law, by holidays, or by any other cause whatsoever, whether it was anything within the control of either or both of the parties, or something entirely beyond their control, or an act of God. You see, I made an option one time with a fellow, way back when they were declaring holidays in order to give the banks a rest, and I got in a big lawsuit over it. When I drew up this option, I made it cover everything."

"Then you didn't get any letter from Stearne accepting the option?"

"Absolutely not."

"The attorney for the estate says such a letter was mailed."

Elwell regarded the district attorney with clear-eyed candor. "I'm going to tell you the truth, Mr. Duryea. Stearne intended to mail that letter all right. I think he had it all written and was intending to mail it, but something happened to him before he mailed the letter."

Duryea said cautiously, "That would, of course, be very important, because it would go a long ways toward fixing the time of death. The copy which Mr. Hazlit showed me bore a notation which I understand is in the handwriting of the deceased, that the original had been dropped in the mail at the post office just before five o'clock. There's a possibility, of course, that the copy was mailed first, and Stearne's written notation related to what he intended to do."

Elwell said, "That's exactly what happened. He mailed the copy from some box here. He intended to take the original to the post office himself. The reason he didn't mail it was that he was murdered before five o'clock."

"You're sure you didn't receive any such letter?"

"Absolutely. It wasn't in the mail. Why, you can ask Martha here—Mrs. Fielding. She's been with us for a good many years. She's the one that got the mail on Monday morning."

Duryea looked at Mrs. Fielding.

She surveyed him with placid eyes and expressionless countenance. "I got to the office Monday morning," she said. "I looked in the door and the mail was there in the letter chute. There were quite a few letters, and they hadn't dropped down to the floor. They were still stuck in the chute. That was because there were so many of them."

Duryea nodded.

"I took them out and looked through them to see what return addresses were on the envelopes. Then I took my paper knife and slit them open, and took out each letter and read it."

"Why did you do that?" Duryea asked.

"To know whether it was a matter I could handle, like an order, whether the letter went to Mr. Elwell, or to Ned—Mr. Fielding."

"That's your usual custom?"

"Uh huh."

"What do you do with the envelopes?"

"Fasten them to the letters with paper clips. Mr. Elwell told me always to do that . . ."

Elwell interrupted to say, "That's my universal business custom. She's done that ever since she started working for us. I always want the envelope preserved until after I've seen the letter."

Duryea said, "I'm going to ask all of you to make written sworn statements."

"Sure thing," Elwell said, "only too glad to do it."

Martha Fielding said, "If you don't mind, Mr. Duryea, I'd like to type my own statement. I guess I've been a stenographer too long not to feel nervous about things that are dictated. If you'll let me have a typewriter, I can write it out, and it will save you the trouble of dictating it."

"Put all the facts in it," Duryea said.

"Oh, certainly," she told him, and smiled.

Gramps Wiggins escorted a light-haired, reluctant young woman into Duryea's outer office. "The district attorney in?" he asked.

Duryea's secretary said, "He's engaged. Was he expecting you?"

"Nope, but I gotta see him right away."

"One of the deputies perhaps could . . ."

Wiggins said impatiently, "You go tell him that Mr. Wiggins is out here and has to see him right away, that it's important. You get me, important?"

She left her typewriter, vanished through a door marked PRIVATE, and returned presently to say, "You may go right on in, Mr. Wiggins."

Gramps took the young woman's arm and said, "Right this way."

She muttered something in an undertone, and Gramps said, reassuringly, "Forget it. There ain't nothin' to it. Just let me talk with him."

Duryea was worried. He was beginning to realize that this murder case, in place of clarifying itself, was becoming more and more complicated. If Elwell and Fielding were telling the truth,—if Stearne had been murdered before he had mailed that letter of acceptance, the district attorney had a valuable clue as to the time at which the murder actually had been committed. If, on the other hand, these men were falsifying the evidence so as to make a second sale of the oil leases, Duryea dare not permit himself to be imposed upon. It would be fatal should he attempt to build a case on the strength of their testimony.

"I can give you only a very few minutes," he said to Gramps, and he placed his watch on the desk.

Gramps nodded. "Got a young woman here that knows something," he said. "Name's Rodman—Alta Rodman."

Methodically, Duryea reached for a memo pad. "Miss or Mrs.?" he inquired, holding his pencil poised.

"Mrs.," the young woman said.

Gramps motioned Mrs. Rodman to a chair, settled himself, and crossed his legs.

"Well. What is it?" Duryea asked.

"Mrs. Rodman," Gramps explained, "is workin' as an usher in a motion picture theater. She's done some stenographic work, though, an' she wanted to get on steady if she could as a secretary somewhere. She left her name around with the different employment agencies, an' she said she was willin' to go anywhere durin' the daytime an' do stenographic work. You see, because she worked nights as an usher, she could have her days free to . . ."

"I'm afraid I'm not in a position to offer Mrs. Rodman any . . ." He broke off abruptly as the look on Gramps' face warned him. "Are you the young woman who went out to the *Gypsy Queen* Saturday afternoon?" he asked, turning to Mrs. Rodman.

She nodded.

"You took some letters for Mr. Stearne?"

"Yes."

Duryea took a long breath, picked up his watch, dropped it back in his pocket, and said, "About what time did you go aboard?"

"I want to keep out of it. I've got to keep out of it. You can't use me as a witness."

"Why?"

"I have my reasons."

Gramps Wiggins piped up, "She's workin' nights. She's afraid that they'll fire her if they find out she's been goin' out daytimes doin' work on the side. I told her mebbe you could keep her name outa the papers."

Duryea said, "I'm afraid I can't guarantee that. I'll do my best, however."

Gramps said in a kindly voice, "He'll take care of you some way. Now just go ahead an' tell him what happened."

She looked, not to Duryea, but at Wiggins.

"You do what I tell you," Gramps said firmly. "We ain't got time for a lot o' monkeyshines."

"But the papers . . ."

"I'll talk 'em out of it," Gramps promised. "I can lie like a house afire when I make up my mind to. You just go ahead an' tell the skipper here about what happened."

She said, in a low voice, "I'd done some work for Mr.

130

Stearne once before, and Saturday he telephoned and asked me to come down to the yacht right away."

"And you went?" Duryea asked.

"Of course. It was good pay."

"And what happened?"

"Mr. Stearne said he had some letters. There were half a dozen."

"What were they?"

Gramps interposed. "I had her bring her notebook. The letters are in there, written in shorthand just as she took 'em down when he dictated. She can write 'em out again."

Duryea said, "My secretary will furnish a typewriter. Mrs. Rodman can do it right here in the office. Now, was there a letter to Elwell & Fielding?"

"Yes."

"And you mailed that?" Duryea asked, feeling that he was at last getting something definite.

"No, sir, I didn't. I mailed a copy of it to Mr. Stearne's office."

"You didn't mail the original to Elwell & Fielding?"

"No, sir. He made a notation on that copy, and told me to address an envelope to his office in Los Angeles. He said I could drop the copy in the mailbox; but the original he said he'd mail personally at the post office. He said he'd have to swear that he'd mailed it himself."

"Now, what time was this?"

"I went aboard the yacht about three o'clock and left shortly after four."

"Was anyone else there?"

"No, just the two men."

"And you mailed some letters from the mailbox near the yacht club?"

"Yes. Mr. Stearne told me to put them in the first mailbox I came to, and I knew that mailbox was there. Before I dropped them in the chute, I took a look to see that there was another collection of mail that afternoon—it being Saturday, you know—and I just thought I'd make sure."

"What time did you mail them?"

"A few minutes after four o'clock. There was a sign on the box saying there was a mail collection at four-twenty-five."

Duryea said, "Now begin at the beginning and tell me just what happened."

"Well, I don't know that there's very much to tell. Mr. Stearne telephoned about half past two and asked me how soon I could be there. I told him in about twenty minutes, and I guess I got there in about fifteen. I was all dressed to go out, and all I had to do was grab my notebook, some pencils, my purse, put on a hat, and go. I . . ."

"Go on a streetcar, walk, or . . ."

"Took a taxi," she said. "He asked me to do that."

"And you discharged the taxi there at the parking place by the yacht club?"

"Yes."

"And then what did you do?"

"Walked out to the float."

"You knew the yacht, of course?"

"Yes. I'd seen it before."

"And someone came out to take you aboard?"

"Yes. Mr. Right."

"You'd met him before?"

"Yes."

"When you got aboard, what happened?"

"Mr. Stearne seemed in a very good humor. He was in the cabin, where the steering wheel is, and card tables, and so forth."

"Then what?"

"He said he wanted to give me some dictation. I sat down at one of the card tables. Mr. Stearne started dictating right away. He dictated those letters, walking back and forth while he was dictating. He's a fast dictator. He knew what he wanted to say, and said it. You know, lots of persons talk rapidly enough when they're just talking, but as soon as they start dictating they'll dictate a word or two, then stop and think, and then dictate another word or two, then stop some more, then ask you what it was they've said, and when you read it to them, they'll say, 'Strike it out.' "

Duryea grinned.

Mrs. Rodman said hastily, "I didn't mean—"

"It's all right," Duryea interrupted. "The shoe fits about nine out of every ten men who dictate."

"Well, Mr. Stearne wasn't that way at all. He knew exactly

what he wanted to say, and he'd say it, giving you eight or ten words at a time, then pausing just for a second, and then giving you eight or ten more words."

"He dictated half a dozen letters?"

"I think so, five or six."

"Were they long?"

"No. This one to Elwell & Fielding was the only long one. The others were short."

"Would you say that he completed his dictation by three-thirty?"

"Before that. Well, wait a minute. By the time he started dictating—well, perhaps it was around twenty minutes past three when he finished."

"Then what?"

"Then Mr. Right took me down into the lower cabin and fixed up a typewriter on a taboret."

"A portable machine?"

"Yes."

"Were you accustomed to it?"

"I can type on anything."

"Wouldn't it have been more convenient to have done the typewriting up in that upper cabin?"

"Probably, but they didn't want to be disturbed by the noise of the typewriter. That's why I went down in the lower cabin. At least, I suppose so."

"How long did it take you to write the letters?"

"Oh, around thirty minutes."

"But you didn't leave the yacht . . ."

"No, sir. I finished the letters and went back to the upper cabin. The two men were talking. I think they were angry. Mr. Stearne told me to go out and wait for a few minutes. I stood at the rail for nearly five minutes, looking over at the other yachts. Mr. Right came out and went down to the lower cabin. Then Mr. Stearne called to me to come in with the letters. His face was flushed, and he was short and curt. He read the letters, signed them, and told me to seal and stamp them. I put them in their envelopes and put on the stamps. Then was when Mr. Stearne said he'd mail that letter to Elwell & Fielding. And he took the carbon copy I'd made for his office and wrote something on it, then put it back in the envelope. He gave me ten dollars and wanted to know if that was satisfactory. I told him very much so, and he said Mr. Right could take me ashore, and I could mail the other letters at the first mailbox. Mr. Right rowed me ashore, and that's all I know."

"Did you notice any change in Mr. Right's manner?"

"Well—not particularly—although I don't think he said a word to me, except to say good-by when he put me ashore."

"You have your notebook with you?"

"Yes, sir."

"I'd like to have you write those letters out so I can study them."

"Yes, sir."

Duryea picked up the telephone. "I'll have my secretary provide you with a typewriter and . . ."

Gramps Wiggins cleared his throat, firmly and significantly. Duryea glanced up at him.

"Mrs. Rodman can use *any* typewriter," Gramps Wiggins said.

"Exactly," Duryea said, reaching for the telephone again.

Gramps coughed, significantly.

Duryea stopped and frowned.

Gramps said, "You was fixin' to ask her about that typewriter, wasn't you, son?"

"She said she could use—oh, yes, the typewriter on the yacht. Do you remember that typewriter very clearly, Mrs. Rodman?"

"It was a portable."

"Did it have a new ribbon or a new platen?"

She thought for a moment, said, "The platen wasn't new, no. The ribbon was all right, I guess. I don't remember about that, but it worked all right."

Gramps grinned at the district attorney. "Now you're gettin' there, son," he said. "You're movin' right along—just a whizzin'."

When the door had closed, Duryea turned to Gramps Wiggins. "I owe you one for that."

"Wasn't anything," Gramps announced. "I just rang up all the employment agencies to ask about stenographers that were free for part time work. I got a whole list of names and on the list there were only three people who had the initials 'A.R.' Shucks, there wasn't anythin' to it. I just got in touch with every one of 'em."

"I thought you were on a wild-goose chase," Duryea confessed. "I thought Stearne had dictated that letter to C. Arthur Right, and Right had put his initials, 'A.R.,' on it. You see, Right had started working for Stearne as his secretary."

"Yep," Gramps said. "I thought about Right as soon as I saw those initials, and then I decided against it."

"You'd already thought of it?" Duryea asked.

"That's right. You see, Right's initials are 'C.A.R.' Everyone calls him Arthur, but he writes his name C. Arthur Right. If he'd put his initials on there it'd have been the same way he signs his name, not just 'A.R.' "

Duryea grinned. "Well," he admitted, "you were right. And it looks as though that typewriter we found was a plant."

"As I see it," Gramps said, "this here Moline woman is the one who stands to make all the profit by having it appear that Right died first. Ain't that right?"

"Well—yes."

"Whoever switched typewriters," Gramps went on, "knew certain things and didn't know others."

"What?" Duryea asked.

"Didn't know that a stenographer had been called in, and sent out letters on Saturday afternoon, but did know that when the bodies were found, there was a typewriter near Stearne."

Duryea frowned down at his desk as he considered the problem, then picked up the telephone, called the sheriff's office, found that Lassen was out, and talked with the undersheriff. "I'd like to have that typewriter which was taken from the *Gypsy Queen* last night sent up to my office right away. As soon as Sheriff Lassen comes in, ask him to give me a ring."

Duryea hung up.

Gramps said, "That Moline woman. Now, she's a deep one. That *Gypsy Queen* was going some place around three o'clock. It wasn't just an ordinary cruise. Stearne wanted Nita Moline along. But why should she have got up here so early on Sunday? She got up plenty early in Los Angeles."

Duryea nodded. "Keep right on, Gramps."

"P'raps two yachts was meetin' out there in the ocean, an' then again . . . And this girl on the *Albatross* may have known all about it an' decided to go out an' keep the appointment instead of the *Gypsy Queen*. Don't overlook any bets on that *Albatross*."

"I'm not," Duryea promised. "Miss Harpler is due at the office late this afternoon. I expect to ask her questions in considerable detail."

"That's good."

The undersheriff opened the door of the office, bringing in the portable typewriter.

Duryea picked up the telephone, said to his secretary, "Ask Mrs. Rodman to come in here. I want her to take a look at a typewriter."

A few moments later, Mrs. Rodman appeared, laid some letters on Duryea's desk, said, "There's only one more, besides that long one about the leases."

"Take a look at this typewriter," Duryea invited.

She studied it carefully.

"Is that the typewriter on which you wrote those letters?"

She shook her head with slow deliberation.

"You're certain?"

"Absolutely."

"How can you tell?"

"In several ways. But this typewriter has rubber cushions on the keys. The one I used didn't."

The silence which followed was broken by a wheezing chuckle from Gramps Wiggins. "Now we're gettin' somewhere!" he said.

CHAPTER 19

PETE LASSEN, the sheriff, was very much in evidence as the diver adjusted his helmet. The group of men clustered on the deck of the murder yacht were tense and silent. The newspapers had been notified and several reporters were there to cover the story. Cameras were held in readiness.

Duryea, always inclined to hold himself aloof when the duties of his office brought him to the attention of the public, remained somewhat detached from the other officers. Gramps Wiggins at his side was puffing furiously at a blackened, disreputable pipe.

The diver lowered himself into the water. The air lines and telephones were tested. Then the diver slipped rapidly from sight, and only a thin stream of air bubbles coming up marked the spot where he had slipped from sight.

Up on the deck of the yacht, two attendants kept the handles of the manual pump swinging with regular monotony. One of the men had earphones clamped on so that he could keep in communication with the diver. From time to time, he relayed bits of information to the little group which clustered along the rail of the yacht.

"Ocean floor's clean and sandy," the man at the pump reported, then there followed an interval of silence while the men worked rhythmically at the pump handles. The little group gathered closer.

"He's found something—a bent gold wire . . . two gold wires. . . . They're embedded in the sand. . . . It's a pair of spectacles. He wants a basket lowered."

Bill Wiegart picked up a steel-meshed covered basket suspended on a rope which had been left in readiness by the rail of the yacht, and lowered it down. A moment later the man with the earphones said, "Okay, pull her back up."

Wiegart pulled up the basket. The men gathered around to examine the gold-rimmed spectacles.

The man at the pumps reported, "Found 'em about fifteen feet off the port quarter, lenses about half an inch deep in sand, the bows sticking up."

Newspaper reporters scribbled furiously.

Slowly the stream of air bubbles worked their way around the yacht. A little manipulation kept the hose and lines from fouling on the mooring as the diver moved.

The man with the earphones reported, "That seems to be all. A few empty tin cans pretty well buried in the sand, but nothing else."

"Tell him to look particularly for a typewriter," Lassen said.

"He has. There isn't anything."

Gramps sidled over to the district attorney.

"Well, he may as well come up," Lassen said.

Gramps took the pipe out of his mouth. "Tide's runnin' out, huh?"

"That's right."

"Comin' in when the bodies were discovered Sunday?"

"I believe so."

"It was low tide Saturday about the time of the murder?"

"What difference does it make?" Duryea asked as Gramps mumbled his mental computation of tide tables.

Gramps said, "I'm just tryin' to find out which way she was pointed. A yacht'll swing with the wind and tide. There wasn't any wind Saturday afternoon, or Sunday morning, so she was swingin' entirely with the tide."

"Well?"

Gramps pushed the coal of tobacco down into the bowl of his pipe with a horny forefinger. "Well now," he said, "the way I look at it, this here yacht's over a hundred feet long. Now you take the moorin' chain an' figure the angle of that. . . . You get it?"

Duryea got it. He stepped toward the group and said, "Wait a minute. Don't have him come up yet. Have him go about a hundred and fifty feet toward shore."

Lassen said, "There wouldn't be anything in there, Frank."

Duryea said, "Notice the way she's swinging with the tide. She's pointing toward the shore now, but, at various times since the murder, she must have been swung around toward land, with the bow pointing toward the ocean."

The sheriff frowned. One of the newspaper reporters glanced quickly at Duryea and scribbled a note on the folded newsprint which he held in his hand. The string of air bubbles which marked the location of the diver hissed upward as the diver moved toward the shore.

There followed some two or three minutes of anxious silence. The sheriff said, "Ain't no use . . ." and was interrupted by the excited voice of the man who was keeping in touch with the diver. "He's found it!" he shouted. "Found a thirty-eight caliber revolver."

"Wait a minute," Duryea said, stepping forward. "We want to mark that place. Have him mark it with a float or something."

"You can send down a float and weight in this basket when we pick up the gun," the man at the pump said to Bill Wiegart. "He'll have to take the skiff and row over there. You can see where he is from the air bubbles." Into the mouthpiece, he said, "We'll be out with a skiff to pick up the gun. Mark exactly where you found it. They're sending out a heavy weight and buoy."

Duryea said, "Also have him go back to where he found the spectacles and mark that place with a buoy."

Wiegart and another man tumbled into the skiff. One of the newspaper reporters tossed them the metal basket. There was a moment of confusion while they were looking for weights, then one of the men came up from the engine room carrying a peculiarly shaped wrench. "This all right to use?" he asked. One of the reporters answered the question. "It's just an oil-well tool." Lassen said, "Okay, boys, use that."

It took a few moments to affix a fish line and a piece of wood, then Wiegart rowed the skiff out to a point nearly two hundred feet from the bow of the yacht. He lowered the basket, raised it with the gun inside, and a few minutes later, the bit of wood bobbing on the water marked the exact point where the gun had been found. The diver walked toward the yacht to mark the spot where he had found the spectacles.

Wiegart rowed back to the yacht, and the group crowded about a thirty-eight blued-steel revolver, in the cylinder of which were two discharged shells. Newspaper reporters brought out their cameras, and Pete Lassen stepped out to stand by himself at the rail of the yacht, holding the gun up in front of him. "Okay, boys," he said. "Get your pictures."

Gramps Wiggins drew Duryea off to one side. "You get it, son?" he asked, his manner excited.

Duryea laughed. "Of course, I get it. Everyone gets it. Pete Lassen is a nice chap, but he always tries to hog the limelight whenever there's any publicity. Not that it makes a great deal of difference. He . . ."

"No, no," Gramps interrupted, his voice becoming high-pitched with excitement. "To hell with that tub o' lard. I'm talkin' about the evidence."

"What about it?"

"You been lookin' up the tides?" Gramps asked.

Duryea shook his head.

"You'd oughta looked 'em up," Gramps said reproachfully. "They're the best clue in the whole dingbusted case."

"What do you mean?"

Gramps said, "It was dead slack low-tide water at 5.06 P.M. Saturday afternoon. The next dead-low water was at 5.34 Sunday morning. She was high water at 11.55 Sunday morning, low water at 5.56 Sunday afternoon, and high water again at

11.48 Sunday night. Gee gosh, come on! Let's get away from here. I got to be where I can get this pointed out to you. We got a clue, a humdinger of a clue, a geewhillikins of a clue!"

Duryea smiled indulgently at the little old man's excitement. "Okay, Gramps," he said, "let's get going."

Gramps started for the skiff, then suddenly turned and pointed a rigid finger at Duryea's buttonhole. "Now you listen to me, son," he said, jabbing away with his forefinger like a woodpecker pecking at a fence post, "no matter what else you do, you keep those buoys markin' the place where they found those glasses an' that gun, an' have somebody from the county engineer's office come out here an' make a map o' that harbor showin' the moorin' of the yacht, an' the place where those things were found by the diver. You get me?"

"I get you," Duryea said. "We'd probably do that anyway—although I don't see why it's so terribly important."

Gramps dragged him by the coat sleeve. "You come along with me," he said.

It wasn't until Gramps had the district attorney in a secluded corner back of the yacht club that he felt free to expound his theory.

"Now you listen to me," he said, pounding his right fist down on his left palm. "We got the very best clue, the best all-fired thing you could get anywhere. It . . ."

"All right, what is it?"

"There weren't no wind on Saturday afternoon or Saturday night," Gramps said. "Wind didn't come up until late Sunday night. Even then it was just a breeze. Saturday night an' Sunday was dead calm."

"Well, what about it?"

"Don't you see," Gramps said, "we got a clock that was run by nature an' tells us just exactly the whole dad blame story."

"I don't get it," Duryea said.

"The way a yacht swings to its moorings," Gramps pointed out impatiently. "Here, take a look at this." He dropped down to sit on his heels while he traced a diagram on the cement with the tip of his forefinger. "You get me? Here's a tide runnin' out. What happens to a yacht that's moored? It swings around on the moorin', an' the bow points toward shore. Doesn't it?"

Duryea nodded, still deriving so much amusement from

Gramps Wiggins' excitement that he failed to pay much attention to the point the old man was trying to put across.

"All right," Gramps went on, "the tide changes. There's a period when the water is just slack, when there ain't no currents at all. Then the incomin' tide starts movin' in, slow at first, but gradually gatherin' speed, an' a yacht that's moored by the bow starts swingin' slowly around. After a while, when the tide's runnin' in good, the yacht's swung around so the bow is pointin' out to sea. Now you take a yacht that's a hundred feet long, an' then figure that the moorin' cable stretches at an angle from the bottom up to the surface of the water, an' between dead low tide and dead high tide there's quite a bit o' movement. The bow moves mebbe around a twenty-foot circle, but the stern swings way around. You get what I'm drivin' at?"

Gramps looked up at the district attorney's smiling face, jumped to his feet, and, fairly dancing in his excitement, said, "No, you don't either. You ain't gettin' it at all. Here." Gramps whipped off his glasses, and said, "How far could you throw these?"

"Not very far," the district attorney admitted.

"That's just it," Gramps said, "an' you wouldn't try to throw 'em. There ain't no reason for throwin' glasses away, but if you was havin' a fight with someone, you'd take off your glasses, wouldn't you?"

"Probably."

"Sure, you would. You'd take 'em off, an' put 'em down some place where you could pick 'em up afterwards. If you was gettin' in a fight with somebody on a yacht, you'd take your glasses off an' put 'em on the rail. It'd be a darn poor place to put 'em, but it would be a place just the same. . . . Then you'd have a fight, an' your glasses would get knocked overboard, like as not. In that case, they'd drop right down to the bottom of the ocean, just about underneath where they was dropped, wouldn't they?"

Duryea nodded.

"Now then, you take a gun," Gramps said. "You could throw a gun a long ways, but if it was daylight an' people were watchin' on the shore, you wouldn't dare to throw it at all. It'd go whirlin' through the air an' reflect in sunlight, an' people would see it."

Again, Duryea nodded.

"So," Gramps went on, "if you was tryin' to ditch a gun that had been used in a murder, an' there was people on the shore, you'd take the gun out to the deck of the yacht, walk around on the side that was away from the shore, an' just quietly drop it over the side, wouldn't you?"

The smile faded from Duryea's face now. His eyes began to show interest. "Yes," he said, "I believe you would, Gramps."

"Sure, you would," Gramps shrilled. "Don't you see what happened? Look at the distance between where those glasses was found an' where the gun was found. You get what I mean? Whenever the fight took place that knocked those glasses overboard, the tide was runnin' out. The yacht was pointin' out to sea. Now that gun was dropped when the yacht had swung way around so the stern was facin' the land. In other words, son, that gun was dropped when the tide was runnin' in, an' them murders took place when the tide was runnin' *out*. Had to be like that."

Duryea was frowning now. "You mean then that the gun wasn't dropped at the time the murder was committed?"

"That's exactly what I mean. That gun was dropped a whole lot later, probably three or four hours anyhow, but more like to be longer. Don't you get it? Everything indicates that this here widow of Right is tellin' the absolute truth. You remember Mrs. Rodman says she left the yacht a little after four o'clock, an' there was kinda a tension between the two men. Something had happened. This here Stearne was in good humor when he started dictatin' the letters. When she brought 'em back to have 'em signed, he was curt an' short with her. Well, she went ashore with the letters, an' Right an' Stearne went out toward the stern o' the yacht, an' got in an argument. There's a deck there on the stern that's covered with an awning, an' at low tide, with the stern pointed out toward the breakwater, people sittin' on the beach couldn't see what was goin' on. Well, they had a fight. One o' the men took off his glasses, an' the glasses got knocked overboard. Then the fight was over, but the hard feelin's weren't. There was a shootin'. I wouldn't doubt a bit if when you check the numbers on that gun, you find it's Right's gun. I'm tellin' you it's a murder an' a suicide just the way that woman claimed. An' what you got to do is find the missin' will, an' that there statement."

Duryea, keenly interested now, said, with respect in his voice, "You've got something there, Gramps."

"You're gol-dinged right I got somethin'! Some time the next mornin' that Moline girl came aboard. She found the bodies sprawled out down there in the cabin, an' the gun was lyin' on the floor, an' probably a long-winded statement that Right had made and signed. Something he'd written on the typewriter, judgin' from the position it was in. An' there was somethin' in that statement she didn't like, somethin' she wouldn't want spread out in the papers, so she ditched that statement. Then she decided she'd better ditch the gun, too. She was afraid to come on deck an' drop it, because someone might see the glint of the sun on the gun barrel as it went overboard. That fainting business was a frame-up. She had that gun stuck in her blouse, an' when she pitched overboard, she just let it slip to the bottom."

"That's making a lot of deduction from just a slender clue," Duryea objected.

"Slender clue, hell!" Gramps shrilled. "It's a natural! You can't get away from it. You take a pencil an' paper an' start figgerin' the position of that yacht, an' you'll find out that the gun was dropped with the tide comin' in, an' the glasses was dropped when the tide was goin' out. An' the murder was committed when the tide was goin' out. Now, tides vary, but you'll find that around Saturday an' Sunday the periods between high water and low water was just about six hours even. So there was quite an interval between the time the glasses were knocked overboard, an' . . ."

"You're pinning a lot of faith on those glasses," Duryea said. "They may have been dropped overboard from someone's pocket. In fact, they might be glasses that have been in the water for a month or so."

"Not glasses," Gramps said. "The way glasses are shaped they'd keep workin' their way down in the sand. But you can find out pretty darn soon. You can get the prescription of glasses worn by those two fellows an' check up on the glasses an' . . ."

Duryea said, "Come on, Gramps. I'll get up to the office and get started on that stuff."

143

Duryea walked rapidly along the macadamized walk. Gramps, tagging along, his short legs taking almost two steps to the district attorney's one, had at times to break into a half-trot in order to keep up. However, despite the tax on his wind and strength, he managed to interpose occasional bits of advice.

"That Moline girl," he said. "I noticed . . . when you was lookin' at Tucker . . . Tucker didn't get your signal right away. . . . But *she* did. . . . She was lookin' . . . at him. An' she was worried. . . . Now listen, why don't you . . . Hey, gol-ding it, stop a minute! I got me an idea, an' I can't . . . tell it to you while the wind's bein' jolted outa me. . . . Stop a minute."

Duryea looked at his watch, then slowed his pace. "I'm sorry, Gramps. What is it?"

"You let me . . . catch my wind," Gramps puffed.

Duryea stopped and lit a cigarette. Gramps quickly regained his breath. "I got an idea that might work," he said. "I was watchin' that Moline girl's face when Tucker an' his wife came into the room. She ain't dumb, that girl. She knew you was bringin' those people in because they was witnesses to somethin'. She kept watchin' your face, an' you kept signalin' Tucker by raisin' your eyebrows an' jerkin' your head over toward the Moline girl. I could see she was havin' kittens, so darned afraid Tucker was actually goin' to identify her."

"Well," Duryea said, "we can't change any of that now."

"Then Tucker shook his head, an' she got smart right away. You could just see the way a load rolled off her shoulders."

"All right," Duryea said, "that's finished. Tucker can't change his testimony."

Gramps rushed on, "This here scheme of mine is a peach of a scheme. I read it once in a detective book, where an officer pulled it on a person he couldn't break no other way. He . . ."

"What is it?" Duryea interrupted.

"Well," Gramps said, "just pick up another couple. It don't make no difference *who* they are, just so the Moline girl ain't seen 'em before. You just put on an act in pantomime. You get her in the office, an' this couple comes in. You go through all this business of raisin' the eyebrows all over again, but this time just have the man an' the woman nod their heads vigorously. Then you smile as though you'd just cut yourself a nice piece of cake, an' tell 'em that'll be all, to wait outside. Then you start talkin' to that Moline woman, an' see what happens."

Duryea said, "I'm afraid I can't very well do that, Gramps."

"Why not?"

"We haven't anything on Miss Moline except a lot of theories. She's represented by an attorney. She's inherited money. She's no one you can shove around. The district attorney can't resort to expedients like that unless he's dealing with someone whom he's morally satisfied has committed a crime. He . . ."

"Doggone it," Gramps said. "Don't be like that. Don't be so damned conservative. Hell's bells, you married a Wiggins. You must have a streak in you *some*where that'll take a chance!"

Duryea laughed at the old man's excitement. "I'm afraid, Gramps," he said, "that's one of the things that works fine in a story but might not work so well in real life."

"The heck it wouldn't," Gramps said. "I tell you I was watchin' her face. When Tucker shook his head, she perked right up. Now suppose Tucker had just nodded, an' then after a minute his wife had nodded, too. Then what would she have done?"

"I don't know," Duryea said.

"Neither do I, but I'm makin' a bet she'd have started explainin', and when you get somebody like that startin' to explain, you . . ."

"Well," Duryea said with a note of finality in his voice, "it's nothing I can do now, Gramps. It wouldn't be in accordance with the dignity of my office. The people I used as stooges might talk, either then or afterwards, and it wouldn't be ethical to . . ."

"All right, all right," Gramps said disgustedly. "Come on, let's go trace that gun."

CHAPTER 20

NITA MOLINE sat across the district attorney's desk. Her gloved hands were clenched into little fists. The color which she had applied to her face no longer blended with her complexion because her complexion had suddenly gone pale, leaving the rouge on her cheeks no longer blended into a smooth luster of color, but as jagged, irregular blotches.

Duryea said, "I will repeat my statement, Miss Moline. You were in a position to benefit by Mr. Stearne's death?"

"I suppose so, yes."

Duryea opened the drawer of his desk, took out the thirty-eight caliber revolver which the diver had recovered from the bottom of the ocean. "I'll show you this gun, Miss Moline, and ask you if you have ever seen it before."

She recoiled from it, and said quickly, "I'm sorry, Mr. Duryea, but I don't like guns."

"Just look at it," Duryea insisted, holding it toward her.

"What . . . what do you want?"

"Have you ever seen that gun before?"

"Not that I know of. I haven't seen many guns. I don't like them. I keep away from them."

"And you don't recognize this gun?"

"No."

"You're certain?"

"Yes."

Duryea said impressively, "This gun was recovered from the ocean by a diver. It had evidently been dropped overboard from the *Gypsy Queen*."

She nodded her head silently, her eyes still fastened on the weapon.

Duryea went on, "That gun has a number stamped on it."

Again she nodded.

"Under the law," Duryea went on, "when a revolver is sold, the dealer must keep a record of the number and the person to whom the sale is made."

"Yes, I've heard of that."

"Oh, you have?"

"Yes."

"Through its number, this gun has been traced," Duryea said. "It was sold by the manufacturer to a jobber in Los Angeles. The jobber sold it to a dealer, and the dealer sold it to—guess who?"

She seemed desperate, as though trapped, but she clenched her lips tightly together, and shook her head.

"It was sold to C. Arthur Right," Duryea said calmly.

"Arthur's gun!" she exclaimed.

"Yes."

"And it was dropped overboard from the yacht?"

"Apparently, but that isn't all, Miss Moline."

She raised her eyebrows.

"By the use of an instrument known as the comparison microscope, we can check bullets and determine definitely whether any given bullet was fired from any particular gun. We have completed experiments with this weapon, and I now have definite proof that this was the weapon which fired the bullets that killed Addison Stearne and C. Arthur Right."

She was silent now, saying nothing.

"A reconstruction of the crime," Duryea went on, "indicates that in place of being a double murder, the tragedy which occurred on that yacht was, in reality, a murder and suicide. Now what do you know about that?"

"Why, nothing."

"How long were you aboard that yacht before you fainted?"

"Just a minute or two. I stood on the pier for several minutes, trying to attract the attention of someone aboard the yacht. Then I noticed that the skiff which belonged to the *Gypsy Queen* was tied up there at the pier. So I felt certain Mr. Stearne, knowing that I would show up early in the morning, probably before he got up, had made arrangements with some other yachtsman to take the skiff over to the float and leave it tied up so I could come aboard.

"I untied the skiff, and got in and shoved off. That took a little while, then I got aboard and called out to see if anyone was up. When I didn't get any answer, I took the skiff back to the stern and tied it. That took a little while. I walked around the yacht, thinking that Addison and Arthur were still asleep. Then I got hungry and decided I'd go get myself a cup of coffee. I went down into the lower cabin, and—well, that was it. I saw the two bodies."

"How long were you there?"

"In the room with the bodies?"

"Yes."

"Just a matter of seconds. Not over a minute at the very longest."

"Then what did you do?"

"I ran through the yacht, screaming and shouting for help,

147

but there was no one in any of the staterooms. I went into the crew's quarters. There was no one there. I came back, and went to the upper cabin. No one was up there. I went out to the rail, and . . . and then I . . ."

"Yes, we know definitely what happened *after* that," Duryea said. "I'm trying to find out what happened *before*."

"Well, that's all that happened."

"And you've told me everything now."

"Yes. Everything."

"There's nothing else you know about this case?"

"No, not a thing."

Duryea frowned. "I have a very definite impression, Miss Moline, that you're holding something back."

She flared into indignation, suddenly pushing back her chair. "I'm tired of trying to co-operate with you, Mr. Duryea. I've told you everything, and I'm not going to submit to any further questioning. I've gone over this time and time again. I'm not . . ."

The door to the reception room opened, and Miss Stevens, Duryea's secretary, said apologetically, "Mr. Wiggins is here and says you're expecting him."

"Tell him to wait," Duryea said irritably.

"But he says that he has those people with him, that you're . . ."

Gramps pushed her gently to one side. "It's all right, my dear," he said in his shrill, piping voice. "These are the people Mr. Duryea wanted to . . . Come right in, folks."

The district attorney stared in surprise while Gramps escorted a man and a woman past the secretary and into Duryea's office.

Duryea regarded the couple with disfavor. They had a somewhat seedy look. The man seemed honest enough, but he was embarrassed and ill at ease. There was definitely something off-color about the woman, a chip-on-the-shoulder attitude of slatternly belligerency.

Gramps moved so that for a moment he stood between the couple and Nita Moline. The woman promptly pushed Gramps to one side so she could get a good view. The man also looked at Miss Moline, his face heavy, unintelligent, and without emotion.

"Well?" Duryea asked, irritated.

The man slowly nodded his head. At the same time, the woman began nodding with such vigor that her coarse, stringy bobbed hair swished back and forth.

Duryea, suddenly realizing the trick Gramps was playing on him, jumped to his feet. "All right," he said irritably to Gramps, "that's enough. Get out! Get these people out of here."

"Yes, sir," Gramps said, and to the couple he had brought in, "That's all the district attorney wants. You may go now."

Duryea's irritation didn't decrease as he realized that Gramps had counted on being abruptly ordered from the office, and was capitalizing on the situation.

Scowling blackly, Duryea watched them leave the office, motioned to Miss Stevens to close the door, and then, still irritated, turned back to Miss Moline.

The haughty shell had dropped from her. Her lips were quivering as she fought a losing battle to hold her self-control, then suddenly, with a wild, half-hysterical sob, she flung her head down on her arms.

"I'm sorry," Duryea apologized.

"Oh, I shouldn't have done it! I might have known that someone somewhere would have seen me. I was afraid of it when you brought that other couple in. As soon as you did that, I knew what you were after. I—"

Duryea rapidly readjusted his mental perspective. "I think," he said, in a voice of kindly dignity, "that you'd better tell me the *whole* truth now, Miss Moline."

She said, "I—when did these people see me?"

Duryea said, "Before I say anything else, Miss Moline, I'm going to give you an opportunity to make a complete statement."

Duryea stepped to the door of his office, said to Miss Stevens, "Will you bring your book, Miss Stevens? I want you to take down a statement."

When his secretary had settled herself with her notebook in front of her, Duryea nodded to Miss Moline. "Very well," he said quietly, "go ahead."

Miss Moline, avoiding his eyes, said, "I didn't tell you the whole truth."

"About the time you first came to the yacht?"

"Yes."

149

"Suppose now, Miss Moline, you tell me just exactly what *did* happen?"

"I was up here Saturday afternoon."

"Saturday afternoon!" Duryea exclaimed, and then, realizing suddenly the necessity of keeping surprise from his voice, said, "Just go right ahead, Miss Moline."

"Do you want me to tell you the whole thing?"

"Yes."

"Well, as I told you, Addison wanted me to come on this cruise. I gathered it was an important affair, that he had something to discuss. I couldn't get away on Saturday, just as I've told you. I had an appointment with my hairdresser and . . ."

"Yes, you've explained that. Go ahead and tell me the rest of it."

"About one on Saturday Addison telephoned me."

"Where were you?"

"At my hairdresser's."

"And where was Mr. Stearne?"

"At Santa Delbarra. At the yacht club, I believe."

"What did he want?"

"He asked me how soon I could get away from the hairdresser's. I told him that it would be around two. He asked me to have the hairdresser hurry things up as much as possible. He said he wanted me to find out where Pearl Right was, and if she wasn't home, to check up and find where Warren Hilbers was, and then get in touch with him and let him know."

"He told you where to get in touch with him?"

"Yes. He said I could call him at the Santa Delbarra Yacht Club, and they'd send a messenger out to the yacht."

"And what did you do?"

"I had the hairdresser hurry through with my appointment and went to Pearl Right's. She wasn't home. The maid seemed rather evasive about it."

"You knew Warren Hilbers?"

"Oh, yes."

"Stearne wanted you to find out if Mrs. Right was with her brother?"

"Yes."

"And where her brother was?"

"That's right."

"What did you do?"

"I found Pearl wasn't at home. I called some friends over at Catalina and found out Warren and Pearl had been over there ever since early in the morning—oh, around nine or ten o'clock."

"Then what?"

"That yachting crowd quite frequently go over in yachts and then rent a cottage. Sometimes one yachting party will have one by itself. Sometimes two or three will get together and rent a cottage between them—a place where they can make headquarters when they're on shore, get baths and so forth. I found out that Warren and Pearl had been seen zipping around the island, and then, later on, Warren had been seen in the boat all by himself, without anyone with him. So I thought he must have rented a cottage and Pearl was there. I asked my friends what cottage Warren usually rented, and they said one owned by a Mrs. Raleigh."

"Did you try to call Mrs. Right at that cottage?"

"Not then. That was later—late Sunday afternoon."

"Warren Hilbers is a yachting enthusiast?"

"Yes. He doesn't care for cruisers. He goes in for speedboats—anything under thirty-five miles an hour he considers slow.—I think his sister likes it, too. She put up the money for his last speedboat."

"And that was all Mr. Stearne wanted to know? Just where they were?"

"Yes."

"Did he say why?"

"No. I thought that perhaps it was because he wanted to be certain—well, I don't know."

"Certain of what?"

She shook her head. "I don't know."

"Go ahead," Duryea said. "What did you do after you'd located them?"

"I tried to get Addison on the telephone. The yacht club said he was out, and they didn't know just when he'd be back. Well, I knew it wasn't going to take very long to run up to Santa Delbarra if I stepped on it, and I wanted to talk with Addison."

"What about?"

"I wanted to find out whether there was going to be any

trouble between Pearl and Arthur, because if there was, I didn't want to be mixed up in it."

"So you drove to Santa Delbarra?"

"Yes."

"Now what time did you get here?"

She said, "That I don't know, Mr. Duryea. It was right around four o'clock, perhaps a few minutes before, perhaps a few minutes afterwards."

"Did you go aboard the yacht?"

"Yes."

"How?"

"I was standing on the wharf when a person from one of the other yachts came out to untie a dinghy. I asked him if he'd drop me off at the *Gypsy Queen*, and he said he'd be glad to. So I jumped in, and he rowed me by the *Gypsy Queen*, and I went aboard."

"And you saw both Right and Addison Stearne?"

"No. I saw Addison."

"You didn't see Right?"

"No."

"Just how did that happen?" Duryea asked.

"As I got aboard the yacht, Addison was just coming out of the cabin."

"Which cabin, the upper one or . . ."

"That's right, the upper one, the pilot house."

"What happened?"

"He seemed very much surprised when he saw me, and I think he was irritated. He motioned with his fingers on his lips for silence, and led me over toward the bow. He said, 'I told you to telephone. I didn't want you to come up.' "

"And what did you say?"

"I told him that I wanted to know where I stood and what it was all about. He said for me not to worry, to come up early Sunday morning, and everything would be all right."

"You told him what you'd found out?"

"Yes. Everything."

"Did he make any comments?"

"He said that under no circumstances must Arthur know I was there."

"That impressed you as being somewhat unusual?"

"Yes."

152

"What did you do?"

"I told him that I must know what was in the wind. He was evasive. After a while he said that he thought that when Mrs. Right left the house, she might have intended to go away for good. If that were the case she'd probably left a letter for Arthur, and that she might have said some things about me in that letter. He said that everything was going to be all right, however, and if I'd just have confidence in him and come up in time to go sailing with him at three o'clock Sunday afternoon, things would all clear up. He asked me to come up early Sunday."

"Did he give you any more details?"

"No. He seemed very nervous. He kept pushing me toward the rail of the yacht. He said it would be fatal if Arthur discovered I had been there. He said there were some things he'd have to explain to Arthur, and he'd have to do it at just the right time."

"Then what?"

"I got into the skiff, and he rowed me to the yacht club."

"And Arthur Right didn't know you were there?"

She hesitated a moment, then said, "I rather think he did."

"What makes you think so?"

"Just as I was leaving the skiff, I heard Addison swear under his breath, and then he said, 'There's Arthur on deck now. Don't look back. Keep right on walking, and duck inside the clubhouse.'"

"You did that?"

"Yes."

"Now, do you know whether this interview took place before four o'clock or afterwards?"

"It was right around four o'clock. I remember stopping on the road back at a service station. I noticed then that the clock showed it was about twenty-five minutes past four. I wanted my oil changed. I left that service station by twenty-five minutes to five. I'm positive of that."

Duryea said, "You telephoned Mrs. Right on Catalina Island Sunday afternoon after you'd learned of the murder?"

"Yes."

"Why?"

"It suddenly occurred to me that if she'd left a statement—and if she hadn't been intending to come back—well, the officers might have got into the house or interrogated the servants and found the statement . . ."

"Go on," Duryea said as she hesitated.

"Well, there might have been something in it which would have made it look bad for Pearl. That is, something that—oh, some dirty linen that it would have been better not to have aired."

"You mean something that would have made things embarrassing for you, don't you?" Duryea asked.

"I didn't think of that so much at the time. I was thinking of what a position Pearl would be in."

"Look here," Duryea said suddenly, "you thought perhaps *she* had murdered her husband, didn't you?"

Nita Moline hesitated for just a fraction of a second, then said slowly, "No. Not that."

"But you thought she might be *accused* of it?"

"I thought the officers might consider that possibility—if they got that statement."

"And you did know that you were mentioned in that statement?"

"Well, I didn't know—it wasn't until later that I recalled what Addison had said. I'm sorry, Mr. Duryea, but I just can't amplify that. Pearl was nervous and upset, and there was a lot she didn't understand."

"Is there anything else you have to tell me?" Duryea asked.

"That's all."

"Nothing about what happened Sunday morning?"

Her eyes widened slightly. "Why? What happened Sunday morning?"

"After you discovered the bodies. Didn't you remove some of the evidence?"

"Why, no, Mr. Duryea. No, honestly. It was just this thing that I'd done Saturday that weighed on my mind—this business of coming up here and being aboard the yacht and not—well, holding out the information on you."

"I see," Duryea said, "and now you've told me everything?"

"Yes, everything. Absolutely everything."

Duryea said, "I think that's all, Miss Moline. I'm sorry you didn't tell me about this in the first place."

"I . . . well . . . you can see what it meant to Mrs. Right

—or what I thought it meant. I'm sorry. I just didn't feel that I should be the one to throw the first stone."

Duryea watched her to the door. When she had left, he said to Miss Stevens, "Get me police headquarters in Los Angeles at once. Rush the call through."

Miss Stevens dashed from the office to put through the call. A few moments later, when Duryea had his party on the line, he said, "This is Frank Duryea, district attorney at Santa Delbarra. Miss Nita Moline resides at six-o-nine Maplehurst Apartments. I want her apartment searched. You'd better get a warrant. It's in connection with the yacht murder case up here. I'm looking for a statement which may have been written by C. Arthur Right and which was taken from the yacht and secreted. You'll have to work fast. Miss Moline has just left my office. It will take her a couple of hours to get to her apartment. You should be able to have a warrant and be there within an hour. That will give you an hour to search."

Duryea hung up the phone.

Nita Moline, trim in her light gray skirt and jacket, waited just long enough after leaving the district attorney's office to make certain she was not being followed. Then she entered a telephone booth in a drugstore. With swift efficiency, she dropped a coin, dialed long distance, and said, "Miss Smith calling from pay station six-four-one-two-five. I want to talk with Mr. Ted Shale at Richgrove nine-seven-three-two-four, with no one else if he's out. Will you please rush the call?"

She was told to deposit eighty-five cents and to hold the line. While she waited, she took a few quick puffs on a cigarette. The slight trembling of her hand as she conveyed the match to the end of the cigarette had been her only indication of nervousness.

When she had taken the second deep drag, the operator said, "Here's your party."

Miss Moline dropped the cigarette to the floor of the telephone booth, placed the sole of her neat gray shoe on the end, heard Ted Shale's voice saying, "Hello."

Miss Moline said, "Ted, do you know who this is?"

"Yes."

"I want you to do something for me."

"What?"

155

"It's very important. I've been appointed administratrix with the will annexed, you know. There are some things I have to do, some very important steps to be taken in connection with the estate. I made a list of some papers I was to deliver to my attorney, Mr. Hazlit, of Hazlit & Tucker. I left these papers in a tan purse which I was wearing with another outfit. When I changed my clothes, I changed purses, but forgot to transfer some of the things. That tan purse is in the upper right-hand drawer of the little dressing table on the north side of my room. I left my key at the desk. I'm going to call them and tell them to let you have it.

"Now, like a good boy, will you run up to the Maplehurst Apartments right away? Ask for Miss Moline's key, and go up to my apartment. Now listen, Ted, this is very important. The apartment doesn't like to have tenants let other persons go to apartments to take things *out,* but it's all right to take things *in.* So will you wrap up a bundle of some sort? It doesn't make any difference what it is. Stop at a bookstore and buy the first two books you come to, or if you have a package of laundry handy, take it along. See that the package is displayed prominently. Do you get that?"

"Yes," Shale said. "What do I do after I get your purse?"

"Hide it under your coat," she said. "Hold it in place with your arm so you won't drop it. Leave the apartment. Go to the office of my attorney and tell him I expect to be there later on, that you had a drink with me, and found I had inadvertently left my purse in your car, that you want to leave it there with them so I can pick it up whenever I come in. Now, have you got that straight?"

"Straight as a string," Shale said.

"A little later on," she said, "we could go out and have a drink and perhaps a dance or two. Would you like that?"

"Very, very much," he told her.

Her laugh was low-throated, seductive. "So would I," she said. "By!"

She dropped the receiver into position and carefully noted the time on her wrist watch.

CHAPTER 21

JOAN HARPLER looked across the desk at Frank Duryea with frank, steady eyes, eyes in which there was the hint of a smile.

"I feel like a notorious woman," she said.

"I'm sorry you've been inconvenienced, but I had no idea there'd been any notoriety. I thought I'd handled that angle very carefully."

"Oh, but you have. I didn't say I *was* notorious. I said I *felt* like a notorious woman."

There was something about this young woman that bothered the district attorney. She had a calm assurance, a poise which almost made him feel ill at ease. Trying to analyze it, he thought that perhaps it came from a complete lack of nervousness. Most of the witnesses who sat across that desk from him had something to conceal, something that was preying on their minds. And, knowing that their consciences had a tender spot, they were in fear that the district attorney's questions might suddenly jab at the sore place—and so they schooled themselves, behind a casual mask, to conceal any little wince which might have come from this sudden prodding. But this young woman apparently regarded her visit as merely an entertaining interlude.

"You look far from being a notorious woman," Duryea said. "You look young and rather unsophisticated."

She laughed at him. "I'll have to remedy that. Young women rather resent being referred to as unsophisticated these days."

"Well," Duryea went on, "what I meant was that you're hardly the type one would expect to find sailing alone in a private yacht. Don't you usually have parties with you when you cruise?"

"Oh, sometimes—when they're congenial. But I get bored with these average yachting parties, men on the make, girls trying to have a fling, too much liquor—and then your yacht's a mess afterwards. I have a yacht because I like the sea. I like big game fishing. I have a few friends who have similar tastes."

157

"Isn't that rather a large yacht for a person who likes to cruise with a small party?"

"She's larger than I would have selected if I'd been building it. I picked it up last year. Naturally, I got it at a bargain. And she's a dream. Now, I'm warning you. I know you didn't get me up here simply to ask me about my yacht and my tastes for yachting. You're sort of feeling me out before you start swapping punches. But if you get me started talking about the *Albatross*, you won't hear anything else. So you'd better come right to the point."

Duryea smiled. "Even conceding that you have the most marvelous yacht on the coast, don't you find it rather inconvenient cruising alone?"

"Yes. I don't very often do it."

"And I gather this trip to Santa Delbarra was an exception?"

"In a way, yes."

"Would it be fair to ask what made it an exception?"

She laughed. "You certainly maneuver very adroitly, Mr. Duryea. For a moment I thought that talk of the yacht was merely a preliminary sparring. You launched your attack so smoothly I didn't see it coming."

He matched her smile, but beneath the courtesy of that smile was a steady insistence.

"A young man in whom I find myself taking more and more of an interest is getting a little—well, a little too independent. No. I don't really mean that, Mr. Duryea. It isn't that he's independent, but that he wants to rob *me* of *my* independence. Our friendship has progressed to that stage where he thinks that he has the right to tell me what I shall do and what I shall not do. And so I found it very convenient to take a trip without telling him where I was going or with whom. Afterwards, when the questioning and protests would come, I could wait until the smoke had blown away, proved to him I had been taking a cruise all by myself, and placed him in the position of being very much in the wrong. I thought it would be good discipline—and if he made too much of an issue, I would realize in time how very unfortunate it would be to have him in the role of a jealous husband."

"Isn't that going to a lot of trouble just to train a young man?"

"Training a young man is a lot of trouble, anyway," she laughed. "However, I suddenly found that I was far more fond of this person than I had realized. I happen to value my independence very highly. So there you are, Mr. Duryea. Rather a bad combination, one which requires thought—more than thought, meditation. And so you have the spectacle of a young woman traveling all by herself on a yacht."

"I see. And your trip Sunday afternoon?"

She made a little grimace. "That trip! I certainly wish I'd kept out of the whole business. I find myself in the position of the innocent bystander who is collecting most of the bruises."

"Hardly that bad, is it?"

"Almost. It's decidedly inconvenient."

"Perhaps you could tell me about that trip with the same frankness with which you've discussed the other?"

"More so because it's so much less personal and because it is so evidently connected with the case."

He smiled. "I'll have to acknowledge that that was rather neatly delivered—even if it was below the belt."

"I'm sorry. It was *such* a temptation. I should have concealed the barb a little more. Well, Miss Moline came aboard to change her clothes. I offered her the hospitality of my yacht. I thought that was the least one could do for a fellow yachtsman under the circumstances."

"And then?"

"This young man—Shale—went ashore. I certainly felt sorry for him, watching him trudging along with his sopping wet clothes clinging to him. He was trying to carry it off with something of an air of nonchalance. I certainly sympathized with him, and yet I had to laugh."

"You enjoy your laughs as you go through life?"

"Frankly, I do—and a good many of them are on myself."

"Miss Moline was changing her clothes while you were watching young Shale?"

"Yes, and then she made me a proposition. She said that it was exceedingly important to her to find out who went aboard the *Gypsy Queen*. Aside from the officers, of course."

"Did she say why she wanted to know?"

"Not in so many words. But she seemed trying to give the impression that some person had been expected to join the yachting party and hadn't. She was anxious to find out whether that person had been delayed or decided not to join up. However, that's merely conjecture on my part. Shall we strike it from the record?"

"Exactly what was her proposition?"

"She wanted to know if I was open to a financial proposition. I told her I wasn't, and then she explained what it meant to her and said that she'd get someone to keep watch, but that there was no place from which they could watch to advantage except from my yacht."

"And I take it you granted her request?"

"Yes, very reluctantly."

"For a financial consideration."

"No. Of course not. I told her I'd be glad to co-operate."

"This, I take it, is explaining that trip."

"It is."

"All right, go ahead."

"Well, it seems she made an arrangement with Ted Shale by which he was to do most of the watching. She wanted to stay aboard and help. Well, that was all right. Then she suggested that Ted Shale go below to get some sleep, which he did. Then Miss Moline decided that there wouldn't be any use trying to do anything while the officers were aboard the *Gypsy Queen*. She wanted to do some telephoning and asked me if I'd wake up Mr. Shale if I noticed the officers leaving the *Gypsy Queen*. I told her I wouldn't promise to watch. Do you know, Mr. Duryea, I suddenly had an idea her whole plea had been because she wanted to have someone aboard my yacht—to look through it, perhaps. I felt very resentful. I told her I wouldn't keep watch to see when or if the officers left, and that I wouldn't even promise to keep the yacht there. I let her see that I left I'd been imposed on a bit.

"Well, she went ashore, and I kept feeling more and more resentful. But curiosity impelled me to look over at the other yacht occasionally. Then I began to think Miss Moline had perhaps merely wanted to have this Mr. Shale where she could keep him out of circulation for a while until she could shape his recollection of what had happened. Well, I got good and mad at the way she'd dumped her problems in my lap. So I decided to show her a thing or two. I just dropped the mooring and went for a little pleasure cruise."

"Now, I believe you kept young Shale locked in his state-room?"

She smiled. "I went down to his cabin and called through the door that I was sailing and he'd have to go ashore. A violent snore was my only answer. I thought perhaps the young gentleman might be putting on an act. Or he might merely have been eager to accompany me on an unchaperoned yachting trip. I can assure you that ambitious young men under those circumstances can become very much of a nuisance. So I took steps to see that he would at least be awake when he left his room. I didn't want him using the old alibi of walking in his sleep."

"How far did you go?"

"Oh, I don't know. I just went out and sailed around and watched the sun on the mountains."

"And young Shale?"

"He woke up around sundown. He made an unearthly racket, and I went down to see how things were progressing. He seemed to be very unaccustomed to being locked in a room."

"What did you tell him?"

"I told him that I was sorry I'd locked the door, but I'd decided to take a little sail, and I felt that an ounce of precaution would be better than a pound of struggle. He laughed and said he'd go back to sleep if I could reassure him he wasn't being kidnaped. And how about his job? Well, he was so nice about it and sounded so thoroughly reasonable that I opened the door and let him out. I didn't even exact any promises. I didn't have to. He's a nice chap, and he knows something about yachting. He helped me bring the yacht in."

"Miss Moline met you?"

"Yes."

"What was her attitude?"

She said, "I'm afraid Miss Moline has been a trifle spoiled. I had to explain to her that I wasn't in her employ, and that I objected to being used as a cat's-paw. Then she begged my pardon, and . . ."

"Did Mr. Shale remain on board to watch—after that?"

"Yes. Miss Moline apologized very prettily. She said she'd had to do some telephoning and it had taken much too long. She asked if I wouldn't please let Mr. Shale watch until morning. She said she'd make other arrangements then, and would I be a good sport and not be too worried about the conventions."

"What did you tell her?"

"By that time, I felt pretty well acquainted with Shale. I felt certain that, while he hadn't taken any vows, a young woman who didn't throw the first stone wouldn't get hit with any rocks. So I told her I'd let it ride until morning."

"What did she do after that?"

"She left to go to Los Angeles. It seemed Mr. Stearne's lawyer had sent for her. Mr. Shale kept watch all night. He was a good soldier about it too. And a perfect gentleman."

"You don't know whether he saw anyone go aboard the yacht?" Duryea asked, more as a matter of routine than anything else.

"Yes. Someone went aboard before I had turned in. It was shortly after Miss Moline had left—oh, I'd say somewhere around one o'clock."

Duryea sat bolt upright in his chair, his back rigid, his eyes hard and cautious. "You mean someone went aboard the *Gypsy Queen?*"

"Yes."

"Who?"

"We don't know."

"Miss Moline wasn't with you then?"

"No. She had gone."

"Was this a man or a woman?"

Joan Harpler hesitated until the very hesitation became significant, then she said, "It was either a man—or a woman dressed in man's clothes."

"How long was this person aboard?"

"Not over five minutes."

"Do you know what he was after?"

"Something that was on the yacht."

"Why didn't you tell me about this?"

"*You* didn't ask me to keep watch. I supposed that if you'd wanted the yacht watched, you'd have arranged to have had it watched. You certainly had plenty of men and plenty of opportunity."

"Yes," Duryea conceded. "I must admit you're right there. Could you give a very clear description of this man?"

"I'm afraid I couldn't. He was rather an indistinct figure to me. He was very clever in handling a skiff. I noticed that. Shale was the one who watched him through the night glasses, and Shale would know more about him than I would. The man was carrying something, both when he went aboard and when he went ashore, a rather small, heavy bag of some sort."

"How did you know it was heavy?"

"By the way he handled it, and then by the noise he made when he put it down in the bottom of the skiff."

"A traveling bag?" Duryea asked.

"It was more like a small, square suitcase."

He studied her face for a flicker of expression which would indicate that she knew the significance of what she was saying, but he could see nothing. "Was it a portable typewriter?"

She frowned as though trying to reconstruct the scene, and said, "It *could* very well have been a portable typewriter."

CHAPTER 22

FRANK DURYEA stretched out in the rattan chaise longue in the solarium and gave himself to the solace of a cigar. It was that mystic moment when the cares of the business world are dissolved in a blue haze of aromatic smoke.

The maid, back on duty now, was getting ready to put dinner on the table. Milred, in a cool print dress that made her seem as clean and dainty as though she had been some choice bit of merchandise wrapped in cellophane, watched her husband speculatively. Her half-closed eyes gave to her face an expression of contentment and of seductive speculation.

Gramps Wiggins, bustling about in the suit of clothes he had dug out of the closet in the trailer, clasped a frosted cocktail shaker in his hands and shook it up and down with the vehemence of a big dog shaking a rabbit.

"What do you call it, Gramps?" Milred asked.

"Well," he said, "rightly it ain't got no name. Heard a fellow the other night crackin' wise about *his* cocktail, said he called it the 'Block and Tackle' because you drink it, walk a block, an' tackle anythin'. Well, this here cocktail, she ain't like that. No, sir. You don't need to walk no block, jus' drink it an' *phss-s-s-s-t!* You take off like a skyrocket!"

"You invented it?" Milred asked.

"Uh huh, an' she ain't got no inert ingredients in 'er. You drink this an' you know you *got* somethin'. The taste is kinda disguised, but don't make no mistake about it. She's like these here women that look mild an' housified, but boy, oh boy, oh boy!"

Duryea said, "I'm willing to try it, but I may have to go to the office this evening."

Milred made a little grimace. "Again! Why don't you let the sheriff work up that case?"

"Because I'm afraid he'll arrest the wrong person," Duryea said, "and then it'll be up to me to go into court with a case that will backfire."

"I gathered from the evening paper that a pretty black case was building up against this Moline girl."

Gramps unscrewed the little cap in the spout of the cocktail shaker. "The way things look right now," he said, "it hinges on that letter to them oil people. Stearne told the stenographer he was goin' to leave so he could get it in the post office before five o'clock. That meant he'd have to leave the yacht by twenty minutes to five at the latest. If he didn't mail that letter, it looks as though he got killed between five minutes past four and twenty minutes to five. An' this here Moline girl was on the yacht an' can't prove where she was next until four-thirty. How'm I doin', Frank?"

Duryea said, "Pretty good. As a matter of fact, Milred, I think I'll have to put Gramps on the force."

Gramps Wiggins looked up with a quick little birdlike jerk to his head. "You meanin' that?" he asked.

Duryea laughed. "No."

"I was afraid not."

Duryea said, "You'd get fed up with it in ten days, Gramps. Nothing but a lot of routine. People commit petty crimes. Kids steal automobiles. Men drive while intoxicated. A burglary here and there. Occasionally some talented crook drifts into town and pulls a job. Mostly those people aren't caught, but if they are caught, it's nearly always a dead open-and-shut case."

"How about murder cases?"

"Murder cases come along about twice a year. Mostly they're emotional killings where a person shoots someone in blind rage, then goes and gives himself up, or commits suicide. It's only once in a blue moon we have any real mystery murders."

"Well," Gramps said, "I guess p'raps I better make arrangements to just come back an' work every blue moon. Here you are, folks."

Gramps passed over the tray with the cocktail glasses. Milred tasted hers, then said, with a voice that held a faint trace of surprise, "Why, Gramps, it's good."

"Of course it's good," Gramps said indignantly. "What you think I been doin' all this time, wastin' elbow grease an' good liquor on somethin' that wasn't good?"

Duryea said, "Tastes as though it had rum in it."

"You just drink it," Gramps said, "an' don't worry about it."

"But it certainly tastes mild. You aren't kidding about its having authority?" Milred asked.

Gramps Wiggins looked at her over the tops of his glasses. "Now, you listen to me, Milred. I've batted around this country right smart. Me an' old John Barleycorn have had many a tough tussle. I ain't never licked him, an' he ain't never licked me. Once or twice he's had me down, but I ain't stayed down. It's just about been a draw so far. But I'm tellin' you this here cocktail is old John Barleycorn's ace in the hole. This is the thing he uses for his haymaker."

"Well, I've certainly tasted lots of cocktails that seemed stronger than this."

Milred turned to her husband. "What are you going to do about that Moline woman?" she asked.

"Darned if I know," Duryea admitted cheerfully. "The sheriff wants to go ahead and charge her. I'm holding off for a while. There are some investigations I want to make. I'd like to go to Catalina tomorrow and check up on some things."

Milred said, "Oh, take me."

"It'd be a business trip."

"I wouldn't interfere. I just want to go along."

He shook his head.

Gramps Wiggins said, "Tell you what you do, sis. You come along with *me*. I was thinkin' o' goin' to Catalina tomorrow, an' you an' I can go along together. If your husband gets on the same boat, we can't do nothin' about that."

"I might fly down," Duryea said, smiling.

"Phooey," Milred retorted. "There's no fun in that. Why

don't you come along with us, get the thrill out of the boat ride, the tang of the salt sea air, see the different types of people? Then you'd have an hour or two over at Catalina after you'd finished your business, and you could really relax. You've been in the office too much lately."

"Are you actually going?" Duryea asked.

"You heard Gramps ask me, didn't you?"

Gramps said with a chuckle, "An' when you ask a Wiggins to go some place, that's all there is to it. No true Wiggins ever stuck around anywhere until he got into a rut. He's a ramblin' son of a gun, the original rollin' stone."

Milred asked her husband, "What are you going to investigate?"

Duryea said, "I want to check up on Mrs. Right and her brother."

"Good heavens, Frank, why?"

"Oh, just a matter of routine."

"Why not let the police do it?"

"I don't want to give it that much publicity."

"But why check up on them?"

Duryea said, almost musingly, "At around four o'clock Sunday afternoon, something *may* have happened. Or perhaps I should say something had been planned to happen."

"What?"

"I don't know. No one seems to know. The *Gypsy Queen* had been intending to put to sea at three o'clock in the afternoon. The *Albatross* was at sea at three o'clock in the afternoon. Now, if it should appear that Pearl Right, in her brother's speedboat, was also ferried out to sea at three o'clock in the afternoon, it would be—rather a coincidence, wouldn't it?"

Gramps said, "Now you're gettin' somewhere, son. I been hopin' the time would come when you'd call the turn on this here Joan Harpler. She's had you plumb hypnotized, an' she knows it.

"She's a cute little package—too darn cute. Somehow, the way she tells her story about sailin' around alone sounds awfully genuine and truthful when you're listenin' to her, but when she goes away an' you don't see those wide eyes anymore, an' don't hear that rich voice purrin' words at you, but just remember the words themselves, they sound kinda fishy."

Milred said, "I guess there really is something in that cocktail. It's got Gramps started talking."

"What do you mean?" Gramps demanded. "I'm always talkin'."

"Telling me secrets about my husband's office. He comes home and talks about the routine legal chores. Then you take two cocktails and I find he puts in his time talking with beautiful women and letting them put him in a state of trance."

"You got somethin' there," Gramps said. "That there Harpler girl is purty as a picture, an' this Moline girl is . . ."

"Oh, I'm not afraid of *her*," Milred said. "Frank doesn't fall for that type. Sophistication, glitter, and the flash of a shapely leg leave him quite cool, thank you; but let a good-looking girl put on the good-sport act, smile up into his eyes, give him a warm handclasp, and he's a pushover."

Duryea said, "So you've been using dictographs again, eh?"

"No, dear. Just studying you."

"When?"

"Before I hooked you, silly. Don't you know that a hunter always studies the habits of the game he intends to stalk."

Gramps started to chuckle. "Heh heh heh. Betcha he thought he was sweepin' ya right off your feet. Didn't know he was just grabbin' the bait an' havin' the hook sunk in him right up to the gills."

Duryea sighed. "As though my job didn't have enough disillusionment."

The maid came to the door. "Dinner is served," she said.

Gramps gulped down the last of his cocktail. "You listen to me, son. Don't let that Harpler girl pull any wool over your eyes. When I'm cold sober, an' think of her lookin' at me with that little one-sided smile o' hers, an' those steady slate-gray eyes meetin' mine, as though she didn't have a thing to conceal, I say to myself, 'Well, now, you may have to watch this Moline woman, but this here Harpler girl is all wool—virgin wool at that.' An' then I get a little bit swacked an' get to thinkin' over what she says an' I'm tellin' ya she don't click. Decidin' somebody was tryin' to impose on her, so she takes a run out to sea. Afraid some man is gonna make a pass at her, so she locks him in his stateroom. She ain't kiddin' *me* none, Frank Duryea."

The district attorney put down his empty cocktail glass, conscious of the fact that Milred's eyes were on him, studying him thoughtfully.

"There may be something she's concealing in connection with her private affairs," Duryea said.

Milred said, "Yes, Gramps, we're going to Catalina tomorrow—definitely. He isn't to be trusted running around loose, not when he begins to get these complexes."

They were halfway through dinner when the telephone rang, and the maid announced that Sheriff Lassen was on the line with some important information for Duryea. The district attorney went to the telephone and returned after a few minutes to face the expectant, eager eyes of Gramps Wiggins.

"I'm sorry, Gramps. It's no go."

"What?"

"Your theory."

"What about it?"

"Those glasses have been in the water for some time."

"What makes you think so?"

"The sheriff got in touch with the oculist who supplied both men with glasses. There's not a chance on earth that that pair of spectacles had anything to do with either of them."

"Why not?"

"The prescription is all wrong. The man who owned those spectacles had a left eye which required an enormous correction. The right eye was nearly normal. It's an unusual combination. The sheriff feels certain they were dropped from some other yacht."

"Well, what other yacht has been there in the last week?"

"Two or three. The sheriff's checking up on them just to make sure."

Gramps grinned. "Well," he said, "it was a good theory while it lasted."

"It was, for a fact," Duryea admitted. "Your theories are all to the good. That diagram you drew of the way the boat swung around with the tide and the position in which the gun was found still indicates something. And the way you handled that third degree of Nita Moline was a masterpiece."

"That Moline girl again," Gramps said. "We keep comin' back to her."

"What about the place where the gun was found?" Milred asked. "I seem to be losing out."

Duryea said, "I don't know whether it's the effect of the cocktail or the fact that the more I think of it, the more I realize how thoroughly logical and clever it was, but Gramps has darned near demonstrated that the gun was dumped over the side of the yacht sometime after the murder was committed. Now the question is, by whom?"

"Nita Moline?" Milred asked.

"It's *almost* a certainty," Duryea said.

Gramps Wiggins' knife and fork clattered against the plate. "By gum," he said. "I've got a theory!"

"No, no," Duryea begged laughingly. "Not another one. Not until after dinner."

"Yes, sir," Gramps said. "I got me a damn good theory."

"Well, what is it?"

"That Harpler girl. When Ted Shale saw her, she was standin' on the deck o' the yacht. Shale says she had on a bathin' suit, an' there was drops of water glistenin' on her arms an' legs. She coulda swum over to that other yacht just as well as not. An' don't forget one thing, son. The skiff that belonged to the *Gypsy Queen* was tied up at the float. That means someone had to leave that yacht sometime after the murders were committed. Now, *if* it had been a murder an' suicide, somebody knew about it an' was on the boat, an' took the skiff an' went ashore."

"The Moline girl," Milred remarked.

"No, it couldn't have been her, because she found the skiff tied up at the float. It has to be one o' two things. Either someone was aboard the yacht an' rowed ashore, or someone in a bathin' suit went over to the yacht, found evidences of a murder an' suicide, ditched the evidence, for reasons best known to himself, an' *then took the skiff ashore* so as to make it look like a murder. A girl in a bathin' suit could have done that. A girl who wasn't wearin' a bathin' suit couldn't. Don't go lettin' this Harpler woman pull a lot o' wool over your eyes, son. You're young an' impressionable, an' you're fallin' for her."

There was an unmistakable earnestness about Gramps' plea.

Milred, watching him thoughtfully, turned to Frank Duryea. Under the scrutiny of her eyes, Duryea felt himself flush. The knowledge that he was flushing, added to his embarrassment and his color.

Milred said, without taking her eyes from her husband's

169

face, "Gramps, before you go, you leave the recipe for that cocktail right here. Mamma is going to need that in her business."

CHAPTER 23

MRS. GIBBS looked up from the newspaper and transfixed her husband with steady scrutiny.

"See by the paper that girl friend of yours was fibbing."

"What girl friend?"

"You know well enough who I mean."

"That Moline girl?"

"That's the one. Looks as though she's in bad now. She was the last person to see those two men alive."

"So far as they know now."

"Well, he was intending to mail a letter shortly before five o'clock, and he never got to the post office with it. You know what that means. He was dead before she was outside the city limits."

"Oh, don't keep picking on the girl. I tell you they haven't anything on her."

"That's just like a man, sticking up for her. Trying to tell me that she was nothing to you, that you were so tired you just went to sleep and let her drive. You didn't pay any attention to her, oh, no. And that picture of her in the paper, why, that was all right, too. 'Don't think anything about it, honey. It's just the way all the women have their pictures taken now. The photographers insist on it.'"

Gibbs went on eating his supper in dogged silence.

"What happened—what really and truly happened? When you found her up in Santa Delbarra and brought her back—did you really leave at three o'clock in the morning?"

"I don't know just what time it was."

"You found her around midnight. Isn't that what you said?"

"I guess so."

"But you didn't get in here until seven-thirty in the morning."

"I stopped and had breakfast."

"Oh, so you had breakfast with her?"

"Of course. I rang her lawyer, and while we were waiting for him to come to his office, we stopped in for a cup of coffee."

"Stopped in where?"

"At an all-night restaurant."

"You had more than coffee, because you weren't hungry when you got home, and . . ."

"I had ham and eggs."

"What did *she* have?"

"The same."

"Then it wasn't just a cup of coffee. You had breakfast together."

"All right, we had breakfast together. So what?"

She was silent for a moment, then she said abruptly, "Where's your typewriter?"

"Why, in my study."

"That isn't the one you had a few days ago."

He paused with a fork halfway to his mouth. "How do you know?"

"Because I know. I wrote a letter on it."

"I've told you I don't want you to use my typewriter."

"Why shouldn't I use it if I want to?"

"It gets it out of adjustment."

"Well, I like that. Why should it get out of adjustment for me if it doesn't for you? I'm not one to smash a typewriter, simply writing a letter on it. But you're avoiding my question. Where did you get that typewriter?"

"Are you sure it isn't the one I've had all along?"

"Absolutely certain. There was a scratch on the enamel on the frame of yours, and you'd just had yours fixed up with a new platen and . . ."

Gibbs interrupted to say hastily, "I must have picked up someone else's typewriter."

"Where?"

"I wouldn't know. In a hotel some place probably."

She said, "That's just the point. You did it in a hotel. I knew it."

"Knew what?"

"That you'd been with that woman."

"What the devil are you talking about?"

"It's *her* typewriter. You switched typewriters with her."

"She didn't have a typewriter."

"Don't be silly. There's a photograph of a typewriter in the paper. They say that it furnishes a clue to the murder of those men. They found it on the yacht. That Moline girl left it there. She killed him. But you picked up her typewriter, and she picked up yours. That's *your* typewriter just as sure as I'm sitting here, Parker Gibbs."

Gibbs said, "Now listen, honey, let's be sensible about this thing. We . . ."

"But you said yourself you'd got it mixed up with someone else's."

"Now listen, hon, that's *not* Miss Moline's typewriter."

"How do you know it isn't?"

"Because I . . . well, it couldn't be."

"But you admit that isn't *your* typewriter."

"I'll have to take another look at it. It may be the same one that I had. You know, those platens get pounded up very quickly. I do a great deal of writing, particularly while I was away on this last trip. I had to write a great, long report."

"You're just trying to fool me now. You're just trying to pull the wool over my eyes. You said before that it wasn't your typewriter. You've just thought of that."

"Oh, forget it!"

"I'm not going to forget it. Unless you can prove to me you didn't stay with that Moline woman, I'm going to ring up the district attorney and tell him that I have her typewriter."

Gibbs said, "You try doing that and I'll—I'll break your neck."

"Oh, you're going to stick up for her!"

"I tell you, I'm working for some lawyers. If you stuck your finger in the pie, you'd ruin my entire career."

"All right, then I'll write an anonymous letter."

"You'll do no such thing," Gibbs said, thinking desperately.

"Oh, no? How do you know I haven't done it already?"

"By George," Gibbs exclaimed, "I remember now what happened. I took my typewriter to the lawyer's office, and left it in the outer room. When I went out, I must have picked up one of the lawyer's typewriters. I'll take this right back and exchange it for mine. I'll start right now."

Mrs. Gibbs stood watching him, her hands on her hips, a sardonic smile playing at the corners of her mouth.

"You didn't eat your dessert."

"I'm not hungry. I don't want it."

"Seems like you're in an awful hurry to get that typewriter exchanged."

"Well, I hate to have the lawyer think—and I want mine back."

"Then you don't think this is Nita Moline's typewriter?"

"Of course, it isn't."

She said, "Go right ahead, Parker. Go right back to the lawyer's office and get your own typewriter. When you bring it back, wake me up and show it to me. No matter what time it is, wake me up. Then I'll let you have this other typewriter. But in the meantime, I've got it locked up. And I'm keeping it locked up."

Hazlit looked up as Tucker came in from the law library, a triumphant grin on his face.

"We've got 'em!" Tucker said.

"What is it, Neldon?"

"The legal ace which takes the whole bag of tricks."

"What?"

"A supreme court decision which has been overlooked by all concerned, one of those peculiar decisions which is logical enough when you read it, but one of which you never think when . . ."

"What is it?"

"A decision that a murder where two or more people are killed is in the nature of a public calamity."

"Well," Hazlit said, smiling, "I certainly wouldn't think it was a public benefit—unless I could pick the victims—in which event it might be a service to all concerned."

"Well, there it is in black and white," Tucker said. "That such a murder is a public calamity."

Hazlit looked at him with scowling incomprehension. "What good does that do? How does that help us?"

"Don't you see?"

"No. I'm hanged if I do."

"It puts us in the saddle, and keeps us there."

"Will you please explain?"

"Don't those words 'public calamity' mean anything to you?"

"Not a damn thing," Hazlit said irritably. "All I know is that it looks as though Gibbs . . . What has a public calamity to do with it?"

"Don't you remember the code sections dealing with disputable presumptions?"

"Well, what about them? They provide that a letter which has been stamped and deposited in a post office is deemed to have been received by the person to whom it was addressed. I remember that."

Tucker laughed. He was as bubbling over with enthusiasm as his partner was immersed in irritation. "Among the presumptions is one which fixes the order of death, in the absence of evidence to the contrary, where two or more persons perish in the same calamity."

Hazlit blinked his eyes. "That code section," he said, "is limited to a wreck, a battle, or a big fire."

"No, it isn't. The words wreck, battle, or conflagration are used as illustration rather than for the purpose of narrowing the purport of the section. It's subdivision forty of section nineteen-sixty-three, and the fourth sub-paragraph of that subdivision provides that where the two persons are both of the same sex, are both over fifteen years of age, and under sixty, the older person *is presumed to have survived longer than the younger.*"

Hazlit thought that over. "Good heavens, Neldon, if that means what it says—if that section is applicable— Great Scott, man, it gives us everything! It gives us the estate. It gives us— Hell's bells, it puts us right in the saddle, and they can't unseat us to save themselves."

"That's it," Tucker said. "That's what I've been telling you. We're sitting pretty."

"That," Hazlit said, "is excellent—provided Gibbs hasn't done something careless."

"What's Gibbs got to do with it?" Tucker asked.

"A private detective is always trying to show the value of his services. He wants to turn in satisfactory reports showing progress. I hope that Gibbs—well, it would be doubly unfortunate, now that we know the law is in our favor, if Gibbs had—oh, well, never mind."

Tucker looked at him curiously. He said, "You talked with Gibbs. I didn't."

He retired to the law library, pulling the door shut behind him with a certain emphatic gesture of finality.

174

Hazlit got up, started pacing the floor, his forehead creased in a deep frown.

CHAPTER 24

THE trim little steamship looked like a miniature ocean liner as it nosed through the blue waters of the channel. A wave hissed up on each side of the white prow, a boiling wake churned up astern. Overhead was a stretch of cloudless blue sky against which seagulls, poised in effortless ease, hung just behind the stern where the suction of air currents carried them forward.

Astern, the coast line of California showed a misty blue. Ahead, the slopes of Catalina, touched with the morning sun, were reddish gold.

Frank Duryea, Milred, and Gramps Wiggins sat in one of the sheltered nooks on the upper deck.

Duryea took from his inside coat pocket a special delivery letter addressed in typewriting to the District Attorney, Santa Delbarra, California. He turned it over in his hands, studying it intently.

"That the one that came at five o'clock this morning?" Gramps Wiggins asked.

"That's the one. Did you hear them ringing the bell?"

"I woke up when I heard you call out asking what it was, and heard a boy say, 'Special delivery letter.' "

"The words 'Urgent. Deliver immediately' are typed on the envelope," Duryea said. He extracted the sheet of paper from the inside of the envelope and spread it out.

Gramps and Milred leaned over to read the words which had been typed on the sheet of paper. "If you want to find out who murdered those two men on the yacht, you'd better find out where Nita Moline spent her time between midnight Sunday night and three o'clock Monday morning. This is a real tip from someone who isn't being catty, but wants the murder solved. After you find out where she was, if you'll put an ad in the personal column of the Los Angeles *Examiner* saying 'Party inquired about was at ———' and *then say who she was with,* I'll write you another letter and let you know something important. But I won't do that unless you put in that ad where she was and who she was with."

The letter was signed simply, *"A Friend."*

"Well," Duryea asked, "what do you think of it?"

"It was written by a woman," Milred said.

"What makes you think so?"

"I should say it was written by a jealous woman," Milred went on. "There are several clues in it. Notice in the first place that she says she isn't being catty. That's typically a feminine expression, then also notice that she wants you to find out where Miss Moline was between those hours and make the information available. She then promises to write and let you know if you are correct. It's a woman, and a jealous or a suspicious woman."

"What do you think, Gramps?" Duryea asked.

Gramps said, "Let's see how much we can tell about the person who wrote it. Somebody that was just a little careless. Notice there are four mistakes in the letter. One has been erased. Down near the end she was too lazy or careless to make an erasure. She simply struck the letter S over. Where she erased, she wasn't careful to do a clean job of it. And this is a good example of how each typewriter shows its individuality. Notice the way that A is tilted over to one side, and the E is . . . Say, son, *wait a minute!*"

"What's the matter?" Duryea asked.

"Great jumpin' Jehoshaphat!" Gramps exclaimed.

Milred smiled at her husband. "Something he ate for breakfast," she said.

"More apt to be something he didn't eat," Duryea said. "This salt air is giving me an awful appetite. I'll bet . . ."

"Ye gods," Gramps shrilled. "You know what we've got, son? You know what this is?"

"No," Duryea said. "What is it?"

"The hottest clue in the whole damn case," Gramps said.

Duryea looked at the old man's excited countenance, and said, "What is it?"

"Don't you get it? The little distinctive oddities of alignment are the same in this letter that they were on the carbon copy of the letter that Stearne's office produced. This here letter, son, *was written on the same typewriter that Mrs. Rodman used on Saturday afternoon!*"

Duryea looked at the expression on Gramps' face, then whipped a photostatic copy of the other letter from his pocket. As he compared the two, his face showed the verdict, even before he said, "You're right, Gramps. Now we've got to find the person who wrote that letter."

"Where's it postmarked?" Gramps asked.

"Los Angeles."

"And she wants you to put the information in a Los Angeles paper. She lives there."

Gramps said, "That envelope is just a plain stamped envelope with a special delivery stamp—"

The hoarse blast of a whistle drowned out his words. He jumped to his feet, ran around to where he could look forward, and came back to say, "We're just comin' into the harbor, son. Better put that letter away. Don't put it back in that wallet. If you run into a pickpocket and he should reef your britch, the first thing he'd grab would be the leather, an' . . ."

"Wait a minute, wait a minute," Duryea said, laughing. "You're using a lot of technical terms, Gramps. When did you know any pickpockets?"

Gramps Wiggins looked sheepish. "Aw, I—just somethin' I read somewhere, I guess, in some of these detective stories."

Duryea laughed with polite disbelief.

"All pickpockets ain't bad, anyway," Gramps asserted. "Some of 'em are nice boys that just got a wrong start, an' once they get in the game, they don't know how to get out."

Milred said, "Well, let's get ashore. And how about eats? Think of the scandal when the citizens of Santa Delbarra pick up their papers tonight and read, 'Special from Catalina. Overzealous official neglects feeding wife. Our readers will be shocked to know that Mrs. Milred Duryea collapsed on the beach promenade at Santa Catalina Island at an early hour this morning. Physicians who attended her said . . . '"

"I surrender," Duryea announced.

"A hamburger with everything," she said.

"Two," Gramps piped up. "Heavy on the onions, too."

"Three," Duryea laughed.

They had no difficulty in finding the house they wanted. It was a small cottage with a sign announcing that it was for rent, furnished, by the day, week, or month. Mrs. Raleigh studied

Duryea's credentials and said, "Why, yes, I remember the party. That was last Saturday, just about noon."

"That's right."

"When Mr. Hilbers, the yachtsman, came here," she said after a moment, "he didn't say how large his party was. He said that he'd come over on his yacht, and intended to be here over the week end. He wanted a place to use as headquarters for his party—where they could have baths. He didn't say how big his party was."

"Can you describe him?" Duryea asked.

"Oh, yes. He's been here once or twice before. He's tall and slender, with dark hair. About twenty-seven or twenty-eight, I should judge, quite attractive. When you've once heard his voice you'll never forget it. He wore a blue serge, double-breasted coat, and a yachting cap."

"Did you see the woman?"

"Why, I saw his sister. She was with him when he checked out."

"Can you describe her?"

"Yes. She's an attractive young brunette, about a hundred and twenty pounds. She has a good figure, and knows it."

"Had you ever seen her before?"

"Yes, but I can't remember just when it was. Incidentally, you might be interested to learn that she left something behind."

"What?"

"A bathing suit."

"Where is it?" Duryea asked.

"I have it over in my house. Would you like it?"

"Very much," Duryea said. "It might be important.—You're sure that it was left by the sister?"

"At least by one of the women in Mr. Hilbers' party. It was hanging in the shower. I'd intended to hold it until Mr. Hilbers happened to be over here again. Just a moment and I'll get it."

She disappeared in the house and returned presently with a rubber bathing suit. A peculiar montage of marine scenery had been worked into the rubber—waves curling into green crests, over which pelicans were flying. Here and there a seal thrust its head out of the water. These seals all had the same facial expression—a whisker-twisting smirk—a leer of cynical triumph.

Duryea held it up to Milred. His wife, studying it carefully and with a practiced eye, said, "Not bad. It looks as though it had been shaped to curves."

Duryea said to Mrs. Raleigh, "I'm going to take this. Would you mind writing your name or putting your initials on a hem somewhere? Some little mark so you can identify it later on as being the same suit which you found in the shower."

He handed her a fountain pen. She scrawled her initials on the hem of the panties.

Duryea took from his pocket a picture he had cut from a newspaper. "Just to make certain—is this the woman?"

"Yes. I hadn't noticed that picture before. How did it happen to be in the paper?"

"Her husband was C. Arthur Right," Duryea said. "He was murdered."

"Was *that* her husband? Good heavens! I knew she was married, but I didn't know what her married name was."

Duryea folded the bathing suit. "Please don't say anything to *anyone* about this interview," he warned.

It was as they were walking back toward the pier that Milred asked, "What about the bathing suit, Frank? You look as grim as an executioner."

Duryea said, "When I went aboard that yacht Sunday morning, there were three witnesses, Miss Moline and Ted Shale, both sopping wet, and Miss Harpler. Miss Harpler was wearing a bathing suit. It was rubber. The ornamental design dyed on it was a series of curling waves, flying pelicans and grinning seals. Now, figure that one out!"

Gramps chuckled. "Now you're gettin' somewhere, son. Now you're whizzin'!"

Miss Harpler managed to appear definitely irritated behind a mask of light banter.

She said, "I suppose being a district attorney must have its compensations—as Emerson would say. However, I think I'd find it frightfully boring—even embarrassing—being forced to inquire into such intimate and trivial matters."

Duryea kept his smile, but leveled his brows in his best cross-examiner manner. "It all depends on what one calls trivial."

"I suppose so," she said, adjusting her hair casually. "I'm afraid *I* couldn't bring *myself* to consider the personal and private wardrobes of the bystanders particularly important. What was it you wanted to know about my bathing suit, Mr. Duryea?"

"Rubber, isn't it?"

"I believe so, yes. It was sold to me as being rubber."

"And the general motif of the pattern is that of life at the beach—grinning seals, pelicans gliding over the waves?"

"Exactly," she said, "and occasionally the pelicans are shown diving. I haven't examined it carefully to see if they catch any fish when they dive. We could, of course, do so. It is, I suppose, a matter of the greatest importance. And the expression on the seals' faces. You think they're singing? I hadn't examined them very closely; but then, I lack the trained legal mind. I wear a bathing suit to comply with the law. It hadn't occurred to me that the expressions on the seals' faces would have anything to do with the solution of a double murder. However, if you think the expressions on their dear little faces will be important, I can't refuse to trot them out for your inspection."

"Oh, I think it's of the greatest importance," Duryea said. "I can't imagine a more significant clue."

"Then we must look at them without delay. I *had* intended to dine out tonight. To be frank, when I received your summons, I felt somewhat put out at having to keep my host waiting. But, after all, if I can make so important a contribution toward apprehending the murderer of two fellow yachtsmen, as to see whether the seals on my bathing suit are really grinning, I'll feel that the sacrifice certainly hasn't been in vain."

Duryea pushed back his chair. "I'm glad you feel that way about it. Suppose we run down to your yacht and inspect the bathing suit right now."

"Do you suppose I'd have to be there?" she asked. "Wouldn't you feel free to inspect it with more professional detachment in my absence?"

"Oh, I should have to see it on you to observe the general effect."

"I see. Unfortunately, Mr. Duryea, I'm alone on the yacht, and while, of course, your keen interest in your professional duties would keep your attention concentrated entirely upon the expressions of the little seals, I'd . . ."

"My wife is in the adjoining office," Duryea interposed, summoning what dignity he could under the circumstances. "I'll ask her to accompany us."

"I think that would be simply splendid! I've often thought the wife of a great detective must take a keen interest in her husband's profession. How nice it will be to let her sit on the sidelines. Then she can see you down on your knees peering at the design on a girl's bathing suit. With her own ears she can hear you say, 'Now, Miss Harpler, you're absolutely certain this is your very own bathing suit? Turn around, please, so I can see the fit in the back.' Oh, I think it's a *splen*did idea having Mrs. Duryea with us! Is that an accident, or did you really plan it that way?"

Duryea crossed through his outer office and into the library. He closed the door behind him and said hastily, "Listen, I'm going to ask you folks to . . ."

Abruptly Milred burst out laughing.

"What is it now?" he asked with some irritation.

"Your face," she said. "You look as though you'd been caught stealing jam."

"And maybe you think I don't feel like it."

"Why? What's the matter?"

"Well, in place of showing her this bathing suit and asking her if it was hers, I thought it might be better to approach the subject indirectly."

"And she thought you were propositioning her?" Milred asked.

Duryea said, "She seemed to have that in mind as a possibility. Obviously, if she has her own bathing suit, this isn't hers. If she *can't* produce her bathing suit, then we're in a position to get her story without showing our hand."

"Well," Gramps said, "what's wrong with that?"

"Quite obviously," Duryea said, "you underestimate Miss Harpler's command of polite sarcasm. She makes me feel as though I were a lecherous Peeping Tom, using my position to . . ."

"And you want me to chaperon you?" Milred interrupted.

He nodded.

"I'm afraid I'd make a poor chaperon, dear. And don't let her bluff you. You have a rather disquieting effect upon attractive young women. I happen to know. And if she has enough intelligence to be politely sarcastic, she's laughing very much at your rather visible discomfiture. Take her over your knee and give her a good spanking."

181

Duryea said, "Unfortunately, I'm not in a position to follow my private inclinations. I'm a public official engaged in rather a delicate matter. If she has her bathing suit, I'm going to have to crawl into a hole and pull the hole in after me. If she doesn't, I'll have to be tactful but insistent in my questions. I can hardly go around pulling people off yachts and accusing them of various crimes just because I have made a mistake in the pattern of a bathing suit."

Milred said, "Come on, Gramps. Let's go rescue him. After all, Gramps, *you're* not a public official. If she gets too snooty, you can act the part of a lecherous old man, and make her think Frank is a paragon of virtue."

Gramps said indignantly, "I don't mind bein' lecherous, but I ain't agoin' to be called old. I ain't old. I've only been here a long time."

Duryea, obviously somewhat embarrassed, piloted them into his private office, and introduced Milred. Miss Harpler, making the usual polite protestations of pleasure when introduced to Mrs. Duryea, added, "It's really splendid of you to come, Mrs. Duryea. I suppose I shouldn't have expressed doubt of your husband's ability to concentrate on abstract problems while watching me change my clothes, but—well . . ."

"Oh, I know how it is," Milred said. "Even county officials have their moments of being human—although perhaps you wouldn't believe it. But you won't need to worry. When *I'm* along, you'll find that he is most discreet."

Duryea said curtly, "And my wife's grandfather, Mr. Wiggins."

Joan Harpler gave him her hand. "Oh, your grandfather, too!" she said. "How nice! Really, Mr. Duryea, you *are* the soul of discretion. Two generations of chaperons! It will be a pleasure to model my suit for . . ."

"I didn't ask you to model it," Duryea interrupted.

"Oh, didn't you? I thought you wanted me to put it on, and . . ."

"I wanted to see it on you to make certain that it fitted."

"Dear, dear," Joan Harpler said. "You'd really be surprised at how thoroughly painstaking the law enforcement officers are these days. And I have a party dress, Mr. Duryea, which isn't quite right across the hips. Perhaps you'd care to look at that too?"

Duryea, flushing angrily, started to say something, when Gramps Wiggins beat him to the punch. "He's purty busy," he said, his eyes twinkling over the tops of his steel-rimmed glasses. "If you're real anxious to show your hips to somebody, try me."

She turned on him savagely. "I'm not anxious to show my hips. I ask only to be let alone. I had a very important dinner date this evening, and I'm being called on to sacrifice my time and convenience because the district attorney of Santa Delbarra is interested in the expression on the face of a seal on my bathing suit!"

"I know *just* how you feel," Milred said suavely. "But do you know, Miss Harpler, my husband is a very determined man."

"I suppose you found that out right after you were married," Miss Harpler said.

Milred lowered her eyes demurely. "And as much as three or four weeks before," she said.

Miss Harpler gave her a quick glance, then decided she had been outflanked. "Shall we go?" she asked.

They drove to her yacht. Miss Harpler asked icily, "I suppose I'll be permitted to change in private."

"Certainly."

Milred said chidingly, "Frank, don't you think that was rather a curt refusal?"

Miss Harpler flared. "I wasn't inviting him to watch me change."

"Oh," Milred said in a tone which intimated she had some doubt on the subject. "He could, at least, have hesitated."

Miss Harpler left them seated in the cabin, retired to the lower cabin, to emerge presently in a tight-fitting rubber bathing suit on which a succession of pelicans were shown soaring along the edges of breaking waves, with occasionally a pelican diving into the breakers. Smiling seals, their heads thrust up from the painted waters, smirked cynically.

Duryea said uncomfortably, "Thank you very much, Miss Harpler. That's all."

"Oh," she said with surprise. "But I thought you wanted to look in the seals' eyes, and investigate whether the pelicans were actually getting fish. Wasn't that one of the important clues in solving your murder, Mr. Duryea?"

Gramps got up and walked over to her. "Yep," he said,

"gotta find out about that," and he bent over, carefully adjusting his glasses.

She looked at him and said chidingly, "Such a fatherly looking man, too."

"Yep," Gramps announced, entirely unashamed. "Lots o' times they call me Daddy. Just a minute now. Hold still, Miss Harpler. I ain't goin' to bite you." He walked slowly around her, surveying the bathing suit.

"Satisfied?" she asked icily.

Gramps beamed down at her. "My curiosity is."

She turned and marched from the room.

Milred said, "Well, that certainly fits her, Frank. You have to admit that."

"Like a rubber glove," Duryea said.

"And," his wife pointed out, "don't think she doesn't know it. After all, Frank, you don't need to be so embarrassed. It was bought for that purpose, you know."

CHAPTER 25

DURYEA pushed back his chair from the table, reached in his pocket for a cigar.

"Heard anything from Gramps?" Milred asked.

He clipped off the end of the cigar and said, "He's probably out prowling. I suppose the comparative respectability of associating with us has been a strain, and he doesn't intend to let it interfere with his weekly prowling."

"Don't underestimate my grandfather," she said. "From the gossip which used to percolate through the Wiggins family and which I was considered too young and unsophisticated to hear about, I gather that Gramps has established a seven-day-a-week prowling record."

Duryea said, "I wish he'd taken me with him. That damn bathing-suit business puts me in a most embarrassing position. I can't get over the way . . ."

"Oh, forget it, Frank," she said. "You just let that girl get your goat. She knew she had it, and was deriving a great deal of enjoyment from hearing it bleat."

"She was really in the right."

"Bosh! She couldn't have stopped Gramps with a line like that, and she knew it."

"Well," Duryea said, looking at his watch, "if we can get started before your estimable grandfather returns from whatever adventure is holding him at the moment, we can get to see a movie which *isn't* a mystery."

She laughed. "That's an invitation?"

"Definitely."

"I'll put on my things," she said, then paused by his chair, bent over and placed her lips to his. When she straightened, Duryea said, "That takes my mind off the events of the afternoon very nicely, thank you."

"That," she observed archly as she swept across the room, "was *one* of my objectives."

Duryea settled back in his chair, lit a cigar, and had entirely recovered his good humor by the time he and Milred were ensconced in loge seats.

He was rudely dragged back to the responsibilities of his job some fifteen minutes later when an usher tapped him on the shoulder. "You're wanted on the telephone, Mr. Duryea. They say it's important."

"Excuse me a minute, dear."

She said, "I'll go with you, Frank, if it should be anything really important and you have to go, I'll . . ."

"I'll see that the seats are held," the usher promised.

Duryea went to the telephone booth, closeted himself within it, and Milred could see his face show surprise, then angry indignation.

"What is it?" she asked, when he emerged.

"I think you'd better come with me," he said. "It seems to concern you fully as much as it does me."

"Will it take long?" she asked. "Can we get back to finish out the bill on the second show?"

"I don't know," he told her. "We have to go to the police station."

Driving down to the police station, she waited at first for him to break his silence. When it appeared that he had no intention of doing so, she said, "What is it, Frank?"

"The police have made an arrest."

"Well, I hope you're going to get that murder case cleaned up now."

"Oh, it's not an arrest in the murder case. It's one of those female impersonators."

"Frank!"

"That's right."

"But will you kindly tell me why we should be dragged out of a movie you've been wanting to see all week, to go to the police station because they've arrested a female impersonator?"

Duryea pulled his car up in front of the city police station. "I think you'll appreciate the reason in a very few moments," he said.

He escorted her into the chief's office. The chief of police, a twinkle in his eyes, said, "I'm sorry I disturbed you, Mr. Duryea, but this is such an unusual case, and he won't say a thing about . . ."

"It's all right," Duryea said. "Bring him in."

The chief nodded to a uniformed officer. A moment later, there were the sounds of shuffling in the corridor, then a figure clothed in a blanket was thrust into the room, and as the officer gave him the final push, peeled back the blanket.

Gramps Wiggins, for once in his life looking completely embarrassed, stood before them, clad only in a woman's bathing suit of rubber, a very scanty and decidedly feminine costume consisting of one piece. Over the bathing suit a never-ending procession of pelicans skimmed the surface of breakers or dived into the blue depths of the ocean, while seals regarded the performance with cynical smiles.

Duryea said, "I'll be damned!"

"Make it double," Milred observed.

Gramps looked at them with agony in his face. "Somebody stole my clothes," he said.

"He'd evidently undressed on the beach, put this thing on, and gone in for a swim," the chief said. "When he came out, his clothes were gone. The officer found him wandering along the beach. In fact, he was quite a center of attraction. You know him?"

"I'm acquainted with him," Duryea said.

"He insisted he was related to Mrs. Duryea, and . . ."

"We'll borrow the blanket," Duryea interrupted, "and take him along."

"I didn't give 'em no name," Gramps said.

"It's all right," Duryea said. "Come on."

186

They bustled him into the automobile, and Duryea started for home. Gramps, swathed in the blanket in the rear seat, leaned forward eagerly, the blanket oozing forth the sickly sweet odor of jail disinfectant as he moved. "Now listen, son," he said, "I got this thing figgered out. I . . ."

Duryea, keeping his eyes on the road, said, "If it's all the same to you, Gramps, just save it."

"But listen, son, this thing makes sense. This all fits together now . . ."

"I think," Duryea told him, "that hereafter the investigation will proceed along more conventional lines. I'd hate to play dirty pool with you, Gramps, but unless we reach an understanding right now, I'm going to call up the chief of police, tell him that you haven't made any satisfactory explanation of your conduct, and have you put back in jail for impersonating a woman in public."

Gramps shrilled, "All right, make a damned fool out o' yourself if you want to! I'm tryin' to tell you."

"I know you are."

"Well, damn it, I'm *goin'* to tell you. If you hadn't been so dumb, an' let that girl get you so flustered and embarrassed, you'd have known that bathin' suit o' hers *had never been in the water.*"

For a moment, the effect of what Gramps Wiggins was saying didn't dawn on the district attorney, then, when it did, he suddenly swerved the car over to the curb and slowed. "What's that?" he asked.

Gramps said, "She had your goat so bad you couldn't see anythin', but I looked her over carefully."

"I'll say you did," Milred said. "What with that rubber bathing suit and your inspection, Gramps, if she has any hidden charms . . ."

"You don't get me," Gramps said. "I hated like hell to do it, but I kept my eyes off'n those things. I was lookin' at the margins of the bathin' suit. There's kind of a hem around the top, sort of a thing that keeps the rubber from startin' to tear, an' if you'd noticed right smart, you'd have seen there was some figures written on that hem, up in the back of the hootnanny that goes around the . . ."

"The shoulder straps," Milred said to her husband.

"Go ahead," Duryea said.

187

"Well, those figgers looked like stock numbers to me, an' I wondered if anyone'd sell a bathing suit with stock numbers written on it that wouldn't come off. You wouldn't think that'd be good sales policy because a person who buys a smart suit like that . . ."

"Go ahead," Duryea said.

"So I went uptown. Sure enough, there was some of these same suits in the biggest department store. They're a branch of a Los Angeles outfit, you know, an' they said these suits had only been in about a week. I asked them if a woman had been in recently and bought one, an' the woman in charge of the bathin' suit department said she'd sold one that afternoon. The description fit that Harpler girl. Well, I didn't say too much, but I bought myself a bathin' suit that would fit me, then I decided I'd go down on the beach an' try it out in salt water, just to see what would happen from *one* swim. You remember when Ted Shale saw that girl on the boat, she'd been swimming, an' right afterwards she jumped in the water an' . . ."

"Yes, yes," Duryea interrupted. "What happened? What happened to the figures on the margin?"

"I'll be gol-darned if I know," Gramps said indignantly. "Somebody stole my clothes, and while I was wanderin' around lookin' for them, everybody started givin' me the merry ha-ha. Then a cop came up an' took me to jail. I ain't had a chance to get the damn thing off to take a look at it. The figures are on the back."

Milred beamed across at her husband. "Home, James," she said, "and don't spare the horses. Drive right through the main part of town."

Duryea slammed the car into speed.

"Us Wigginses always come through in a pinch," Milred stated.

Duryea swung through the residential district at high speed, slid his car to a stop in front of his house. "Come on, Gramps," he said, bundling the spare figure in the blanket and rushing him across the curb to the house.

The maid, hearing the sound of Duryea's latchkey in the door, came bustling forward, only to stop in horrified amazement at the sight that greeted her eyes. The district attorney, standing in the hallway, stripped the blanket from Gramps' bony shoulders. Gramps turned around, twisted his head, trying in vain to see down between his own shoulder blades. Duryea said, "Hold still. . . . Here. . . . My gosh, you're right, Gramps! The figures were here, weren't they?"

"Uh huh."

"They've all run together now—just a little blur of ink. That's an ink which dissolves in water, and . . ."

"There you are," Gramps said triumphantly to Milred. "I knew that girl was concealin' somethin'. She didn't want Frank to make a close examination of that suit, an' that was why she was puttin' on that snooty act."

Milred said, "But *why*, Gramps? Why's the bathing suit so important?"

Gramps said, "That's where you got me. I'm just an amateur. Frank's the professional."

Duryea's eyes narrowed as he contemplated the problem.

"Go ahead, son," Gramps said. "What is it? Was it this Harpler woman that was over at Catalina Island with him and . . ."

"No," Duryea said. "It was Mrs. Right. It had to be. But it could have been Joan Harpler's bathing suit. Then Mrs. Right must have been aboard the *Albatross* with Joan Harpler. Let's see. The *Albatross* tied up around six o'clock Saturday afternoon. That would make it."

"Make what?" Milred asked.

"Give Mrs. Right plenty of time to commit the murder, and then get back aboard the *Albatross*. Joan Harpler can well be an innocent accessory. Mrs. Right could have told her some story which would lull her suspicions—probably that she wanted to be where she could watch her husband and see who came aboard the *Gypsy Queen*. Miss Harpler probably went uptown to get provisions right after she tied up. Mrs. Right could have rowed over and killed her husband—and it was probably premeditated murder because she must have taken Arthur Right's gun out of his bureau drawer and then fixed up this story about how he'd gone up to grab the gun."

"Go ahead," Milred said. "You're doing fine."

"You're danged tootin' he's doin' fine," Gramps said proudly. "He's goin' places now! He's just a whizzin'!"

"Well," Duryea said, "as soon as the murder was discovered, Miss Harpler realized that it would take a lot of explaining to account for Mrs. Right being secretly present on her yacht, so she said absolutely nothing about that when she told me her story. She then went aboard the yacht, knowing that Mrs. Right would keep under cover. Probably in that starboard stateroom with the door locked. But Nita Moline realized someone else was aboard the yacht—perhaps the scent of some perfume, or perhaps she saw and recognized Mrs. Right's compact on a dressing table, or some other clue."

Gramps nodded vigorously. "Atta boy! Stay with it."

"And so," Duryea went on, "Miss Moline wanted to trap Mrs. Right aboard that yacht. So she asked Miss Harpler what seemed to be an innocent enough request that she be permitted to use the yacht to watch the *Gypsy Queen* and see who went aboard. And then, having planted Ted Shale aboard the yacht, she calmly went out to check up on Pearl Right."

"But wait a minute," Milred said. "Pearl Right was over at Catalina Island Sunday afternoon because Miss Moline talked with her on the telephone."

"Certainly," Duryea said. "That's the point. As soon as Miss Moline went to telephone, Joan Harpler locked Shale in his stateroom, went over to the yacht club and did some telephoning of her own. Miss Harpler got Warren Hilbers over at Catalina, told him to jump in his speedboat, set a course for Santa Delbarra, run wide open, and meet her at sea. Then she went back to her yacht, cut loose her mooring, started the motor, and headed out toward Catalina. Hilbers had calm water, so he could send his speedboat at a fast clip. And Mrs. Right and her brother concocted an alibi after they got together. They did it very nicely—that little touch when Hilbers told me that his sister had been with him all the time, except for a few short intervals; and she conscientiously reminded him that there'd been a time when she was taking a nap in the cottage Saturday afternoon. That was positively artistic."

"But how about the bathing suit?" Milred asked.

"Don't you see? When the speedboat caught up to the *Albatross*, Mrs. Right had made a bundle of all of her clothes. She could toss them aboard, but she couldn't very well jump aboard the speedboat from the deck of the *Albatross*—not without having the speedboat stand in so closely that it would bump against the yacht and waken Shale. So she put on Miss Harpler's bathing suit and jumped overboard. Then Miss Harpler swung the yacht in a wide circle, and Hilbers picked up his sister, turned around and made tracks for Catalina."

"If the killin' was at six o'clock," Gramps said, "then Stearne must actually have mailed that there oil letter."

Duryea nodded.

The old man said, "By gum, that accounts for it."

"What?"

"That young oil man marryin' his secretary."

Duryea thought for a moment, then smiled. "I think you've got something there," he said to Gramps. "Well, I'm headed for Los Angeles."

"Oh, I'm going, too," Milred said.

"Me, too," Gramps shouted. "I'll get some clothes on an' . . . Oh, my gosh a'mighty!"

"What's the matter?" Duryea asked.

"The trailer's plumb locked up," Gramps said. "The key to the trailer was in my clothes they stole. An' you can't bust those locks because I've got some contraptions of my own on the thing, burglar alarms that go off, an' . . ."

"You can wear—no, you can't," Milred said, surveying the difference in stature between her husband and Gramps. "It looks as though you're out of the race."

"No, I ain't neither out o' no race," he shrilled. "I'll go in these here clothes . . ."

"Don't be silly. You can't do that. It would ruin Frank's case, and you can't wear Frank's clothes. You'd drop out through a coat sleeve, or slip through a pant leg at the most exciting moment."

"Well—"

"No," Duryea said. "I've jeopardized the dignity of my official position enough as it is. I can hardly go to Los Angeles to call on a widow and accuse her of murdering her husband, taking along my wife's grandfather, attired in a woman's tight-fitting rubber bathing suit."

"Well, by God," Gramps sputtered. "Of all the ingrates, of all the . . ."

"Come on, Milred," Duryea said, grabbing her arm.

"Listen, Frank, Gramps is entitled to . . ."

"I tell you, he can't," Duryea interrupted. "Seconds are precious. I've got to get down there in time to close this case before something happens. I'm starting right now."

"Sorry, Gramps," Milred said.

They dashed out of the door and down the steps, jumped in the car, and went tearing away down the boulevard. Gramps Wiggins, attired in his rubber bathing suit, stared after them with speechless indignation, then an idea struck him. "By gum," he said, "I can't get the trailer open 'cause I ain't got no keys, but I can drive the car all right, because it ain't locked."

"What's that?" the maid asked.

Gramps wrapped the blanket around his shoulders, said, "Nothin'," and sprinted out of the door. A moment later, the motor on his rattletrap car roared and sputtered into life, loose connecting rods and slapping pistons setting up a cacophony of discordant protest.

Without waiting for the car to even warm up, Gramps slammed in the gear, jerked the trailer into a swift start, and went rattling out of the driveway, the homemade trailer bouncing and swaying as the old man urged his car into reckless speed.

CHAPTER 26

AN aura of death surrounded the house, an intangible, mystic miasma of violent demise. Other houses in the neighborhood were either brilliantly lighted or completely dark, giving the impression of life and gaiety on the one hand, or dignified slumber on the other. But in the house of C. Arthur Right two or three windows glowing with the sickly emanations of subdued light managed to convey an impression of death.

Duryea, who had stopped at police headquarters to pick up a police escort, pulled his car to a stop in front of the house. A few feet behind him, the police car glided in close to the curb. Officers debouched to the pavement, formed with Frank Duryea and his wife into a compact group.

Duryea said, "I don't want her to commit suicide. If she asks to be excused, you'll have to go with her, Milred, and if she should make any attempt to . . ."

"Go right ahead, Frank. I'll back your play by doing whatever's expected."

Duryea said, "All right, here we go, boys," and rang the bell. A maid answered the bell.

"Mrs. Right," Duryea said. "This is the district attorney of Santa Delbarra County."

"I'm sorry. Mrs. Right simply can't see anyone. She . . ."

"She'll have to see me," Duryea said, pushing his way on through the door.

The maid started to protest, but gave ground as the determined little group pushed past her.

"Where is she?" Duryea asked.

"Upstairs lying down in her bedroom—the one in front."

"Is she dressed?"

"Yes."

"You come with us," Duryea said.

They made noise as they ascended the steps, the boards creaking in protest as heavy bodies, keeping in the closely compact companionship of a group which is called upon to discharge a disagreeable duty, climbed the carpeted treads.

The maid indicated the room.

Mrs. Right looked up as Duryea opened the door. The expression on her face ran through a rapid series of changes from surprise to indignation, indignation to dismay.

Duryea said, "I'm sorry to have to bother you, Mrs. Right, and sorry to take this unconventional method of calling, but there are some questions in connection with your husband's death which you'll have to answer in person, and immediately."

"Why . . . why, I . . ."

Duryea whipped out the rubber bathing suit. "For instance, Mrs. Right, I'm going to ask you to make a frank statement concerning the circumstances which caused you to borrow Miss Harpler's bathing suit."

"Why, I—I can't understand . . ."

Duryea said, "Remember that anything you say may be used against you, that I have means of checking up. Miss Harpler telephoned you, didn't she?"

"Well, yes, she . . . I . . ."

"Miss Harpler walked into a trap," Duryea said with the assurance of a man who is bluffing and knows that he must make his bluff carry weight, "I'm afraid her attempt to rush out and buy a duplicate bathing suit, in place of putting you in the clear, has put both of you in a very bad light."

Mrs. Right faced the circle of accusing faces, said, "I don't know what you're talking about. Miss Harpler telephoned me upon an entirely different matter, and, as for that bathing suit, I . . ."

"Wore it," Duryea said, "when you jumped overboard from Miss Harpler's yacht when Warren Hilbers picked you up in his speedboat and took you back to Catalina so you could manufacture an alibi. I'm afraid, Mrs. Right, it's going to be necessary for me to ask you to accompany me to police headquarters."

She studied his face for a moment, then made a little gesture of surrender. "All right," she said wearily, "I was afraid it wouldn't work. That's right. I was on Joan's yacht. She was keeping me concealed. Then Nita Moline wanted to use the yacht. We were afraid that if we withheld permission it might make her suspicious. She was nosing around too much anyway. I guess you know just about what happened."

Duryea said, with dignity, "Perhaps you'll tell us exactly why you killed your husband, Mrs. Right."

"But I didn't kill him. That's just the point. I . . ."

"You want us to believe that you went to all this trouble to manufacture an alibi and yet knew nothing of your husband's death?"

She said, "I was suspicious of my husband. I thought that he and Addison Stearne were planning to do something that would jeopardize my interests. I felt he was going to fix it so Nita Moline would consent to marry Arthur after he'd secured a divorce. I wanted to follow them and see what happened. Well, I fixed it up with Warren. He has a speedboat. As soon as my husband had sailed, Warren and I followed along. Joan had consented to put her yacht at my disposal. So when we found they were headed for Santa Delbarra, Warren put me aboard the *Albatross* and we went to Santa Delbarra. I kept out of sight, of course.

"Joan moored her yacht where it was possible to watch the *Gypsy Queen*. We wanted to see who went aboard."

"Who did?" Duryea asked.

"That's exactly the point. No one. Mr. Duryea, that crime couldn't have been what you think it was. Addison shot my husband, and then committed suicide, and someone who didn't want it to appear that he had committed suicide, picked up the gun and tossed it overboard."

"Which accounts for the reason you went to all this trouble to build an alibi?" Duryea asked sarcastically.

"I admit that was a mistake, but Miss Moline must have been suspicious. She kept prowling around the *Albatross*. And, after all, as Joan pointed out, I *could* have swum across to the other yacht at almost any time during the night, killed Arthur and Addison Stearne, and returned. Joan said the officers would probably think of that if they knew I was hiding on her yacht. So she got Warren on the telephone, told him to come out with his speedboat and stand by. I guess you know the rest."

"What time did you first get to Santa Delbarra?" Duryea asked.

"Right around six o'clock Saturday. Saturday morning we tagged along in the speedboat long enough to find out that Stearne was taking his yacht to Santa Delbarra. Then Warren took me over to Catalina so he could pick up Joan. She was waiting there in the *Albatross*. We couldn't find her right at first, because she was out fishing. When we finally located her, she had to go in to Catalina to take aboard some gasoline and do some telephoning. It was shortly before six o'clock when we got to Santa Delbarra. And no one went aboard the *Gypsy Queen* after that."

"And I suppose your alibi for that is Miss Harpler?"

"Yes."

"Then you must have killed your husband almost immediately after the yacht was moored," Duryea said.

"I tell you I didn't. I . . ."

"I'm sorry, Mrs. Right, but, according to your own admission, you were within a hundred feet of the place where your husband was killed. You had every opportunity to kill him. You had every incentive to kill him. You concocted a fake alibi. According to your own admission, you knew about his death, yet proceeded to deliberately fabricate a lot of evidence to throw the officers off the trail. Under the circumstances, Mrs. Right, I'm going to have to take you into custody. If you'll get your things together . . ."

Duryea broke off as the house echoed to the sound of struggle. The impact of jarring thuds shook pictures on the walls. A revolver shot crashed punctuation to the sounds of struggle. For a moment following that shot, the noises ceased, then they started again.

"Watch this woman," Duryea said to one of the officers. "This may very easily be a trick. Come on, men."

The rest of them ran across the corridor, down the stairs toward the back of the house from which the sounds were proceeding.

Duryea jerked open a door. A chair, thrown with great force, crashed against the door just as he had it partially opened, jerked the door out of his hand.

Duryea jumped into the room, the officers behind him.

Gramps Wiggins, attired in his rubber bathing suit, a broomstick in his hand, was dancing nimbly around, striking out with quick, sharp blows. Warren Hilbers, his face distorted with rage, one arm dangling at his side, was picking up everything movable which seemed to offer possibilities of a lethal nature with his other hand.

"Hold it!" one of the officers said, raising a revolver. "Hold it or I'll shoot!"

The men stopped. It was as though a motion picture had suddenly frozen on the screen. Gramps shrilled to Duryea, "Take him, Frank! Take him! Don't you get it now?"

"Get what?" Duryea asked.

"He's the one who killed Right and Stearne. Nab him. Those were his spectacles. An oculist can . . ."

Hilbers turned and made a wild dash for freedom.

One of the officers made a flying tackle, and grabbed his legs.

Gramps ran his fingers through his graying hair. "Yep," he said, "I got to thinkin' it over, drivin' down. Shucks, son, that other yacht didn't get in there until about six o'clock. The murder might have been committed before then. S'pose it was? Well, I got to thinkin' that if Mrs. Right left the house with Hilbers an' showed up in Santa Delbarra aboard Joan Harpler's yacht, then Hilbers must have put her aboard the *Albatross*. His speedboat would do thirty-five or forty miles an hour. What was to prevent him from puttin' Mrs. Right on the *Albatross*, then pretendin' to go back, but instead circlin' around, an' goin' up to Santa Delbarra?

"Hilbers had been gettin' money from his sister. She had

paid for part of the cost of his last speedboat. You get it? If Mrs. Right an' her old man split up, Hilbers was goin' to get pinched. But if Right an' Stearne should get bumped off, Mrs. Right was goin' to inherit a whole flock of iron men.

"Then Mrs. Right told him about how she'd made that crack about Nita Moline to Arthur Right—an' that was Hilbers' chance. He'd already got Right's gun. Right might have gone to the bureau drawer for it, but it was gone when he got there.

"But when Hilbers got aboard the yacht, Right smelled a rat. P'raps he saw the gun in Hilbers' pocket. He an' Hilbers had a fight. Hilbers' glasses went overboard. Then they fell down the cabin stairs an' Hilbers shot. He had to do his shootin' inside so the noise wouldn't attract attention.

"When Stearne came back from mailin' that letter, Hilbers was waitin' for him. It was that simple, just a murder an' suicide frame-up, an' then a lot o' dough. He didn't know the law wouldn't have let Right inherit from Stearne—that would have been a laugh—if his scheme had gone through.

"Then Hilbers sneaked back an' went over to Catalina an' was the devoted, loyal brother when the murder came out. You see he knew his sister would be hidin' on the yacht, an' he knew darn well that havin' done that, she couldn't afford ever to let the authorities know she'd been there. He just co-operated in manufacturin' her alibi, an' he was laughin' up his sleeve all the time, because if everythin' went right, he was goin' to get his hands on a fortune, an' if anythin' went wrong, he had it fixed so *she'd* take the rap for the murder.

"I came down here as fast as I could. I couldn't make such good time with my old jalopy, what with the trailer on behind. But I got here in time. He'd been in with his sister. When he heard the cops come up, he tried sneakin' out. He was goin' to leave sis to take the rap."

Gramps ceased talking, looked at Duryea, then at his grand-daughter. "How'm I doin', Milred?" he asked.

"Swell," she said. "Right according to the best Wiggins traditions."

Hilbers said angrily to Gramps, "You're cockeyed. Don't think I'm so dumb I left myself that wide open. I staged that whole thing to look like a murder and suicide. I left a type-written statement with a darn good forgery of Arthur Right's signature. You poor hicks never would have had anything on me if something hadn't happened to *that* evidence."

Gramps grinned at the district attorney. "That is where we shoulda got wise sooner, son. We had it all doped out, but we didn't have guts enough to follow our convictions. About the only one who coulda ditched that confession and tossed the gun overboard was the Moline woman, but after she did that, she went to a lot o' trouble to try an' watch the yacht. Get the sketch? She knew the confession was a fake, an' that it was a double murder. How did she know it? Because she knew Addison Stearne an' Right could never have quarreled over her, because the minute Right made a crack Stearne would have told him the true facts, that he looked on Nita Moline as his daughter. So when that Moline gal found the confession an' the gun, an' found her name was mentioned the way it was, she knew it was a murder. But even so, she didn't want her name to get smeared, so she tossed the gun overboard, pocketed the confession, an' then tried to keep watch to see who went back aboard the yacht."

Gramps swung back to Hilbers. "But don't think we wouldn't have got *you* now. We was checkin' up on everybody in the case. By tomorrow at the latest we'd have had a report on *your* eyes. When you dropped those glasses overboard, you as good as left your callin' card."

Duryea said, "I remember now, Hilbers, how much trouble you had finding the end of your cigarette with a match. You had to move the match back and forth."

Gramps grinned triumphantly. "What'd I tell you?" he said to Hilbers.

One of the officers turned to Duryea. "Listen," he said, glowering suspiciously at the weazened old man in the woman's bathing suit, "who the hell *is* this guy?"

"That," Duryea said, "is a relative by marriage who aspires to become a detective."

"Aspires, hell!" Gramps Wiggins wheezed. "I've graduated."

>>> If you've enjoyed this book and would like to discover more great vintage crime and thriller titles, as well as the most exciting crime and thriller authors writing today, visit: >>>

The Murder Room
Where Criminal Minds Meet

themurderroom.com

www.ingramcontent.com/pod-product-compliance
Ingram Content Group UK Ltd.
Pitfield, Milton Keynes, MK11 3LW, UK
UKHW022314280225
455674UK00004B/302

9 781471 909504